"Don't think these modern Austenites are any less fun to read about than their nineteenth-century counterparts just because they're wearing golf pants instead of Empire dresses."

—*Newsday*

"Borrowing from Jane Austen with witty panache, Cohen shows us a social world percolating with its own brew of prejudice and mistaken assumptions."

—*The Philadelphia Inquirer*

"[An] amusing, kvetchy take on *Pride and Prejudice*."

—*Publishers Weekly*

"Finally, a love story involving characters with grandchildren, Social Security checks, and membership in AARP! Her novel, set against a Jewish retirement community in Boca Raton, is both satirical and touching. Snowbirds in Florida will be glued to every page, but 'Golden Girls' everywhere are sure to get a big kick out of the book."

—Jane Heller, author of *Secret Ingredient*

"Clever and fun."

—*Kirkus Reviews*

"Will amuse readers everywhere."

—*Library Journal*

"Cohen offers gimlet-eyed and uproariously funny critiques of everything from the significance of the color turquoise in Jewish home décor to the dynamics of trying on clothes at Loehmann's."

—*Albermarle* magazine

"Fun poolside reading."

—*Palm Beach Post*

P9-DMV-971

# JANE
# AUSTEN
## —*in*—
# BOCA

JANE
AUSTEN
— *in* —
BOCA

PAULA
MARANTZ
COHEN

ST. MARTIN'S GRIFFIN
NEW YORK

*For Gert, who laughed,*
*and*
*Ruth, who would have laughed*

JANE AUSTEN IN BOCA. Copyright © 2002 by Paula Marantz Cohen. All rights reserved. Printed in the United States of America. No part of this book may be used or reproduced in any manner whatsoever without written permission except in the case of brief quotations embodied in critical articles or reviews. For information, address St. Martin's Press, 175 Fifth Avenue, New York, N.Y. 10010.

*Book Design by Jonathan Bennett*

www.stmartins.com

Library of Congress Cataloging-in-Publication Data

Cohen, Paula Marantz, 1953–
    Jane Austen in Boca / Paula Marantz Cohen.—1st St. Martin's Griffin ed.
        p. cm.
    ISBN 0-312-29088-8 (hc)
    ISBN 0-312-31975-4 (pbk)
    1. Boca Raton (Fl.)—Fiction. 2. Mothers-in-law—Fiction. 3. Jewish women—Fiction. 4. Widowers—Fiction. 5. Retirees—Fiction. I. Austen, Jane, 1775–1817. Pride and Prejudice. II. Title.

PS3603.O49J36 2003
813'.54—dc21                                                        2003046838

10   9   8   7   6

# ACKNOWLEDGMENTS

I would like to thank the following people for their advice on early drafts of the book: Ian Abrams, Rosetta Marantz Cohen, Alan S. Penziner, Gertrude Penziner, and Lauren Weinberger. I would also like to thank Albert DiBartolomeo for encouraging me to take the leap into fiction writing and Don Riggs for staging the Drexel University Writing Gala, in which the germ of this novel was first presented. Additional thanks go to my agent, Felicia Eth, who saw something in the earliest draft, and to my editor, Hope Dellon, at St. Martin's Press, who guided me in shaping the book into its present form.

*Take it from me. A nice widower with a comfortable living can be nudged into settling down by a not-so-young woman who plays her cards right.*

—Lila Katz to Flo Kliman and May Newman

# JANE AUSTEN
# —*in*—
# BOCA

# CHAPTER ONE

"MRS. GRAFSTEIN IS DEAD!"

"Uh-huh." Alan Newman nodded without raising his head from the stock market page.

"Hel-lo!" Carol Newman leaned toward her husband, her face, like a small, high-intensity lamp, positioned above the top of his paper. "Can I have your attention, please?"

He looked up.

"Listen to this—" Carol cleared her throat and read aloud crisply from her section of *The Star Ledger*. " 'Norman Grafstein, former owner of Grafstein Leather Imports, will be honored for his generous gift to the South Orange Beautification Committee in memory of his late wife, Marilyn. Grafstein, formerly of South Orange, now resides in Boca Raton, Florida. His son, Mark, of Scotch Plains will be present at the committee breakfast to receive the plaque in his father's honor.' " Carol put the paper down and looked meaningfully across at her husband.

"So?" Alan responded.

"Did you know Norman Grafstein had lost his wife?"

"How would I know? I haven't seen Mark since our last high-school reunion."

Carol sighed. "Honey, don't you get it?" She tapped a long, mauve fingernail on the table between them. "Norman Grafstein. Boca Raton. Your mother."

"Carol, please . . ."

"Alan—" Her voice took the sharper tone generally reserved for their seven-year-old. "Do you want your mother to be

1

loved, to be happy, to have someone to take her to dinner? Why don't you exert yourself? Call up Mark Grafstein, tell him you're sorry about his mother"—she gave her hand a wave to suggest the routine preliminaries that would need to take place—"and tell him your mother's in Boca. Arrange a meeting with his father."

"Carol, my mother doesn't want to meet anyone. She's fine the way she is. Leave her alone."

"She's not fine," countered Carol. "She's miserable."

"She's fine."

"She's miserable."

Alan began to feel dizzy.

"You want her to be miserable"—Carol picked up a magazine and began to thumb through it—"let her be miserable."

Alan shifted uneasily in his chair, anticipating defeat. It was possible to be irritated by Carol, but it was hard to oppose her for long. The fact was that she had a big heart—literally (the result of twice-a-week classes in high-impact aerobics at the JCC) and figuratively. Carol not only felt for the plight of others, she saw it as her mission to set things right for them. Last year, she helped the homeless in their town by organizing crisis career workshops and a low-fat soup kitchen in the library annex. The year before that, she raised math scores by 60 percent in the district by taking charge of the after-school homework program (even poor Jimmy Hahn, said to be ineducable, buckled down so as not to have her fingernail poked in his shoulder one more time). Carol was not one to sit idly by in the face of adversity, human weakness, and error. She was constantly striving to improve the lives of those around her, whether they liked it or not.

Alan vaguely understood that Carol carried a great weight of responsibility on her small shoulders. It fell to her to sustain that network of human relations called civilization—at least as it existed in the northern New Jersey suburbs. She was forever sending her friends to her hairdresser, passing the word about a new caterer, and arranging large family gatherings that involved hunting down estranged cousins and convincing them to let go of the grudge they'd been holding for thirty years and attend. She had been committee chair of last year's most successful event at their synagogue—an interfaith hootenanny in which Methodists, Baptists, and Jews, all wearing yarmulkes, crowded inside the cavernous blond-wood sanctuary, whose astronomical cost her herculean fund-raising efforts had helped pay for.

You could take one of two tacks upon finding yourself married to someone like Carol. You could resist and be caught in a debilitating struggle that you could not win. Or you could succumb and discover the pleasures of being managed by an expert.

Alan Newman, an accountant by profession, was a philosophical man. Life was hard. Life was short. He saw no point in swimming against the tide of this powerful and well-meaning force that was his wife. And so he succumbed and was, as far as such things are possible, happy.

# CHAPTER TWO

MAY NEWMAN, WIDOWED FOR ALMOST TWO YEARS, HAD BEEN living undisturbed in her Florida condominium until the day the previous spring when her son and daughter-in-law, arriving earlier than expected, had found her in her kitchenette in a housecoat. Alan had seen nothing noteworthy in this, but Carol insisted that it could only mean one thing: His mother was lonely and depressed.

"Any woman wearing a housecoat at two in the afternoon is depressed!" she declared. "And why shouldn't she be?" she added when Alan attempted to argue on behalf of the comforts of a housecoat. "It would be more surprising, given the circumstances, if she weren't!"

From then on, May's case had been a theme in the Newman household to be picked up and examined at those odd intervals of the day or night when Carol found herself with nothing else to do.

"Your mother needs to move in with us," Carol announced one night, just after Alan had fallen into the deathlike slumber that preceded his six A.M. wake-up to catch the early commuter train into the city.

"Wuh?" mumbled Alan groggily. He had been enjoying a dream of skiing down a mountain in Aspen.

"Your mother. It's our duty to take her in."

"Fine," he said, rolling over to continue the downward run, the wind whipping at his face. He was in no mood to put up even the semblance of a fight.

But the next day, when Carol broached the idea with her mother-in-law, she was surprised to find opposition from this quarter.

"No, dear," said May, "I'd rather stay where I am."

"But Mom, you'd be happier with us. You'd get to see the children all the time."

"I'm not sure the children would want to see me as much as that," demurred May gently. And though Carol cajoled and bullied, May would not budge.

This left Carol with a definite challenge. If her mother-in-law were nearby, she could drag her to senior functions, sign her up for art appreciation classes, and take her on as an assistant to her own numerous charitable and community activities. But directing May's social life from a distance of a thousand miles was another story. It required more elaborate intervention.

"Did you see the announcement about the senior bagels-and-lox brunch at the Reform temple?" Carol asked her mother-in-law over the phone as she ran her eye over the *Sun-Sentinel* spread out on the kitchen table (she had the paper expressed up so as to keep abreast for May's benefit). "Go! You never know who you'll meet."

May always said she would check things out—it was easier to say yes to Carol than to say no—but she rarely followed through on her promises. When her daughter-in-law called for a report, she always had an excuse: an attack of dyspepsia, a heavy rain, a made-for-TV movie that she wanted to watch. For someone like Carol, used to having her initiatives stick, May's mild-mannered but unwavering refusal to cooperate was frustrating to say the least.

"We need to go down," Carol announced one day to her husband soon after the newspaper had drawn her attention to a widowed Norman Grafstein. "We need to visit your mother and get things moving."

"We were just there in December, and we'll go again in

June," said Alan wearily, for he detected the fateful note of determination in his wife's voice. "You know I can't take off again until tax season is over."

"June is too far away," pronounced Carol. "This is the plan"—for, of course, she had one. "I'll go down with the kids next week; you can meet us for a long weekend. I've already reserved the tickets. But you'll have to call Mark Grafstein before we go. Tell him we'll stop in on his father, to pay our respects, when you arrive."

Alan knew it would all be done.

# CHAPTER THREE

MAY NEWMAN SAT IN HER KITCHENETTE WITH LILA KATZ AND Flo Kliman, fellow residents of the Boca Festa retirement club. Boca Festa was one of many clubs in Boca Raton, Florida, former scrubland developed in the early 1970s as a haven for modest-to-well-to-do retirees. The population was mostly Jewish (though with a definite sprinkling of Italians) and mostly from the tri-state metropolitan area (though with a vocal minority from Chicago, Cleveland, and Montreal).

Boca Festa was built on a plan that resembled the other clubs in the area. It was set on a large expanse of manicured grounds with a Tara-like clubhouse at the center and an Olympic-size pool alongside. The surrounding complex was divided into three "estates," each reflecting a superficially different (but structurally similar) architectural style. Each estate was in turn divided into ten "pods," and each pod into fifty condominium units. At the center of each pod was a small pod-pool and pod-clubhouse.

The entire complex was thus parsed and organized like a collapsible set of mirrors—a mix of the quasifuturistic and the quasihistorical. The estate names—Fairways, Eastgate, and Crestview—suggested the stylish manor houses featured on popular 1980s TV series like *Dynasty*. May lived in pod 3 in the Crestview Estate; Lila and Flo in pod 9, Eastgate.

It was to her daughter-in-law that May owed her company. Lila's niece was a friend of a member of Carol's coffee group, and when the coincidence of the women's mutual residence had been unearthed, a meeting had been inevitable. Lila and Flo were neighbors in their pod and had known each other for several years.

"So what are we doing tonight?" asked Lila as the three women sipped their Sankas at May's kitchen table.

"Why do we have to do anything?" countered Flo.

"We have to do something. It's Saturday night!"

"Oh my God!" cried Flo. "Saturday night and I don't have a date!"

"At our age it's important to get out and mix," said Lila impatiently. "Otherwise, they say, you lose interest in life."

"Don't worry; I haven't lost my will to live."

"You joke, but it's not funny."

"Okay," said Flo, relenting as she always did after teasing Lila. "I'll tell you what we'll do: I'll rent a Clark Gable movie and make some popcorn. You can both come over and watch."

"Sitting home and watching television is not my idea of Saturday-night entertainment," declared Lila. "I like human company."

"Clark Gable is better than human company."

"Well, you can stay home," said Lila huffily. "I'm going to go out. May, will you join me? The JCC has a talk by one of those guru doctors on lowering your blood pressure through stress management. They say it will be very well attended."

"Well . . ." said May. "I was feeling a little tired—"

"May wants to watch Clark Gable," interrupted Flo. "He does more for stress management than a guru doctor."

"Flo, mind your own business. Just because you have no interest in meeting anyone doesn't mean you have to influence May."

"I'm not influencing May."

"You are!"

"Please," interceded May. "I wouldn't mind going to hear the guru doctor with you, Lila, only I'm feeling a little tired. Flo isn't influencing me. I do like Clark Gable."

8

"All right," said Lila, sighing. "I like Clark Gable, too. We'll watch the movie tonight, but you have to promise to do something tomorrow, even if it's only going to the clubhouse to hear Pinkus Lotman on parking violations in the pods. If we don't do things, we might as well be dead."

"Agreed," said Flo. "We'll go hear Pinkus Lotman tomorrow. That is, if May's phlebitis doesn't flare up."

May laughed. She marveled at the amount of time she had come to spend with the two women and how much she enjoyed them. Even their bickering, which was fairly constant, was entertaining, and she never left their company without being amused and engaged.

Until meeting Lila and Flo, May hadn't realized how lonely she'd been after Irving's death. For almost a year, her only regular companion had been her neighbor Carla Rossen, a woman of seventy-eight who lived in the adjacent condo. They had gone to lunch and dinner at the clubhouse almost every day, and May had sat by quietly while her friend rehearsed an endless series of complaints.

"Do you call this a piece of veal?" Carla would demand, putting down her fork and looking around her in amazement. "It tastes like cardboard! How dare they expect me to eat cardboard instead of veal!"

Everything for Carla was a personal affront. The mailman, in placing *her Boca Times* in May's box, was clearly intending to insult her. "I know what he's up to," she explained knowingly to May. "He gave me the fish-eye the first time I saw him. Murray"—Murray was her husband, once a focal point of irritation, now, in being dead, a saint—"wouldn't have stood for it."

Carla's ability to find fault was at times so vast and inventive that it approached the level of a literary gift. Nothing was too small to evoke her disfavor, from the quality of the plantings next to the pool to the odor of the air freshener in the club bathroom. May dutifully listened to Carla's complaints, nodding and offering explanations as far as she could, until the friendship was finally severed when May failed to send a thank-you note for a dozen *rugelach* that Carla had baked for her birthday. May had not seen the necessity of a note since she lived next door and had given her thanks in person, but for Carla the omission had been a gross breach in etiquette.

"A thank-you note shows respect," declared Carla indignantly; it was a dictum her mother had taught her when she was ten years old, and she had held to it unwaveringly for nearly seventy years. "It's clear that you do not respect me."

May assured her that she did, but Carla would not be convinced and eventually ceased speaking to her neighbor altogether. Now, when they passed each other, Carla looked away with exaggerated disdain, so that Lila and Flo, who knew May's gentle nature, were mystified as to what could have elicited such a reaction. For May, Carla's hurt feelings were a source of pain, though she was also secretly relieved—being audience to so much constant complaining had been a trial. She felt fortunate to have met Lila and Flo, women with opinions and ideas who did not take themselves too seriously and who liked to laugh.

The friendship was odd in its way. Though all three women were Jewish and over seventy, they were also very different in disposition and style. Lila Katz was the shortest, barely five feet, with a trim, bosomy figure and a mass of red-orange hair that she kept carefully lacquered through weekly trips to the premier Boca stylist. It was her one indulgence, since she was on a fixed income and obliged to be vigilant about expenses.

"If Mort, the schnook, had had the good grace to leave me something, I wouldn't have to worry about the mortgage on the condominium and go around in rags."

"Rags?" queried Flo, looking doubtfully at Lila's Nicole Miller top and Ralph Lauren skirt.

"Well, they might as well be, for what I paid for them," explained Lila. "Why shouldn't I be able to buy retail? I'm not saying that I would, but I should be able to if I want." Lila's sense of what should be had the incisive clarity of the best utopian philosopher.

"I think you look lovely," interjected May.

"I don't want to look lovely," protested Lila, "I want to look glamorous."

May Newman listened to Lila's tirades with amusement. She had none of her friend's flash or sense of frustrated entitlement, and her unassuming manner might have rendered her invisible were it not for an unusual sweetness of disposition and a definite if faded prettiness that gained by the novelty of her unawareness of it. She dressed conservatively, dyed her hair the light brown of her youth, and wore little jewelry. She was zaftig, as she liked to say, and was forever turning down the offered piece of cheesecake by explaining that she needed to lose twenty pounds. Flo argued otherwise: "If you ever lose weight," she said, "you'll look like a movie star and be shipped off to Hollywood to compete with that skinny half-Jewish Gwyneth Paltrow—so eat the cheesecake."

Florence Kliman, the most educated and acerbic of the three women, was also the hardest to categorize. She was taller than the others—"Five-seven on a good day," as she put it—and had the lean, long bones of the former athlete and expert tennis player that she was. Her face was angular—sharp features, long nose, large, dark eyes, and a wide mouth with prominent teeth made more so when she laughed, which was often. She had worked as a librarian at the University of Chicago until she and her husband moved to Florida three years before. He had been a successful real-estate lawyer, a workaholic whose doctor had urged him to retire and move south.

"But the sunshine and leisure immediately did him in," explained Flo. "Eddie used to go out in twenty below and make ten deals in a morning; but eighty degrees and a game of pinochle, he couldn't handle."

She had considered moving back to Chicago after her husband's death but had decided in the end that she liked Florida—not a chic position among the academic-type women she had worked with back home. "Those women all wear Dr. Scholl's and like films about Tibet," she declared.

May and Lila enjoyed Flo's wit but were also a little afraid of it. There was no telling when she might turn it on them.

Having resolved the issue of the evening's entertainment, the women moved on to other topics. Lila's interest in socializing inspired Flo to describe the men in West Boca.

"They're all alike." She expounded: "Pastel shorts, little caps, deaf in one ear, and a joke up the sleeve for culture. I used to look out the window and see twenty who could have been my Eddie, and who knows, but I may have gone to bed with two or three of them."

"Flo, you're terrible!" protested May, though she couldn't help laughing.

"I think it's a top-secret government plot," continued Flo. "All the men over seventy in Boca have been turned into identical clones of each other."

"Well, I'd take one with a nice pension in a minute," declared Lila. She had announced to her friends that if she didn't snag a husband this year, she would be forced to take a more modest place, maybe move out of the complex altogether.

Lila had embarked on the subject of the dreaded move when the doorbell rang. The three women ran to the window: A Bermuda-shorted, capped man of seventy-five was holding a bakery box in front of May's door.

"It looks like May has an admirer," said Lila.

"Oh, Mr. Marcus." May was embarrassed. "He lives in Fairways. He once gave me a ride to the clubhouse."

"Aha!" observed Lila with interest.

"Is he nice?" asked Flo.

"I suppose so," said May, sounding unsure. "Well, I'd better see what he wants." She rose and left the room.

There was a murmur of voices near the door, and Hy Marcus, having apparently escaped May's attempt at a barricade, fairly jumped into the kitchenette.

"Ladies, ladies. I brought some Danish from New York City. I was visiting my son, Steven, a gastroenterologist with an office off Central Park, very successful, with a beautiful brownstone and a house in the Hamptons. My wife and I used to spend most of the summer there." He now waved the box and put it down in the middle of the table. "May said she liked prune Danish when I gave her a lift to the clubhouse last week—saw a lady in distress, thought much better to ride in a Lincoln than schlump along and swell up the ankles—so when I saw these in the Boolangarary, which is the best French bakery in New York City where my daughter-in-law shops, I had to bring her back some. A prune for a princess," he proffered gallantly.

May, looking overwhelmed, had pressed herself near the wall and watched with combined fascination and horror the progress of Hy Marcus's monologue. Flo rolled her eyes, but Lila made an effort to respond:

"How nice that your son is doing so well."

"Well, he went to the best schools and it cost enough, but I can't complain." And there proceeded a detailed description of the colleges, medical schools, and professional schools that his two children and their spouses had attended.

"Do you have grandchildren?" persisted Lila.

"Two little superstars! Ashley, as smart as a whip and what style; and Michael, throws a ball like a pro."

Lila nodded and drew out their visitor with a series of questions that elicited more gleeful boasting, until finally, depleted of subject matter and with no questions forthcoming from the other two women, he felt obliged to take his leave.

"God help us," exclaimed Flo as the door closed behind him. "Can you imagine being married to that?"

"No!" May laughed.

But Lila was more philosophical. "I think you're being unfair. You happen to have enough to live on, but the fact is that for most women, a man who has some money and can give some security is not so ridiculous. This man is a decent man. Look, he brought May the Danish she liked from New York City."

"Well," said May, "I think he said he liked prune Danish and asked me if I did, too, so I agreed to be polite."

"You see," said Flo, "she doesn't even want the Danish."

"Not the point," said Lila. "He thought of her. He was, in his way, considerate. So he's proud of his children's accomplishments. Is that a crime?"

"Only when we have to serve as the audience," said Flo.

"It's a woman's lot to listen. If the men are more educated, they use fancier words and boast about fancier topics. But it's all the same. They talk, we listen. That is, if they have the money and we don't."

"Well, I'd rather be on my own," said Flo, "wouldn't you, May?"

May, who had never thought to think comparatively this way, failed to respond, but Lila did.

"Well, I haven't that luxury," she declared. "If you're not interested, May, give me his number—I am."

# CHAPTER FOUR

ONCE TAKEOFF FROM NEWARK AIRPORT HAD BEEN ACCOM-
plished, Carol Newman set to work, a confined space thirty
thousand feet above sea level being the ideal forum for her networking skills. Her operative strategy was to bump up against
and ask questions of anyone within any proximity of her. Since
she moved around a lot, this came to include the entire plane.

A man in a leather jacket with a large gold *chai* around his
neck assisted her in stowing her valise and, in the process, recounted how he owned a condominium with his wife in Boca
Vista, only a few miles up the road from Boca Festa. Carol explained about her mother-in-law, recently widowed and alone,
and the man clucked and thought he knew a nice widower, a
little deaf but otherwise in good shape, who might love meeting
May.

A young woman trying to appease a cranky two-year-old was
invited by Carol to share her Alison's crayons. The two children
were soon battling over a box of Chiclets as Carol and the
mother discussed their respective mothers-in-law. The woman's
mother-in-law lived in Century Village but was looking around
for something different. Perhaps she'd want to stop by and see
May's place? Carol would speak to her mother-in-law and arrange it.

Seven-year-old Adam, on his way to the bathroom, stepped
on a man's foot, and Carol insisted that he return, herself accompanying, to apologize. This led to a conversation and the
discovery that Adam's victim, a man in his eighties, lived in Palm

Beach—which meant he probably wasn't Jewish and thus was of negligible interest. Carol didn't pursue the conversation.

Alan had called his old high-school classmate Mark Grafstein and discovered that his friend's father inhabited the fashionable Broken Arrow Club. Carol was impressed. Only the biggest *machers*—Park Avenue dermatologists and real-estate moguls—could afford to live there.

"What I wouldn't give to have your mother settled in Broken Arrow," Carol declared, her determination now greatly intensified.

Carol, it must be emphasized, was not mercenary in any conventional sense. Although she could appreciate a Gucci handbag as well as the next woman, things in themselves did not interest her so much as what they stood for. Above all, she relished a challenge and was always prepared to direct her considerable energy and cunning to meet it.

It had been arranged that when Alan came down on the weekend, they would pay their respects to Norman Grafstein at his club. Carol was not entirely sure how she would proceed from there, but she had a talent for improvisation and enjoyed working under pressure. By the time she and the children landed in West Palm Beach, she had amassed a slew of names from her encounters on the plane that she could add to the contacts her Jersey friends had given her. She hoped to organize something— a little brunch, perhaps, on the Sunday they were scheduled to return home—in which Norman Grafstein, if everything went according to plan, would be present among a bevy of other prospects. With any luck, her mother-in-law would soon be launched on an exciting and productive social life. Luck, as Carol knew, was a euphemism for rigorous calculation, unswerving vigilance, and continual, relentless nagging. The combination had always worked for her in the past; there was no reason to doubt it would do so again.

# CHAPTER FIVE

MAY WAS WAITING FOR HER DAUGHTER-IN-LAW AND GRAND-
children by the luggage pickup. As always, retrieving the valises
and loading them on the carts took considerable time. Though
only down for a week, Carol had not stinted in the packing
department. The children had been well provided with games
and toys and an assortment of coordinated outfits, complete with
vests and cloche hats, that the designers might have concocted
with the express purpose of making small children feel uncomfortable. Carol was one of the few mothers capable of actually
getting her children to wear them, her talent for bribery and
threat being more advanced than that of her peers.

She had also brought two large suitcases of her own that contained a wide range of clothing calibrated to small variations in
the weather. A hot, moderately humid day and a hot, very humid day were two different things with entirely different wardrobe specifications. She had also bought her mother-in-law two
cute outfits that she was hoping to bully her into wearing. May
tended to gravitate to the same off-white pantsuit, and Carol was
determined to get her into something more glamorous.

"You see," Carol declared as she greeted her mother-in-law,
"look at all the work I've done for you—a whole padful of
names. We're going to have a party! Get you into the swing."

"Carol, dear, relax. Stop with the parties. Let me enjoy the
children." May tried to sound forceful, but knew she was no
match for her daughter-in-law. She had recently had a nightmare
in which a large predatory bird, scarily possessed of Carol's face,

had descended from the skies and plucked her up in its very long and apparently very strong talons, carrying her to the top of a tall tree. There had been a vague prospect of painful and embarrassing operations to follow, but May had awakened with a start before they could begin. The dream had probably been inspired by her visit to a spa a few months back—part of a birthday gift that Carol had arranged long-distance through her emissaries. May had been placed on a treadmill for half an hour and had had to be rescued by a young man with an earring. Her poor flaccid muscles, used to nothing more than the short walk from her apartment to the clubhouse, had been thrown into a panic at the prospect of moving briskly for a sustained period on a rolling piece of rubber. The "day of beauty," as it was called, had included an application of acrylic nails, which Flo had helped her to remove the next day, and a deep-tissue massage that had given her aches and pains that lasted a week. Like her son, May was both in awe of Carol and afraid of her, a combination that allowed her daughter-in-law's particular brand of bullying to proceed.

"I don't know . . ." began May tentatively.

"Mom, just leave everything to me. Why do you think I'm here? For my health? I need a Florida vacation like I need a hole in the head. Adam, get over here this minute. Stop kicking Alison, and take the gum out of your mouth—how many pieces are you chewing, anyway? Tie your shoelaces and hold your grandmother's hand." May clutched her grandson's hand for dear life.

"How big is your counter space?" asked Carol as she maneuvered in front of a group of businessmen waiting for a taxi and snatched it away from them with a curt, "My mother-in-law has phlebitis."

"We'll go informal," she continued. "Sloppy Joes. Or maybe bagels and lox. Sunday brunch or Saturday afternoon. Brunch is better. No one has anything to do Sunday and it breaks up the day. You take me to the best deli around and we'll choose together what to serve."

Carol exuded the authority of a general taking stock of troops and artillery before an important battle. It would be hopeless, May realized, to try to resist. She let herself be pushed into the pilfered taxi and sat docilely while her grandchildren fought beside her. For the next week Carol would be taking over her home and her life, and she might as well sit back and accept it.

# CHAPTER SIX

BOCA'S RETIREMENT CLUBS CONFORM TO A DEFINITE SOCIAL HI-erarchy. At the top are the elite residences like Broken Arrow, whose impressively landscaped grounds are hidden behind clipped shrubbery, where a golf membership costs in the tens of thousands of dollars, and where the waiters are never seen without their white gloves and special shoes resembling spats. At the bottom are the more austere, no-frills residences where a large pool and a cavernous card room constitute the major amenities. In between lie a plentiful array of graded facilities, their position in the hierarchy as carefully noted by the local population as the Great Chain of Being by medieval scholars or the circles of hell by the readers of Dante. May Newman, for example, occupied a club somewhere slightly above center—neither ritzy nor shabby, in Boca parlance.

Yet although the hierarchy exists and is scrupulously noted by all residents, there are also extensive linkages among the various levels. In Boca, the degree of separation between any two individuals, instead of holding to the conventional six transitional bodies, never exceeds two, and generally involves only one. As a result, the possibilities for the development of relationships are enormous, as two people sitting next to each other at a restaurant, in a movie theater, or poolside will, in striking up conversation, soon discover that they belonged to the same synagogue in Edison, New Jersey, or enjoyed the rye bread at the same bakery in Jersey City.

There are also the secondary linkages provided through children and grandchildren up north. An unofficial matchmaking operation of grandchildren and divorced children is one of the major industries of Boca Raton—and the number of disastrous blind dates that have resulted from Mrs. Schwartz telling Mrs. Levine about her darling nephew with a degree in theater arts has filled countless therapy sessions on New York's Upper West Side.

The subtleties and intricacies of the West Boca landscape were of extraordinary interest to Carol Newman. She loved meeting new people and was tireless in excavating their lives, mining for the ore of some shared association. Standing next to a middle-aged woman in orange capri pants with a gold and turquoise belt at the Clinique counter of the Saks in Town Center, she moved quickly to establish a connection.

"I love the belt," she said. "I saw one like it in Chico's when I was in Cherry Hill last month. Seeing it on you, I should have bought it."

"You think so?" said the woman. "I wasn't sure. Maybe the gold looks a little cheap."

"Not at all," said Carol. "You were right to buy it. And you couldn't beat the price."

"That's true," said the woman. "You look familiar. You're from Cherry Hill?"

"No, North Jersey, Morristown; I grew up in Bayonne. My husband's from South Orange."

"I'm from Long Island," said the woman, "my husband, too." She seemed disappointed. "But he went out with a girl from Bayonne, if I recall. A Robin Fleishman."

"Robin Fleishman!" screamed Carol. "I went to summer camp with Robin Fleishman."

"You did? Phil said she was a bitch."

"She was!" exclaimed Carol happily.

And so a connection was established and cultivated from there.


Now, as Carol pulled into the parking lot of Mizner Center, the site of Boca's premier boutiques, she surveyed the pink expanse of upscale consumerism as though it were a vast canvas awaiting the imprint of her creative vision. She was fired with the energy of the artist and the questing pilgrim: She would find May Newman a husband or *plotz*.

# CHAPTER SEVEN

CAROL HAD DROPPED MAY AND THE CHILDREN OFF AT A DISNEY film and had come to Mizner to browse. The party she had planned would bring new people into May's ken who were likely to troll for signs of her position in the elaborate pecking order of Boca society. Carol was determined that her mother-in-law's apartment should make a good presentation, and this meant some emergency sprucing up. To this end, she was seeking the shopper's muse.

Shopping in Boca is an activity that falls somewhere between a vocation and a sacred rite. Everyone shops regularly; everyone is a good shopper. This means that the merchandise is copious and, on the whole, reasonable—except, that is, in the area of art and crafts, where notions of value, which Boca women hold to assiduously when it comes to clothing and kitchen appliances, go out the window.

Art objects in West Boca consist, primarily, of distorted-looking pottery in earth hues and large abstract paintings in bright colors—both inspired by installations at the Met and the Modern in the late 1960s, the period when Boca residents first began to see profits from the family business and move to the suburbs. Visits to these museums then became the professed reason for excursions back into the city, though the real reason was the chance to proceed afterward to Peter Luger's in Brooklyn for a good steak or Sammy's Roumanian on the Lower East Side, where one could gorge on twenty-ounce veal chops and *grivenes* with chicken fat on mashed potatoes.

The Boca esthetic is also shaped by the floating apparitional figures and pastel washes associated with the most Jewish of modern artists, Marc Chagall. Everyone in Boca has a signed Chagall print in a place of honor in the living room, and the population is forever trekking off to see special Chagall exhibitions in museums up and down the East Coast.

Finally, there is the importance of the color turquoise as the keynote in Boca-favored artwork, especially for the larger pieces showcased in synagogues and community centers. This color is believed to be evocative of Israel.

Paintings with turquoise accents and Chagallesque thematic motifs are everywhere displayed (alongside ochre earthenware) in white-and-chrome-decorated shops throughout Boca, and are continually snapped up at astronomical prices.

Irving and May Newman had never acquired the taste for Boca art favored by their contemporaries. They had furnished their condominium with objects from their South Orange home and left the walls bare, except for a few modestly framed family photographs over the dining-room table and a more ornate Bachrach photo of the whole family—a kind of *Addams Family* grotesquerie—set flush over the sofa. Carol had been struck by the unprepossessing effect when she first laid eyes on the place.

Carol was thinking about May's apartment during her expedition to Mizner Center. Although shopping among her set was generally an activity severed from the concept of need, Carol, in a form of self-imposed handicapping, preferred to imbue it with a purpose. She liked to have something in mind that she was looking for: a better loofah to remove the dry skin on Alan's back, a binder that would keep Adam's math worksheets in better order, a red-orange bag (with less red and more orange than the one she had) to go with the tie-dyed sequined top that she planned to wear to the Hadassah breakfast next month. The possession of a shopping goal did not prevent the purchase of a myriad of other items, fortuitously discovered in the course of that search, but the goal had a way of focusing and fueling the expedition in a way that was personally satisfying. To find the item in question was to achieve a success, modest though it might be, while not to find it was simply to leave it open for some future expedition and to add to the eventual pleasure of finding it. Either way, there was satisfaction.

On this occasion, Carol was looking for something to add a little style to May's apartment. She wasn't exactly sure what she was after, but she knew she'd know it when she saw it.

Entering one shop specializing in lacquered murals, Carol was greeted by a youngish woman in black stretch pants and a long sweater embroidered in silver thread.

"Gorgeous stuff," said Carol, nodding toward one large canvas in gold and hot pink with turquoise accents on the far wall. "I'd kill for that one."

"My favorite, too." The proprietor nodded. Her name was Sylvia Cantor and she might, given her dress and speech, have been taken for Carol's sister, or at least a member of Carol's synagogue.

"Your place?" asked Carol, looking around, with a glance at the lighting fixtures and the recessed office space at the rear.

"All mine. My life's dream. I said to my husband, It's now or never. Mizner's a natural place. And he supported me a hundred percent. We've been here a year and business couldn't be better."

"Mazel tov," said Carol.

"So what are you looking for? For the living room, the bed-room? Tell me colors, fabrics."

"Not for me," said Carol. "My mother-in-law. She's got a cute little condo in Boca Festa, but no style. Even the bed-spread's a solid."

"I know the type. Jeffrey's mother was the same. She didn't care. I'd say, 'Mother, how can you stare at blank walls? Don't you need some visual stimulation?' It didn't occur to her. With women like that, you've got to remember, they've had a hard

life. Then I brought a couple of my things in, hung them—
didn't even ask her—and what a difference. She loved it. Gave
her a whole new lease on life."

Carol was pleased to have found a kindred spirit, but then,
she found them everywhere. It was as though she exuded a
highly specific odor or emitted a sound outside the range of
normal auditory perception that communicated with a vast army
of like-minded sisters. The two women soon discovered that
they knew several people in common who had gone to the camp
in the Poconos where Sylvia had gone and who belonged to the
Hadassah in Morristown where Carol was vice-president.

Carol assured Sylvia that she would bring May to visit the
shop and urge her to purchase the gold-and-pink canvas. She
also invited Sylvia to the party on Sunday with her husband,
Jeffrey—also an accountant—who would give Alan someone to
talk to, they agreed.

# CHAPTER EIGHT

On Friday afternoon, Carol went back to the airport to pick up Alan. She had arranged for them to drop by Norman Grafstein's club that night, when she planned to invite Norman to the brunch on Sunday. Norman was by no means her only prospect for May; she had met a group of widowers tending grandchildren in the shallow end of the pool yesterday, and they had eagerly agreed to come. At least two of the four had looked to be in good health and prosperous.

Alan opened his eyes when Carol mentioned her plan for a party. "But won't my mother be embarrassed, not knowing anyone?" he asked. He would certainly be embarrassed, and his mother would be in the worse position of serving as apparent hostess. He had a vague suspicion that his mother was shy—not through any real knowledge of her personality, but given that he himself was excrutiatingly so. He assumed he'd inherited large doses of timidity from both parents.

"I'll take care of her; I'll take care of everything," pronounced Carol with a wave of her hand, which she then tucked securely under her husband's arm, steering him confidently toward the airport exit and out to May's car in the short-term parking.

Although Carol had been to Boca only a few times before, she seemed to have memorized the terrain and already knew the best routes to get places. Her capacity for navigation, both literal and figurative, never ceased to amaze Alan, who always needed a map to find his way anywhere.

Alan held his wife's resourcefulness in awe and, in his own

grudging way, loved her for it. Her ability had been forcefully brought to his attention during their first meeting at a Syracuse University mixer seventeen years earlier. The band had been very loud, making it impossible to talk. After the requisite dance, in which she had thrown her arms around his neck as though staking a claim (or, at least, the right of first refusal), she had taken a file card out of her purse and scribbled "Name? Number?" and handed it over. He dutifully provided the information, and she took back the card and walked away. She called the next day and arranged their date—drinks at the Ramada Inn lounge off campus. They were engaged three months later and married a year after that (the engagement being half the fun, according to Carol, and not to be cut short under any circumstances).

It had taken a while for Alan to get used to being married to someone who was always at least three steps ahead in planning his life. But once he did, he found the arrangement distinctly consoling, like inhabiting a world in which predetermination had finally gotten the jump on free will. It helped, of course, that what was predetermined was invariably in support of his best interest and his highest impulses. As aggressive as Carol could be, she also had an instinct for the good and the just.

At the present moment, Alan was counting on his wife to bring her managerial skills to bear on what to him seemed an awkward meeting with Norman Grafstein. His memory of his friend's father was dim, though he vaguely recalled a large and imposing man with an air of prosperous good humor. Mr. Grafstein had owned a leather importing company that had required frequent trips to Italy, of which his son Mark was the beneficiary in the form of pencil cases, belts, briefcases, and other expensive-looking items that Alan had vaguely envied. His relationship with Mark had been largely confined to math class during their sophomore and junior years in high school, where they developed a modest competition as two of the better math students. Alan could still recall the thrill, after receiving back a test with a high grade, of leaning over to Mark and whispering "Whadju get?" in competitive camaraderie. This did not appear to be a sufficient basis on which to found a visit to Mark's father. But Carol was confident, and he could only trust in her better judgment and resign himself to her direction.

# CHAPTER NINE

NORMAN GRAFSTEIN SAT IN THE BROKEN ARROW LOUNGE AWAIT-
ing the arrival of the Newmans. He was puzzled when his son
told him to expect a call from Alan Newman, whom he vaguely
remembered as a shy boy who had sometimes telephoned Mark
to discuss the math homework. But Norman was a genial, not
deeply contemplative person, and the prospect of a visitor hark-
ing back to an earlier life seemed pleasant.

Norman was of a generation of men for whom the condition
of marriage had existed as a given—a kind of neo-amniotic fluid
that it was impossible to imagine withdrawn. One day, two years
ago, it had been withdrawn, leaving Norman on his own for the
first time in his life.

The initial adjustment was difficult but, having adjusted, he
wasn't sure that the idea of marrying again appealed to him.
Over the past year, he had discovered the joys of a belated bach-
elorhood, only now his popularity was greater than it would
have ever been at an earlier stage in his life. From almost the
first week after the funeral, women had descended upon him in
an avalanche. He had discussed the phenomenon with a number
of fellow widowers.

"I never knew so many women existed," remarked one
friend, shaking his head in amazement. "If I want to take a nap,
I have to unplug the phone. It used to be I'd go to the library
or the supermarket and see maybe one or two to say hello. Now
I go to check out a book or buy a loaf of bread, and ten come

up to suggest what to read or that maybe I should get the pumpernickel instead of the rye."

"It's true," said another, "they appear out of nowhere. You're minding your own business, eating your breakfast, and suddenly there's one on top of you, asking you to lunch."

"My advice," said a third, a seasoned widower whom Norman respected for his sagacity, "don't even take their numbers for six months. You're too confused in the beginning. That's what they count on. Later, once you've got your bearings, then you can start going out and having a good time. But play the field. Marriage is a wonderful thing, but once is enough. Who needs the nagging, the complaining, the 'How do I look,' the 'Eat this' and 'Don't eat that.' There's something to be said for the single life. So you don't have the regular meals at home? You go to the clubhouse; these women don't want to cook anymore anyway. Weigh your options; enjoy yourself. There are plenty of fish in the sea."

Norman had taken this advice to heart. His own marriage, though it had its points, had been far from ideal. He'd had little in common with his wife, a frivolous woman who was continually off at the beauty parlor or the mall. She had evinced not the slightest interest in his inner life (though admittedly, until the concept became popularized by TV specials, he hadn't realized he had an inner life). Like so many of his peers, he had married very young, and, as he liked to say when considering the "irreconcilable differences" in his daughter's short-lived marriage, "We made it work." Norman had accommodated himself to Marilyn's habits and personality in the way that he accommodated himself to his most demanding and unreasonable clients.

He missed her—they had shared so much, and there were the children—but was in no rush to return to the benevolent bondage of matrimony. Now that his widowerhood had passed the two-year mark, he had settled into a pleasant social life that included fielding numerous phone calls from women he hadn't

31

seen in years (or had never seen at all) and scribbling appointments in a little black book, the purchase of which had given him a definite thrill.

He had not associated Carol and Alan with further female attention until midway into their visit when, after some reminiscences about Mark and Alan in the tenth grade—stories that Carol had recalled and suitably embroidered—the subject of Alan's widowed mother, May, was casually raised.

"She has a lovely little place in Boca Festa," offered Carol. "Not like Broken Arrow, of course"—she cast her eyes admiringly around the well-appointed club lounge—"but fine for a single woman with modest tastes." She had learned from childhood that all men, especially Jewish men of prosperous means, were wary of fortune hunters and liked women with modest tastes. She herself, during the first weeks of her courtship of Alan, had taken pains to display such modesty as she could muster and had left her flashier outfits in the closet.

Norman Grafstein nodded his head and expressed regret over the death of Alan's father, whom he had met several times at school functions. He had a vague impression of May as a quiet, sweet-natured woman—pretty, in a simple sort of way.

The prospect of the brunch, which Carol delicately proffered as the final piece to her mission, appealed to him not just for himself. Last year his daughter-in-law's father had lost his wife. Stan Jacobs was a man he respected and had come to love, and Norman had watched him suffer a powerful, seemingly bottomless grief. He had tried to console his friend, and had recently begun to urge Stan to pursue a more active social life.

"We can double-date," he had suggested a few months ago. "That way, if you don't like her, you always have me."

"Who says I like you?" said Stan. "But don't give me double-date. The terminology nauseates me. We're not in high school."

"It's a chance for a second youth."

"I don't want one."

"So you just want to brood. Bury the dead, Stan, move on."

"Norman"—Stan gave his friend a penetrating professorial stare, the kind of look that instilled fear in his students—"mind your own business."

Norman had said he would, not entirely meaning it. He continued to use various pretenses to entice Stan out of the house and into meeting new people. The other day he had taken him to a ballgame with a group of lively men and women, friends from his card group, only Stan had excused himself after the third inning and taken a cab home. Here was a chance to try again. A Sunday brunch at the home of an old acquaintance was something that Stan could not easily object to, and Norman was determined to drag him along—an extra man, as he knew, being always welcome at such events.

He looked over at the woman whose mouth, carefully delineated in cranberry lip-liner, was moving in eager solicitation, and at her husband, who clearly would have preferred to be somewhere else, and smiled at them both in the amiable way that had sold all those department-store buyers in New York and Connecticut:

"It would be a pleasure to see May again after all these years. I'm touched that you thought of me. I wouldn't miss it for the world."

# CHAPTER TEN

PROMPTLY AT ELEVEN A.M. ON SUNDAY MORNING, THE GUESTS for the brunch began to arrive. Coming late for a party is an affectation that senior citizens, with abundant time on their hands and a heightened consciousness of carpe diem, have no use for. Carol had positioned May at her side near the door, though it soon became clear that her presence there was superfluous. May was the technical hostess, but Carol was the party planner and *tummler*; she did all the work, welcoming everyone and matching people by background and interest.

"This is Toby—help me with your last name, dear? We met on the plane; and this must be your mother—I'm so glad you could make it. Take a look around. I know you're looking for a place, and Boca Festa has a lot to recommend it. This is Lila, my mother-in-law's friend. She lives in Boca Festa, too, on the other side, pod nine, Eastgate. If I remember, your husbands were both in retail. Lila's from Philadelphia." Carol had the gift of retaining seemingly negligible details about people and summoning them up in unexpectedly useful contexts.

Soon the room was abuzz with talk. A group of women were admiring the pink-and-gold canvas over the TV unit; Carol had insisted on buying it for May, who, no match for the combined bullying of Carol Newman and Sylvia Cantor, had quickly acquiesced. Now Carol grasped Sylvia by the arm and led her over to May to describe other paintings in her shop. Alan, Sylvia's husband, Jeffrey, and a third man with a hearing aid were huddled over Alan's laptop, scanning investment possibilities. Lila was nodding her head encouragingly while Hy Marcus spoke about his daughter-in-law's gourmet-cooking course. A widower in a cap (one of the healthier ones that Carol had sighted by the pool) was making a penny disappear behind seven-year-old Adam's ear and then extracting it from the child's nostril, while two women whom Carol had met yesterday on the supermarket line looked on. Another group of widowers, who had taken possession of the sofa and whom nothing short of a fire bombing were likely to dislodge, were trying to arrange a golf game around the obstacle course of their respective doctors' appointments.

After talking with Sylvia for a while, May retreated with Flo to the side of the room where they stood together, surveying the scene and hoping to escape Carol's notice. If she saw them together, she would step in and separate them. Carol saw no point in talking to someone you already knew at a party.

"Who are these people?" Flo wondered to her friend.

"People Carol found. What can I say?" said May with a resigned shrug.

"Don't explain—I know the type. I had a daughter-in-law like that, only my son divorced her. She made him do calisthenics before they had sex. She was a health nut. Ran ten miles a day, macrobiotic food, special breathing exercises. One day he ordered a hamburger and she had a tantrum. She said she wasn't going to live with anyone who ate a hamburger."

"That doesn't sound like Carol," said May doubtfully. "She eats hamburgers. And she's devoted to Alan—in her way. But she *is* a fanatic."

"Of course she is," pronounced Flo. "Just look at her waving her arms. She's a fanatical arranger. And it looks like we're about to be arranged." She gestured toward the knot of golfers on the sofa, whom Carol was clearly eyeing in the view of hauling them over to meet May and Flo.

"I think you're right," sighed May.

"It's not such a bad thing, you know. It shows concern for you, in a way. My daughter-in-law—the new one—has almost no sense of my existence. The other day she asked me if I was coming up for Yom Kippur. That's eight months away! Of course, she may have Yom Kippur mixed up with Passover. Her grasp of the holidays is weak—to my son's delight."

May was still surprised by Flo's willingness to criticize those close to her. It was a novelty, schooled as she was in the idea that it was undignified to ridicule one's family. Yet Flo somehow managed to get away with doing it without compromising her dignity. May did not think that she could do such things herself, but she appreciated Flo's gift and admitted that it made people seem much more interesting. She was looking forward, for example, to meeting Jonathan Kliman ("my son, the *vantz,*" as Flo called him) and his second wife ("the ice goddess").

"You don't like your daughter-in-law?" May asked, not altogether innocently. She was eager to hear Flo expound further on the subject.

"Like? What's to like? My son goes and marries a girl who is everything I'm not, and I'm supposed to like her? What's he running away from? He says he likes her quiet elegance. Let him buy a piece of furniture. He tells me I'd like her if I'd get to know her. But how can I get to know someone who rides a horse? It's an impossibility. I am never going to get to know someone who rides a horse."

"Flo, you're terrible," laughed May.

At this moment, Norman Grafstein and another man entered the room, and Carol, abandoning the widowers near the TV, rushed to meet them.

"Norman, so glad you could make it." Carol placed her two hands over Norman's one. "Just a few friends. Come, I want you to meet May." The two men were dragged to May and Flo.

Norman Grafstein, who had the rare gift of enjoying himself

in all company, approached May with characteristic expansiveness: "May Newman, you haven't changed a bit. As pretty as ever."

May blushed. She remembered Norman Grafstein as a vocal presence at PTA meetings, where she and her husband always sat toward the back and never participated. How could he remember her? But he did, and seemed genuinely glad to see her.

May introduced Flo.

"Another South Orange fugitive?" asked Norman.

"No," explained May, "Flo's from Newark by way of Chicago. We met through Lila." She pointed to their friend who was sitting across the room and listening, with the patience of Job, to the relentlessly voluble Hy Marcus. Hy appeared to have mastered the technique of certain gifted trumpeters and trombonists who can play on and on without seeming to pause for breath.

"Yes," added Flo, "we three 'hang out' together, as they say. You may have noted that you never see fewer than three widows together in Boca. We travel in packs, like teenage girls. It's an adaptive behavior, since we outlive you men three to one."

Norman laughed, then turned to introduce his friend, who had been standing silently by his side, apparently not amused by Flo's wit: "Oh, this is my friend Stan Jacobs." Norman placed his hand on the other man's shoulder as though he were bringing a large, possibly dangerous dog to heel. "Stan has the dubious honor of being my *machuten*—his daughter married my son. We play tennis every Sunday and I can sometimes beat him, but he always ends by making me feel like his intellectual inferior. I dragged him along to buck up his spirits. He had that hang-dog widower's look, and I thought he needed to go to a party."

Stan Jacobs was a large man with a mop of white hair and a picturesquely lined face. He ducked his head in greeting.

"Stan's an odd bird," continued Norman. "He actually lived down here before he retired."

"Really?" said Flo. "Does Boca have a Jewish population under sixty?"

"My wife wasn't Jewish," said Stan curtly. "She was a Boca native. I moved here to be near her."

"Well, there you are. I knew my statistics couldn't be wrong," said Flo triumphantly. "The lure of a non-Jewish woman is a wholly unforeseen element. It throws off the whole system."

Stan was silent, but Norman chimed in good-humoredly, "Are you saying Stan's a glitch in the system?"

"Absolutely. I can tell he's not a businessman or a lawyer or an accountant. He probably doesn't even have grandchildren living in New Jersey."

"You've got it!" laughed Norman. "Except for the grandchildren—we share one and he lives in Scotch Plains. But you're right about the job description. Stan's an English professor, of all goddamn things. He teaches literature at Florida Atlantic."

"Only one course a year now," said Stan stiffly. "I'm what they call *emeritus*. I teach an elective in the spring to keep me out of trouble."

"An English professor is unforeseen enough for my taste," said Flo.

"What do you teach?" asked May.

"Oh, a range—all of equal indifference to my students, I'm afraid. Mostly eighteenth- and nineteenth-century literature: poetry, prose. This spring I'll be teaching a course on Jane Austen."

" 'It is a truth universally acknowledged that a young man in possession of a good fortune must be in want of a wife,' " recited Flo crisply.

"Are you an Austen fan?" Stan asked, less impressed than Flo felt he should be by her on-the-spot recitation of the first line of Austen's most famous novel.

"I suppose. Really just a reader. When I was young, I read to escape my family. Now I read to escape not having one. I became a librarian because I always felt safest in the library."

"I don't think I've read a book—I mean from cover to cover—in years," announced Norman. "I read the papers and the book reviews. I keep up with ideas, or so I like to think, eh, Stan? But I don't seem motivated to read books, do you know what I mean? I don't have the discipline at my age." He looked at May, who nodded. "And for godsakes, you can't tell what they're about from the covers anymore."

"Do you notice a hidden boast?" Stan responded, gesturing toward his friend with a bit more animation than he had shown until now. "I think he's really proud of not reading. He likes to think of himself as a quick study who doesn't need to pore over books to keep informed."

"Excuse me. I wasn't boasting at all. I'm genuinely ashamed of how little I read, especially when I'm around you."

"If that were true, you wouldn't be telling us about it. You'd be trying very hard to keep us from finding it out."

"Perhaps he's simply trying to reduce the embarrassment by telling us about it before we find out," offered Flo. "I think it's a very effective strategy, and I don't think any less of him for doing it."

"Thank you," said Norman cheerfully. "I hope you don't either." He turned to May.

"Not at all," laughed May. "I agree with you. I wish I read more. I just don't like the books being written now, that's all."

"Then read the older books," said Stan. "Read George Eliot and Henry James and Dickens."

"But what did they think about the Jews?" quipped Flo (she was herself quite partial to these writers but determined to give this pompous man some opposition). "George Eliot, as a woman, understood what it's like to be kicked around, but Dickens and James were anti-Semites to the core."

Stan looked annoyed. "I wouldn't say that. You have to consider when they wrote—and the nature of the characters involved."

"I see," said Flo, "they only hated Jews when it came time to write about money-grubbing, greasy shysters; otherwise they didn't have a problem."

"I think you're intentionally missing the point. Dickens and James wrote great literature that happened to reflect the prejudices of the society in which they lived."

"Prejudices that helped create a climate for the pogroms and the Holocaust."

"Yours is the kind of attitude that has helped keep us in the ghetto, intellectually speaking."

"And their attitude helped keep us there, literally speaking."

"Now, let's not get political," cautioned Norman. "I think you've met your match in this one, Herr Professor." He turned to May, whom he could see was relieved to have him stop the debate, and was about to ask how long she'd been in Boca when he was interrupted by a shout from halfway across the room.

"Norman Grafstein, as I live and breathe!" One of the women whom Carol had met on the supermarket line pushed her way toward them. She was wearing purple harem pants and an enormous quantity of mascara, and might have put serious film enthusiasts in mind of the great silent-screen vamp Theda Bara (really, Theodosia Goodman, daughter of a Jewish tailor from Cincinnati), albeit a good ninety years after her screen debut.

Norman looked confused for a moment and then showed signs of recognition. "Gloria Fox, how are you?"

"Fine," corrected the woman. "I'm fine, too, but it's Gloria Fine."

"Of course," said Norman. "Gloria Fine. Janet's sister. I saw you last at the Weissman bar mitzvah last year."

"It was the Janoff wedding, but never mind," said Gloria, waving her hand. "All I know is that you were one good dancer."

"Years of lessons," said Norman. "No aptitude, but practice makes perfect."

"Well, I remember you had me out of breath that evening," said Gloria, looking sideways at May, who instinctively took a step back. Norman, however, seemed intent on keeping May in the conversation.

"I suppose you know our hostess, May Newman," he said. "Gloria—"

"Fine," said the woman, glancing again at May without much interest. "I can't say I've had the pleasure. Your daughter-in-law invited me. A lovely woman."

"Carol's very friendly," agreed May.

"You're at Broken Arrow," said Gloria, turning back to Norman, as though telling him something that he might have forgotten.

"Yes, for longer than I'd like to admit. We moved down almost ten years ago, and it's two since my wife passed away."

"Time flies," observed Gloria, scrutinizing Norman closely, as though trying to determine where she might fasten herself onto him. "I'm in Boca Lago," she volunteered. "Down the road. You'll have to come visit."

Before he could frame a response, Stan, who had been standing next to Flo without saying a word, suddenly interceded curtly, "Norman, we should get going."

"Ah," Norman exclaimed, pleased to have his attention diverted, "I was wondering when that yank would come. This is my keeper, Stan Jacobs." Norman presented Gloria, but looked over at May and winked. "He keeps me on a very short leash. Whenever I start to have a good time, he knows to butt in and spoil it for me."

"We have a court reserved at five," said Stan without smiling, "and we promised Stephanie we'd call this afternoon to see how she's feeling."

"Stephanie is Stan's daughter and mother of our grandchild," Norman explained to the women. "She's expecting again, and Stan likes to check in to be sure she's taking her vitamins and drinking enough milk. He clips articles out of the paper for her on nutrition and has a whole file on up-to-date birthing techniques."

"That's wonderful," said May, looking respectfully over at Stan. "Most men don't take an interest in such things."

"Stan takes an interest in everything," Norman declared proudly, putting his arm around his friend, who winced slightly. "He's unusual that way. A veritable fountain of knowledge. That's why I let him boss me around."

"I'm his whipping boy," said Stan, showing the trace of a smile. "He can blame me for anything he does that he doesn't like. The devil made him do it, you see, only the devil is his *machuten*."

"You misinterpret. I do what you say because I respect your opinion."

May nodded. "It's part of friendship, like marriage, to give in."

"A woman should try to please a man as much as possible," offered Gloria, staring fixedly at Norman.

"Nonsense," interceded Flo, unable to restrain herself any longer. "A good friendship, like a good marriage, is based on speaking your mind and maintaining independence. I can't see how anything good could come out of one member giving in to the other."

"It depends on how you're brought up," said Gloria with a supercilious look.

"Giving in isn't always bad," said May gently. "Some things aren't worth fighting about."

"But some are," said Flo. "I say"—she addressed herself to Norman—"you should tell your friend to take care of number one and trust your own judgment."

"But I couldn't do that," said Norman. "Stan is always right, so I ignore him at my own peril. You see, we do have a court reserved at five, and we did tell Stephanie we'd call. What's more, little Ben expects it, and one thing a grandparent can't do is disappoint a grandchild."

"Now, there's a point I won't argue with," acknowledged Flo.

"Norman . . ." Stan looked at his watch again.

"Well, it's been a pleasure," said Norman, smiling at them all, but turning quickly from Gloria's penetrating gaze to May's sweet, more timid one. "I know we'll be seeing each other again soon—that is, if I can escape my keeper long enough." He looked at Stan, then tapped his head in a sudden illumination. "Wait a minute—I have an idea! We'll all take Stan's course in the spring. He can't object, since he'll have us under his thumb. He'll even have the satisfaction of getting me to open a book. We'll read—who is it? Jane Austen—together, and Flo here can quarrel with him in front of a group of undergraduates."

May's face lit up. "I'd like that!" she responded happily. Flo caught Stan's eye and smiled, too, but for a different reason: It amused her to imagine how little the idea appealed to him.

# CHAPTER ELEVEN

CAROL DECLARED THE PARTY A GREAT SUCCESS. EVERYONE ATE everything, including the tuna sandwiches, which, she said, were soggy, a fact she intended to relay to the deli owner ("If you don't tell them, how can they know to improve?"). The poolside widowers had even posed a problem in not wanting to leave. They had burrowed into comfortable positions on the sofa, and it had taken a pointed "excuse me" from Carol, as she squeezed by to get her valises, to flush them out.

"I think," said Carol to her mother-in-law, "that you have some wonderful raw material here. It's a matter of working it up." She ran over to straighten May's sofa pillows. "You need a throw to liven up this corner." She gestured toward one of the armchairs near the TV unit. "I'll pick one up and UPS it down."

"Please," said May, "don't bother."

"As for follow-up, let's see: Arrange a little card game for Friday night; have them all over again, or at least those with real possibilities. I saw you talking to Norman Grafstein—well-preserved, rich—pursue him; let him know you're interested. If only I were around here to push you. But you're on your own. I've done what I could."

"And you've been wonderful," said May, kissing her daughter-in-law and gently steering her toward the door. "You need to go lead your own life now."

But Carol seemed to feel that she hadn't covered everything. She stood in the doorway, holding the Vuitton overnight case in one hand and Alison's trainer potty in the other, resisting departure. "Did I leave you Sylvia Cantor's number? She absolutely wants to see you about recovering the sofa. She says she knows just the fabric to pick up the pink in the painting."

"Yes," said May. "I have all the numbers. You've done a wonderful job getting me in the swing."

"Carol—the limo's here. We'll miss the plane." To May's relief, Alan was calling up from the parking lot.

"I want you to use the momentum we've got going," Carol added rapidly. "Call Norman Grafstein tonight. Ask him to lunch. It's not threatening to go to lunch. People go to lunch here like they get a glass of water." Alan had come up from the parking lot and was steering Carol out the door like a guard with an unwilling prisoner. "I'll call you tomorrow to check up . . ." Carol's voice grew faint as she was led down the stairs into the waiting car.

And then, thank God, thought May, she was gone.

# CHAPTER TWELVE

FLO AND LILA STOPPED BY THAT EVENING FOR WHAT FLO RE-
ferred to as a "debriefing."

"Has your daughter-in-law left?" asked Flo, peering in the
door. "I sense a power outage."

"Gone," said May. "They took the five-twenty plane to
Newark."

"That woman has a mind like an overstuffed freezer," noted
Flo. "I've never seen so many ideas packed so closely together."

"You know, she collared me and asked me why I never had
children," commented Lila. "She wanted to know why I didn't
plan better for my old age."

"I'm sorry," said May, "how rude."

"No, no, coming from her, it wasn't rude. I had the feeling
that she was genuinely concerned. More than concerned. Ready
to solve the problem. I thought maybe she could find me a few
spare children for my old age."

"I wouldn't put it past her," sighed May.

"Well, she dug up that Norman Grafstein for you," noted Lila
with approval. "I'd call that a nice gesture. And the other one
didn't look so bad, either."

"Awful," pronounced Flo. "Norman was fine, but the other
one, Stan Jacobs, was a pill."

"Flo was upset because he didn't laugh at her jokes," observed
Lila.

"You were a bit direct," agreed May. "You might have hurt
his feelings."

"Feelings—at his age? It's an affectation to have feelings at our age."

"Men don't like to be made fun of," cautioned Lila, "at any age. Or to think that you might be smarter than they are."

"Well, I thought Stan Jacobs was nice," said May.

"You think everyone's nice."

"Norman said that Stan lost his wife only a year ago."

"So we all lost a spouse recently, give or take a year. I don't see anyone walking on eggshells with us."

"But Flo dear, you come at them with a sledgehammer," said Lila. "A little gentleness is seductive."

"Gentleness does not come as easily to me as it does to May. She's gentle by nature. And I could see that she captivated Norman Grafstein—to his credit."

"Oh, please," said May. "He was only being polite."

"From what I could see, he was very attentive to May," agreed Lila.

"Yes," laughed Flo, reverting to her usual tone, "when a man of that age actually registers your existence and doesn't simply expound to the furniture, you know you've made a strong impression."

"Oh, Flo, you're terrible!" protested May, but it was clear that she was pleased. Norman Grafstein *had* noticed her, and she had to admit that she liked being noticed.

# CHAPTER THIRTEEN

THERE WAS NO CALL FROM NORMAN GRAFSTEIN THAT WEEK, BUT on the way out of the movies at City Place on Friday night, Flo and May (Lila had gone to dinner with Hy) bumped into him with a woman on his arm. May caught sight of him first and tried to maneuver to avoid a direct encounter, but Norman, apparently unembarrassed, hailed them down.

"Ladies, I was going to call," he said jovially, looking at May in particular, "and I will, I promise. Excuse me, this is a friend: Dory Feldman."

"Feldstein," corrected the woman.

"My mistake, Feldstein. She lives at Broken Arrow. We're neighbors." He continued to smile at May with apparent unself-consciousness, as if to say that it was only natural that he would be at the movies with a woman, there being so many of them around.

"Well, we better hurry or we'll miss the movie," announced May, dragging Flo by the arm. Norman had seemed eager to chat, but she hardly felt up to it. She was more pleased to see him than she expected, and more disappointed to see him with someone else.

Once inside, Flo looked at the flustered face of her friend and shook her head. "You're too upset, you know."

"I'm not upset," said May, trying to regain her composure.

"It's not his fault," said Flo. "I'm sure *she* asked *him*. He's been widowed two years. The attention must be over-whelming."

"I'm sure it is," said May sadly. "I don't see why he'd want to go out with me."

"Because you're sweet and modest and delightful to be with," Flo explained. "Because you don't wear bugle beads and your fingernails aren't going to send him to the hospital for stitches."

"I'm not flashy," agreed May, "if that's what you mean. But maybe he likes flashy." She thought of the woman Feldman or Feldstein whom Norman had been with. She was wearing a cape and leather pants.

"I'm just saying that you're naturally attractive, and if I'm any judge, he likes that."

May blushed. "Do you think so?"

"I do. I'm guessing he'll call you tomorrow—unless, of course, he's too busy fielding calls from his admirers. But if he does call, you have to promise to be casual and not take it too seriously. I'm sure he'll want to see more of you, but a man like Norman Grafstein isn't ready to settle down again soon. He's enjoying his popularity."

Flo was right. Norman Grafstein did call May the next day.

"I'd been meaning to ring you up ever since the brunch," he said, "only things got hectic. You know how it is. Obligations and so forth."

May said that she did—though she didn't. Her days, outside of the outings with her friends, were generally empty of commitments, and most of her time was spent, as she said, "puttering around." She had a vision of Norman's life as cluttered with elaborate social commitments of the kind featured on *Entertainment Tonight*.

"I just thought maybe you'd like to come over to the club for a bite on Thursday," he continued in his easy tone. "You can bring your friend, since I know you don't like to drive."

He'd recalled the conversation they'd had at the party in

which May admitted to being one of those dangerous Boca drivers who went under thirty on major thoroughfares. It was the sole area where Irving, her late husband, a man who rarely raised his voice, had lost patience with her. "Put your foot on the gas, for chrissakes!" he used to scream whenever there was a lane merge and she and another car engaged in a tortoise race as to who would get behind whom.

Driving up to speed was a source of stress that May carried with her whenever she took her Ford Escort to the Publix supermarket or the Glades Multiplex, her two principal destinations. The Escort was another project that Carol was working on.

"It's unsafe," her daughter-in-law had declared. "If you have to go American, why not a Cadillac or a Lincoln? Personally, I'd have you in a nice, solid German car—the war's been over for more than fifty years and everyone in Boca has one, even the professional Jews, so don't give me any excuses."

It was on Carol's list that she and Alan would buy May a BMW for Mother's Day. May was against it. She hated to drive, so why spend money on a new car? And with Flo, a confident if reckless driver (they had actually done seventy last week on a trip the three friends had taken to South Beach), she hardly drove at all anymore.

"Bring Flo," Norman repeated, "and I'll try to drum Stan up for another tongue-lashing. Boy, did I get a kick out of hearing her give him what-for."

Flo was more than ready to drive her friend, and May knew enough not to tell her about Stan's possible attendance at the luncheon.

"I'm taking my role as chaperone very seriously," Flo said. "And I admit I'll take enormous pleasure watching the two of you together. From the little I've seen of Norman Grafstein, I'd say that he has a disposition almost equal to yours, which is an amazing accomplishment, if you ask me, for a seventy-five-year-old Jewish man who's been successful in business. Usually, the combination produces someone with the looks of Zero Mostel, the ego of Alan Dershowitz, and the temper of a small, poisonous snake. Norman Grafstein is an exception on all counts."

Driving through the manicured grounds of Broken Arrow, having been properly vetted at an ivy-covered guard-house, May was dazzled.

"It's like one of those old English estates!" she breathed admiringly.

"Please, spare me," groaned Flo in a rare display of irritation with her friend. She credited May for her sweet nature and general good sense, but it was hard not to lose patience when confronted with this kind of esthetic judgment. Granted, Broken Arrow was a top-of-the-line club in Boca Raton, but it was no Blenheim Palace. In fact, it was merely Boca Festa on a grander and lusher scale, with every building material, every decorative object, every amenity ratcheted up to its most expensive version: Where Boca Festa had veneer on the staircases, Broken Arrow had mahogany; where Boca Festa had Corian in the bathrooms, Broken Arrow had marble; and where Boca Festa had a manicured yenta seating guests in the club dining room, Broken Arrow had a tuxedoed maître d'.

Flo was aware of the incongruities of life in the surreal nirvana that was West Boca, but she was of two minds on the subject. Sometimes, as at this moment when confronted with May's schoolgirl effusions, she felt herself rebel against the mock-esthetic grandeur, the weird hierarchical distinctions, and the often provincial mentality of the residents. At others, and particularly when she heard Boca attacked by some of her "intellectual" friends up north, she rose stridently to its defense, arguing that its inhabitants were decent, often fascinating people, passionately devoted to their families, who had worked very hard all their lives and in some cases survived the worst atrocities in world history. They had earned the right to live comfortably together in retirement and enjoy whatever luxuries they could afford. Turning up one's nose at club life in Boca Raton always struck her as a disturbing brand of snobbism that harbored its share of anti-Semitism (or self-hatred, if coming from Jews). That is, except when she indulged in it herself.

Norman was waiting at a table for four near the window as May and Flo entered the dining hall. May was literally agape as they made their way across the intricately parqueted floor and past the tables with embroidered tablecloths and ornate center-pieces of fresh flowers.

"Close your mouth," murmured Flo. "This isn't Chartres Cathedral, for godsakes."

"Flo, be nice," whispered May, seeing that her friend was in one of her moods. She was glad to note that Stan Jacobs wasn't there. Flo was in a state May knew could be dangerous; if she saw Stan and thought she'd been put on the spot, there was no accounting for what she might do.

Norman rose to greet them and, by the miracle of his disposition—a disposition that accounted for his business success more than any particular savvy when it came to calculating the need for leather goods in East Coast department stores—managed to make May feel immediately comfortable and even take the edge off Flo's mood.

"I always say that there are two styles of decor in Boca Raton," said Norman after May complimented him on the beauties of Broken Arrow. "There's the Atlantic City casino look for the more with-it crowd, and the English country gentry look for the old-money types. Old money, by the way, means it's actually been in a bank and not in a pillowcase. That's what we have at Broken Arrow. All the furniture here looks like it's been hijacked from one of those *Masterpiece Theatre* productions. You know how it is—Jewish men really want to be English country lords.

Our fathers wanted it for us, which is why they gave us first names like Arnold, Murray, and Norman—and your husband's, May, wasn't it Irving? All these very pedigreed British *last* names suddenly become upwardly mobile Jewish *first* names. The fact of the matter is that our fathers missed the point. It's the last name, not the first, that counts. We're talking landed gentry, not the gent behind the deli counter."

Flo and May both laughed.

"I can see you've given this a lot of thought," observed Flo.

"I have," conceded Norman. "And personally, if I weren't so lazy, I'd move to the South of France."

"Stop sounding like Flo," said May, with more animation than was common for her. "I think it's beautiful here." It was apparent that she did, Norman noted happily, since he, too, for all his protesting (much of it learned from his friend, Stan Jacobs), liked it enormously. Broken Arrow was pretty much his idea of heaven on earth.

They seated themselves and began to peruse a calligraphied menu that to May was as impressive as an illuminated manuscript when Stan Jacobs walked in. He was wearing tennis shoes and was holding a racket, and had the air of someone who had wandered into the clubhouse by accident and happened to find three people he vaguely knew assembled in front of him.

"Oh, hi there," said Stan. He shook May's hand, but then seemed to lose interest in the amenities of greeting and only nodded to Flo. "I heard that you might be here, and Norman and I usually have a tennis match on Thursdays at two, so . . ."

"Good old Stan, gracious as ever," laughed Norman. "Join us for lunch. Tennis today is off. I plan to drink at least two glasses of wine and give these two fascinating ladies my undivided attention all afternoon. Why the hell would I want to play tennis with you?"

"The court's reserved," said Stan in a tone of mild irritation. "You know how hard it is to get a court here."

"Almost as hard as an audience with the pope," laughed Norman, "and about as desirable, as far as I'm concerned right now. Though perhaps the ladies think otherwise." He turned inquiringly to May and Flo. "We can play doubles if you like. The shop will outfit you in a jiffy." He snapped his fingers. "That's the kind of service we pay an arm and a leg for here."

Norman offered the idea without much enthusiasm, and May, who rarely went into the water above her knees and for whom tennis was as foreign as skydiving, demurred quickly.

"I don't play," she explained, hoping that her athletic incapacity would not diminish her in Norman's eyes. He looked as if he probably did all the sports like tennis, golf, and skiing that she associated with a lively, moneyed strata outside her ken. "But Flo is a wonderful player," she added, hoping that her friend's abilities might compensate for her own lack of them.

"Well, we'll eat first," said Norman, "and then Flo can decide if she wants to play. I hope she does. That'll get me off the hook, and maybe she can beat Stan's ass and really make it worth my while."

Stan looked doubtful about the idea of playing Flo, but he sat down and said nothing. Flo, who preferred the prospect of playing Stan to talking to him, remarked with exaggerated cheerfulness that she was "game for a game," and didn't need anything but a racket from the pro shop since she was wearing her shorts and tennis sneakers.

"I always come prepared, since court time is at such a premium in Boca," she announced. "You know you're retired when you're 'on call' for tennis." She gave Stan a dazzling smile, which, if one didn't know her, might have passed as an attempt to be friendly.

In fact, it had always been a rule with Flo Kliman not to let unpleasant people register on her or cow her into submission. It was a compensatory strategy, she knew, that came from growing up in an era when women were supposed to defer to men. Hers was not a pliant nature, as she had demonstrated fifty years ago when she refused to entertain the banal dronings of the dental student judged by everyone in her circle to be a good catch. She could still recall the tearful pleadings of her mother, mystified by how her daughter, hovering on the brink of spinsterhood at twenty-four, could reject such a prospect. Fortunately, Eddie had come along soon afterward, a man secure enough to withstand a strong woman's opinions and with a taste for combat that made spirited argument part of their marital sport. Flo felt she'd been lucky in her husband, as she had been in her career, but she still suffered pangs of envy when she saw women a generation younger who'd been able to embark more aggressively on their own paths. And her envy turned to awe when she looked at the present generation of young women, as exemplified in her great-niece Amy. Amy was twenty-one, a film student at NYU with an unshakable sense of her own worth and an openness to the possibilities of life that struck Flo as breathtaking. If she could be born again, she often liked to say, it would be as Amy's best friend. Amy, for her part, responded that her great-aunt *was* her best friend, not to mention her most dependable resource for all information (she'd been reaping the benefits of having a librarian for a great-aunt ever since the third grade). The two women maintained a lively e-mail correspondence on topics ranging from shopping to books to the eccentricities of various family members, whom both tended to look upon with a similar mixture of amusement and dismay.

"Have decided that you and I only sane members of family," Amy had written the other day, after a particularly nasty confrontation with her father (Flo's nephew), a successful tax attorney whom both women agreed was sadly lacking in imagination and humor. "Have traced father's problem to failure to learn haftorah portion at his bar mitzvah. Has made cryptic mention of this over the years and always looks depressed afterward. Postulate that teenage shame accounts for years on the couch and inability to have fun."

"Was at said bar mitzvah," wrote Flo in her return e-mail. "Recall no failure with haftorah, though do recall very old rabbi with very bad breath (memory of which may have precipitated depression). Must insist that father/nephew's problems reach back to earlier period. Possibly related to trauma of having insane father, driven so by ball-breaking older sister (i.e., yours truly)."

Flo and Amy found such exchanges endlessly amusing, reinforcing their affinity in a family besieged by rivalries and antagonisms, and giving them a solid anchor outside the turbulence of their own generation. It was a relationship that Flo, for one, valued greatly. Often, while in the midst of an experience, she would find herself thinking about how she would describe it in her next e-mail to Amy.

Such was the case now as she sat over lunch at Broken Arrow. The setting itself, with its look of Windsor Castle as re-created by Aaron Spelling, was good fodder, as was the situation—Norman and May conversing sweetly while she and Stan glared at each other over a sea of cut glass. Surely there was enough material here for a week's worth of entertaining e-mails.

And that was before getting into the food. Flo and Amy had always enjoyed trading descriptions of memorable meals, and the lunch at Broken Arrow was decidedly memorable. The gazpacho was wonderfully piquant; the veal, exquisitely tender; and the apple crisp, quite simply the best apple crisp she had ever eaten— and she had eaten a good deal of apple crisp in her day. Flo had to admit that the meal was worthy of the better restaurants in Chicago and New York.

But since when was this surprising? Food was a prominent feature of life in west Boca Raton. All the senior residences in Boca had noteworthy food: copious, frequent, and lavish in presentation and variety. Food, after all, was interesting. In the elderly Jewish lexicon, it was not just a source of gustatory pleasure and an excuse for getting together and schmoozing; it was a subject for intellectual analysis and debate in its own right, a kind of digestible seminar topic.

"So do you think the potato salad is as good as the potato salad at Don's Drive-In?" a wife would ask her husband, referring to an eatery in northern New Jersey, where they had formerly lived.

"I don't know," he might respond, pausing to ruminate on the question. "This one seems a little grainy."

"I wouldn't say grainy, but there's less mayonnaise. I like mayonnaise in potato salad, as long as it's not mayonnaise-y."

"This isn't mayonnaise-y."

"Did I say it was mayonnaise-y? I said there was less mayonnaise than at Don's."

"Don's was kind of mushy."

"Mushy, no, one thing it wasn't was mushy, but it had more mayonnaise"—and so on, with such conversation expanding to take up an entire lunch and, in some instances, many subsequent lunches. In point of fact it was an exercise in critical exegesis like any other, no different in kind from the study of Renaissance portraiture or the metrics of John Milton. No doubt it had its origin in the hair-splitting commentary that Jews had performed for millennia in their reading of the Torah and the Talmud. Add to this natural analytic inclination the fact that most of the residents of West Boca had esoteric dietary requirements—the result of health problems, bizarre taste preferences, and in some cases, the vestiges of religious dietary law—and the intricacy of food-related conversation could become veritably labyrinthine.

Given the importance of food to Jewish seniors, it was logical that the quality of food would increase as one moved up the hierarchy of residences in Boca, supporting the dictum "You get what you pay for." Where large portions and a varied buffet table were standard fare everywhere, quality of preparation and ingredients marked the vast divide between the lower-rung clubs, where even the non-Egg-Beater eggs were powdered, and the top-of-the-line establishments. Broken Arrow, being at the very zenith, boasted a genuine French chef, trained in both traditional and nouvelle cuisine, who had gotten tired of battling over his second Michelin star and decided to relax in semi-retirement supervising the kitchen in this food-conscious corner on the eastern coast of Florida.

"These people are not chic, but they know their food," explained the chef to his friends, who enjoyed jetting over for a long weekend to sit on the awninged balcony overlooking the golf course, surreptitiously sucking on Gauloises cigarettes and watching the bizarre parade of orange-haired matrons drive by in golf carts. God forbid he should try to pass off a lesser-quality fish in his quenelles; some irate patron, hardly more than four feet tall but with a very loud voice, was sure to storm into the kitchen with the complaint that she was not paying $x$ amount in club dues to be served gefilte fish.

"The meal gets three stars," Flo commented appreciatively to Norman now as they sat sipping their coffee over the remains of the apple crisp.

"That's a great compliment," said May. "Flo is a gourmet and very critical. She walks out of restaurants if the bathroom is dirty." Stan Jacobs looked up from under his bushy eyebrows as if to take the measure, or so Flo thought, of an aging Jewish American Princess.

Norman nodded good-naturedly. "My wife was the same way. Not me. My father used to tell us that a little dirt helps build the resistance. When we were small, if we dropped a piece of food on the floor, we'd kiss it to God and eat it."

"That sounds familiar," said May, laughing.

"The food is good here," said Stan brusquely, "but it's wasted on the likes of you, Norman. You could just as well be eating at a hot dog stand on Coney Island."

"Well, that's true." Norman seemed to give the comment

some serious thought. "Nothing ever beat a good Nathan's frank. But did I hear Stan Jacobs correctly? Has my friend actually something good to say about Broken Arrow? It's a first, so let me enjoy it." He turned to the women as he put his arm around his friend's shoulders and continued, "For all that he spends half his time here, I've never heard him do anything but complain about the place."

"You don't live here?" asked May.

"He lives in a house about two miles away," explained Norman. "You know, that traditional form of shelter where you have to mow the lawn and take the garbage to the curb? It's a nice house, too, though he owes that more to his wife than to him. She had taste. Stan's contribution was the books. He can't move out; the books won't let him. They've taken over, like a nasty weed. Come to think of it," Norman added, winking at Flo, "he could use a librarian. It's gotten to the point that you can't get to the bathroom without tripping over stacks of poetry that lifting would give you a hernia. That's why he's always hanging around here, along with the fact that he has a natural, overwhelming love for me."

"Let's face it," said Stan, smiling at his friend's teasing, "I'm a schnorrer, and you indulge me."

"What's this?" shouted Norman. "Has the refined Stan Jacobs stooped to a Yiddishism?"

"You forget I was the son of a cantor," said Stan, "and weathered ten years of Orthodox Hebrew school."

"Yes, but then you washed your hands of it," protested Norman, "what with 'Mary romping through the heath' or whatever that English literature stuff is about. I know you only love me for my food"—Norman motioned to the remains of the meal before them—"but I don't care. I'll take you on whatever terms you want."

"Meshuggener," laughed Stan, tapping his head and addressing May, who seemed to find the exchange delightful, "and if

he weren't so damn sweet, I'd have nothing to do with him."
They all laughed. May seemed as though she might float away.
The expression on her face, the way she sat, leaning in a little
to listen to Norman's jokes, the ease and liveliness with which
she responded to his quips, made Flo, who had the protective
affection toward her friend of an older sister, feel at once
charmed and concerned. She did not want May to get hurt.

Stan had stood up and, speaking directly to Flo for once, asked
if she was ready for a game of tennis. "I can't sit still in these
clubhouses for too long. What with the food and the atmosphere, I'm afraid they're going to mount me on the wall like a
piece of moderately big game."

And you'd be more appealing up there, Flo thought to herself,
but she got up, too. They'd been sitting for almost an hour after
finishing the meal, and she was ready for some vigorous exercise.
She was also looking forward to the opportunity of beating the
arrogant Stan Jacobs at tennis.

"Let me know if you get tired," he cautioned as they made
their way to the French doors at the back of the dining room.
Although the courts were only about a hundred yards away, the
club had gone all out in the landscaping, and they crossed a small
stream and a little bridge that Flo thought for the life of her was
a dead ringer for the bridge in Monet's garden in Giverny. "Feel
free to call it quits whenever you want," he continued. "It can
get hot out here if you're not used to it."

"I'll be sure to let you know," said Flo with a mock-earnest
smile. She felt a little (but not too) guilty about her bad faith,
and was glad that May, who liked to boast about her, had not
mentioned that she was the Boca Festa tennis champion, that
she played regularly with the club pro, and had even been asked
to play in senior tournaments, though the prospect of going into
training at her age had not appealed to her.

She beat Stan without much effort in the first set, 6–3, and,
as she saw his surprise and the mere grunt that he gave her

afterward, she exerted herself and whipped him more completely in the second, 6-1. She would have gone on for a third but saw that he was seriously out of breath and his white hair was matted with sweat. As much as the man annoyed her, she wasn't about to have his heart attack on her conscience. Instead, she walked forward and stretched out her hand.

"Good game," she said. He shook but said nothing.

"I've said 'Good game,' and now you should say 'Good game,' " she instructed. "Clearly it hasn't pleased you one bit to lose to me, especially since you expected to win easily, but seeing as you did lose and I played exceptionally well, natural courtesy requires that you say so."

"I'm sorry," said Stan, "you're right. I'm just a bit winded, that's all. And it was a good game. You're an amazingly intelligent player."

"So I've been told," said Flo. "Playing tennis is one of the few things I can say that I do well."

"I doubt that."

"Doubt all you please. It's true."

"Then we'll have to play again, so I can get the benefit of one of your few talents," said Stan.

"Perhaps," said Flo archly. She was relieved to see Norman and May strolling toward them, and she raised her hand to urge them forward. Flo considered her match with Stan Jacobs effort expended in a good cause if it would assist the happiness of her friend. But having done her part in allowing May personal time with Norman, she now felt perfectly within her rights to head back to Boca Festa.

"So how did the sparring partners do on the tennis courts?" called out Norman as he approached with May on his arm. "Looked to me like she was beating the pants off you."

"She did," said Stan. "She's a damn good player. You should have told me." He directed this to May.

"I'm afraid I don't keep up with tennis," May apologized.

"But I could have told you that Flo does everything well."

"That's not what she said," said Stan. "She claims to have very few talents."

"Well," said Flo, who felt the discussion had gone on long enough, "if you must know, I'll give it to you succinctly: I play tennis, I read, I do the *Times* crossword in ink, I write a good letter, and I know the Dewey decimal system inside out. But that about covers it. Now, May here has a far more useful and extensive array of skills. She cooks and sews, she's a sympathetic and tolerant mother, and an even better mother-in-law—quite an accomplishment under the circumstances; she's an excellent and supportive friend, a superb bargain shopper, and she grows the best tomatoes I've ever eaten in a planter on the balcony of her condo, in direct violation of club rules—which I take to be a sign of healthy rebelliousness within the proper limits."

"Really?" said Norman to May. "I hope you'll save some for me."

May blushed. "They're just plum tomatoes. Nothing special. I like to garden, that's all, and that's about all I can do here, short of the flowers in the window boxes."

"I know what you mean," said Norman. "We had friends who used to complain about it all the time. They used to say how much they envied Stan and Elsa. Stan's an excellent gardener—his wife taught him, of course, like everything else he can do. He has a wonderful garden in his backyard, though it's not what it was since Elsa died. She made the best rhubarb pie to boot."

"Strawberry-rhubarb," said Stan softly.

"Well, I hate to garden," said Flo, "and I hate to cook."

"I never met a woman who hated to garden," murmured Stan.

"How exciting—now you have," announced Flo, then turned abruptly. "May, we've got to get going. I can feel myself fading as we speak. All I need is to get behind a Lincoln Town

Car going twenty miles an hour, and what with the lunch, the sun, and the tennis, I'll be asleep behind the wheel and Norman will be saying kaddish for us."

"I wouldn't like that," said Norman.

"Then let us go." She turned for a moment to Stan and, extending her arm in a mock-dramatic gesture, declaimed, "Parting is such sweet sorrow." Startled, he took her hand and seemed to be considering what to do with it when she removed it from his grasp, grabbed May, and strode off toward the Broken Arrow parking lot. The liveried attendants quickly brought their car. It was the Escort—Flo's Volvo had overheated after the South Beach trip and was in the shop—and it looked like a poor relation among the imposing Lincolns, Lexuses, and Mercedes. An attendant helped them in and waved them through the iron-and-bronze-filigreed gate onto the highway.

Norman and Stan stood where they had been left, looking after the two women. "Delightful!" Norman declared happily. Stan said nothing. It was unusual for Stan Jacobs not to make a summary comment, but Norman was too content to probe, and the two men sauntered back to the clubhouse in search of a *New York Times* and a cold beer.

# CHAPTER FOURTEEN

ALAN NEWMAN COULD HEAR HIS WIFE ON THE TELEPHONE WITH his mother in the other room. When Carol spoke on the phone, she always yelled, so it was no problem picking up the conversation. He had once asked her, while she was in the throes of a high-volume conversation with one of her friends, to "please speak in a normal voice," and she had replied tersely, her hand spread over the mouthpiece, "This *is* my normal voice." He had not seen fit to raise the subject again.

He could hear her now, excitedly pumping his mother for details: "How many dates? Three?" Carol's voice grew even louder. Norman Grafstein had been her idea. She had done all the legwork. To see the thing coming to fruition this way, and to have it happen at a distance, was a stupendous feat—better even than getting Wendy Wasserstein as the keynote speaker for the Hadassah luncheon last year. Alan sensed that Carol's pleasure would only have been increased had the whole thing been more arduous and taken place in some even more remote locale—had she set up, say, a trappist monk with a nice Jewish girl in the outer reaches of Mongolia.

"Have you had him to dinner yet?" Carol had entered into phase two: planning the capture. "You must have him to dinner, May. You cook so well, you're a natural in the kitchen. The way you bustle around—wear the pink apron with the macramé—it'll make him realize what he's been missing."

There was a silence for a moment. May was obviously explaining her disinterest in catching Norman Grafstein in the way Carol had in mind.

"Don't be silly!" Carol's voice grew irritable—and louder, if that was possible. "Of course you want him to pop the question. You want to live alone in that little condo for the good years you have left when you could be gallivanting around the best Boca club, jetting to Europe twice a year, and taking weekends in New York? I know Norman Grafstein's type. Men like that know how to live. Don't give me that you don't want a commitment. What woman doesn't want a commitment? And don't give me friends. Your friends are there for you because they don't have a man of their own. You let Norman slip through your fingers and, believe me, one of them will snatch him up before you can blink an eye."

Listening to Carol's authoritative pronouncements made Alan feel vaguely uneasy. Clearly he had been snapped up and must therefore have appeared to his wife to be hot property. This came as news to him. It made him wonder if he had assessed his own worth properly and possibly sold himself short. The thought, however—a momentary twitch of vanity—passed quickly. Carol's notion of value was so rarefied that no one, short of one of her equally yenta-ish friends, would have been privy to his qualities. Since he saw no advantage in having one of them over her (indeed, within her circle, Carol was acknowledged to be the best), the notion that he was worth more than he thought quickly dissipated. If anything, Carol had produced the value-added effect. By choosing him, she had greatly enhanced his resale worth. Were she ever to leave him, she would be able to say in good conscience that he would thereafter be advantageously viewed as Carol's ex.

It was strange for Alan to hear Carol speak to his mother about catching a husband. May, married at nineteen to the most dour of men, was unlikely to have an interest in the commodity aspects of marriage. And yet the conversation did not appear to be flagging.

"Lila Katz?" he heard his wife scream. "She's dating that *vantz*, Hy Marcus? Well, she could do worse. Give her my congratulations. You take Norman with you to the wedding. And make him dinner tomorrow night. Something substantial. Use lots of butter—worry about his cholesterol after you're married. I'm going to be expecting both of you up here for Passover. You want to say a few words to your son? He's dying to talk to you. Alan! Alan!"

Alan lumbered to the phone. He always felt that his own conversation with his mother, which circulated through a number of standard questions and answers, was particularly leaden and superfluous after Carol's spirited exchanges.

"Hi, Mom. How're things going?"

His mother's voice was surprisingly animated, more surprisingly in having weathered conversation with Carol. "I'm fine, Alan. I'm feeling well, knock wood. How are the children?"

"The children are fine. Adam has his school play next week." There was an awkward pause. "We're having a cold snap here, so you're lucky to be where you are. Business is the same. Carol's been redecorating the den." He could think of nothing more to say and, impetuously, decided to break from the expected pattern of signing off. "I hear you've been seeing quite a bit of Norman Grafstein," he offered shyly.

"Yes . . ." His mother's voice sounded pleased. "He's a very nice man. We talk a lot about you and Mark. Mark's living in Scotch Plains, you know, not far from you. And Norman's niece lives in Morristown—the name is Schecter, I think; she belongs to B'nai Or . . . I told Carol." She paused. "He's a nice man," she repeated.

Alan, who had initially resisted his wife's plan of introducing his mother to Norman Grafstein, heard the animation in her

66

voice and realized, once again, that Carol had been right. The thought of his mother's happiness cheered him, and his own voice became, if not exactly animated, warmer in tone.

"I like him, too," he said. "I'm glad for you."

# CHAPTER FIFTEEN

"FLO'S IN LOVE!" ANNOUNCED LILA AS SHE AND FLO JOINED MAY at the clubhouse one day.

The idea of Flo in love struck May as unlikely, and, given Lila's penchant for the dramatic, she merely looked over at Flo to have the statement refuted. Flo rolled her eyes but, to May's surprise, also seemed to color slightly.

"She'll deny it," continued Lila, "but I saw it myself. She was actually flirting."

"Lila, calm down," said Flo with irritation. "Just because I respond politely to a man who speaks to me with civility and intelligence doesn't mean that I'm flirting."

"There, what did I tell you!" said Lila triumphantly. "She's saying something nice about a man instead of tearing him to pieces. She must be in love."

May, not altogether in disagreement with Lila on this, turned to Flo expectantly. "Please," she said, "fill me in."

Flo waved her hand as though the idea of describing such things was beneath her, but Lila eagerly took up the challenge. There was nothing she liked more than telling a juicy story.

"Well," she began now, buttering a roll as she started in, "I had stopped to pick Flo up on the way here, and just as we were getting into the car, she realized she'd left her watch at the pod pool this morning. I said she could always get it later, but she said no, she'd rather now, since some *alter cocker* might swipe it and send it as a present to his grandchild. Typical Flo, thinking that way—though I'll admit that if we hadn't gone to get the watch, she might never have met him. *That*"—Lila's voice took on an emphatic tone—"is what they call fate." She paused at this point to take a bite from the roll and order a diet Pepsi from the waiter behind her.

"So," she continued, wiping her mouth carefully, as though preparing it to embark on the next lap of her saga, "we walked down to the pool to get it, and ran into Rudy Salzburg talking a blue streak to another man. You know how Rudy likes to take prospective buyers around the place, show the highlights, and get the rich ones to fork over something for the landscaping fund? Well, there he was with a very handsome gentleman."

Flo snorted. "You think anyone in pants is a handsome gentleman."

"This was a handsome gentleman," countered Lila stubbornly. "You know it, so stop trying to trip me up."

"Okay, okay," said Flo, "he was a handsome gentleman. I'll grant you that."

"Tall, full head of hair, nice shape, well spoken. Rudy introduced us. He said, 'This, ladies, is Mel Shirmer, he's thinking of taking a place in Boca Festa. Perhaps you could say a few words on its behalf.' I, of course, said how wonderful it was here, but Flo, being Flo, said, 'If you want me to tell you it's paradise, I won't. It's more like the waiting room for paradise'—something morbid like that. Rudy looked upset, but Mel thought she was funny. He said, 'A witty lady,' and Rudy seemed relieved and said that Flo was a witty and beautiful and generous lady."

"Yes," said Flo, "my praises were sung."

"Mel seemed to be very interested in Flo right away after that. He said she looked very familiar." Lila nodded as if to say she knew what that line meant.

"Lila, you're jumping to conclusions," Flo interrupted. "He said he worked for the *Chicago Tribune* for many years and so had occasion to use the library at the university. Who knows, but he might have seen me there."

"Flo, be quiet, I'm telling this. So we chat, and he tells us he was a big-time reporter first in Chicago, then bureau chief or something for one of those news agencies. Foreign correspondent, spent time abroad, et cetera, et cetera." Lila waved the hand holding the buttered roll in the air as if to say that this was impressive but boilerplate material, no need to provide great detail. "Not a lot of money—he was up front about that—but since when does Flo care about money?" Lila added this as an aside, since it placed Flo in a different category from herself and therefore outside the realm of competition. "He loves to read," she continued, pressing down a finger on one hand for each point that followed, "speaks several languages, enjoys travel, very cosmopolitan, very knowledgeable. It's a perfect match, if you ask me."

"No one asked you," said Flo.

Lila paid no attention. "He explained that he'd retired a few years ago, though he still does some consulting for the big PR firms, to keep his hand in, as he put it. But he thought it was time to finally get a place down here: enjoy the sun, relax, maybe write his memoirs." Lila gave a particularly knowing look as she delivered this last point—memoir-writing being, she knew, just the sort of thing likely to impress Flo. "Anyway," she concluded briskly, "he's joining us for lunch. He seemed so taken with Flo that he as much as invited himself, though she kept her claws in for a change and was gracious about it."

"All right already," said Flo. "I'll admit that he seemed nice, and with the added novelty of being able to make intelligent conversation."

"And he's coming to lunch?" asked May. She was eager to meet the man who had impressed her fastidious friend.

"He said he just needed to make a few calls and, if we didn't mind, would join us in a few minutes," explained Lila. "It will give him a chance, he said, to check out the food. He and Flo had some jokes about how we Boca-ites live for food. As I say, they were very sympatico." She raised her eyebrows meaning-fully while Flo rolled her eyes again.

"A widower?" asked May delicately.

"That or divorced," said Lila. "But certainly available. No ring. I looked."

"Of course you did," said Flo.

"And very solicitous of Flo."

"You said that," said Flo.

"And I'll say it again."

The women were halted in their exchange by the sight of an imposing-looking man with a thick head of salt-and-pepper hair entering the dining room. Lila put her hand up in the air and waved. "Mel, over here!"

"He sees us," said Flo. "No need to make a scene."

Mel smiled and walked over to the women. He was an ex-tremely good-looking man in his early seventies, with an easy, graceful manner and a warm smile. He moved to the chair near Flo, but not before extending his hand to May. "I've met your companions, but I've not had the pleasure." May introduced herself. "I must say that I wasn't expecting to have lunch with three ladies," said Mel. "Not that ladies are in short supply in Boca"—he smiled wryly at Flo—"but good company and good conversation, I'm afraid, often are. It's what's been keeping me from moving down for several years now."

"I know what you mean," said Flo. "If it weren't for my friends, who enjoy poking fun at 'our people'—or at least in-dulge me in poking fun—I don't know what I'd do."

"Well, I can see I'll have to become an honorary member of your group," said Mel, "if you'll permit me."

"You can join right now," said Lila. "Sign on the dotted line."

Mel laughed. "I confess that I'm thinking seriously about buy-ing a place in Boca Festa. I'd looked at Boca West several years ago. It's expensive, but not entirely out of my range. But the place is too pretentious for my taste. Boca Festa seems less so."

"Yes," said Flo, "we're very 'down home' here."

Mel laughed again. "I'm told that the differences between the clubs really aren't that great. But you learn to distinguish, I'm sure. Freud called it 'the narcissism of minor differences'—rivalries and such that break out between peoples that are very much alike. I suppose that it's that way here in Boca."

"Exactly that way," agreed Flo. "We are having an ongoing war with our neighbors in Boca Lago. We fear that they may have a step up on us in the quality of their aerobics instruction. We have spies and counterspies trying to get at their secrets and steal their instructor, the curvaceous Kim, and there's a move underfoot to redecorate the workout room since they did theirs last spring."

"Well then, maybe I can be helpful," joked Mel. "I did some intelligence work—very small scale—when I was stationed in Saigon years ago."

"Were you really a spy?" breathed May.

"Well, they asked me to ask a couple of extra questions in an interview I was scheduled to do, that's all. It doesn't quite qualify as spymaster, but there were some cables from the CIA and a debriefing in Washington afterward. More exciting, I'm afraid, in the telling than in the doing."

The women looked impressed by the telling.

"Have you checked out all the clubs, then?" asked Lila. "It's flattering to think that you're inclining toward Boca Festa."

"As I said, I've spent time at Boca West and I know people at the Polo Club and St. Andrews."

"Broken Arrow is very nice," volunteered May.

"Nice, yes," agreed Mel, "but I hear it's one of the snobbier ones. If you don't wear the right shoes with your tuxedo, they boot you out—excuse the pun."

"May's partial to Broken Arrow," explained Lila. "She has a friend there."

"Norman Grafstein is not a snob!" declared May more adamantly than was usual for her.

"Norman Grafstein, is it?" said Mel.

"Do you know him?" asked Flo, noticing that he frowned slightly at the name.

"Not really," said Mel. "I've heard of him, but we've never met."

Hy Marcus arrived at the table at this point and began pelting their guest with tales of his family. When Mel mentioned that he was looking at Boca Festa as a possible home, Hy's boasting turned in that direction:

"They do a good job with the food, the decorating is top-notch, and the grounds couldn't be better," declared Hy. "Take it from me; it's the best club for the money."

"I believe it," said Mel. "Some friends of mine in the area spoke highly of it. I'll admit that for someone like me, used to the large cities"—he nodded at Flo, as if assuming she shared his view—"this will be quite an adjustment. But I'm ready for a rest, and it helps to know that I'll find some lively minds if I decide to settle down here." He glanced at Flo again, and May noted that, for the second time, Flo colored.

"Let me invite you to check it out further," urged Hy magnanimously. "Breakfast, lunch, dinner, come when you please. Just say you're my guest and look for us. I usually spend two hours here at every meal, noshing and making the rounds, so you can't miss me."

"You're too generous," said Mel, putting his hand on Hy's arm but directing a quick smile at Flo. "I may take you up on that offer."

Flo had to admit that for once she was grateful to Hy Marcus for being the voluble fool that he was.

# CHAPTER SIXTEEN

THE APPEARANCE OF MEL SHIRMER AT MEALS IN THE BOCA FESTA dining room over the next week was a source of pleasure to Flo. They were rarely alone; what with the constant presence of Hy, Lila, and May, not to mention an assortment of others whom Hy was always asking to take a seat, there was less occasion for prolonged talk than she would have wished. Still, they spoke enough to confirm Flo in her initial opinion that Mel was an unusually educated and worldly man for Boca Festa. One day he came in with John Le Carré's *Tailor of Panama* under his arm.

"Do you like it?" asked Flo. "I found the movie intriguing."

"Missed that, I'm afraid, and haven't started the book yet, but I've been meaning to read it for years. Did a brief stint way back when I was bureau chief for AP in Panama, and I'm curious to see if Le Carré got it right."

"It sounds like you've led a very exciting life," noted Flo. "You must miss the travel and the personalities that you met as a foreign correspondent."

"Yes and no," said Mel. "It was an exciting life, I'll grant you, but hollow in many ways. It was skimming the surface, never penetrating to the deeper stuff that calls for time and commitment. I regret that I never really worked at a relationship."

They were interrupted at this point by a question from one of the women at the table about whether Mel had really been a spy, a fact that had spread like wildfire through the club after Lila had mentioned it casually to Pixie Solomon. There followed an animated conversation on Jewish spies, many residents having read the book about the baseball player, Moe Berg, who had been a spy during World War II. The reference to Berg elicited at least three repetitions of the familiar joke: "He could speak ten languages, but he couldn't hit in any of them" (a quarrel ensued as to whether it was ten or thirty languages).

The next evening, when Mel appeared at dinner again, Flo found their conversation moving in the same direction as it had the day before.

"I feel myself a bit out of water here, I must say," he confided as pictures of grandchildren were passed around the table. It had happened, as it always did, very quickly: No sooner was one photo extracted from a wallet than the rest at the table had theirs out, as though they were all members of some secret society and had been asked to show identification.

"Yes," agreed Flo, "I've considered clipping pictures of a few cute kids out of a magazine so that I can take part in the ritual. Of course, I'd have to provide the supporting commentary on Little League and ballet lessons, and IQs that are off the charts, but I think I have enough gift for fiction to be able to do it. Given free reign, I could concoct something that would blow the competition out of the water."

Mel laughed, but then continued more seriously: "It's a regret I have, I must say. A grandchild would be nice to carry on the Shirmer legacy—whatever that is. But then, I would have needed a child as a prerequisite, and that, I fear, was beyond me when it would have been feasible. I didn't want to be pinned down. That's what doomed my marriage. The poor woman wasn't up to packing off for Costa Rica or Zanzibar every few years, though she had no trouble, I must say, with Paris and London."

"I'm sure it's difficult for the person who has to tag along," admitted Flo, "but if you're blessed with the opportunity to lead such a life, it would be hard to give it up for more domestic pleasures."

"That's how I felt, of course," said Mel, "only now I see more to those domestic pleasures than I did."

"It's not unheard of for a man your age to start a family," said Flo innocently. In point of fact, she was among the most vocal critics when men upped and had children in their sixties and seventies—"trophy children," she called them when speaking of this with Lila and May. "It's disgusting." But she was interested in hearing how Mel would respond to the idea. As she saw it, he was certainly attractive enough to hook a much younger woman.

"Nah," said Mel, in response to her suggestion that he have children now, "that's not for me. First, I may like the idea in theory, but if I didn't have the patience when I was young, I certainly wouldn't have it now. Second, I'm immune to the attractions of the younger woman. I find that I like mature conversation; it's something I'm unwilling to give up."

Flo said nothing. She was secretly glowing with pleasure.

"And you?" asked Mel. "You've said that you don't have grandchildren; what about children? You hardly look like a woman who would deprive herself of—what should I call it?—that great adventure. For women, I often think, it is an adventure, while for men it's simply a spectator sport."

"I have one child," said Flo, laughing. "One of those adventures was enough for me. And you're right, I have yet to be graced with the glory of a grandchild. Jonathan, my son, has the good sense to realize that he needs to mature a bit before inflicting himself on some innocent child."

"He's still finding himself, I assume?" asked Mel sympathetically.

"Oh, no, on the contrary. Perhaps he found himself too soon. He made a fortune with one of those new Internet companies right after college. He'd been what they call a nerd in high school; suddenly he was the most popular man at the party. He's thirty-eight now—chucked his first wife from the nerd days and married a debutante, to the envy of his high-school friends. I think he married her to provoke that envy."

"Well, it must be nice not to worry about him, financially speaking at least," noted Mel.

"I suppose you're right," reflected Flo, "but it's hard to know what to worry about with Jonathan. He spends half his life playing video games. He says it's the future of mass entertainment, and it's where he plans to make his next investments. He may be right, but then again, as I told you, he's not mature."

"The world belongs to the immature," observed Mel, "but counsel him to be careful. A bad investment can wipe you out. Fortunately, I haven't had the kind of income that would lend itself to those problems. I've never wanted for anything, but rich I'm not—you don't go into my line of work for the money."

Flo nodded. "I admire you for that. Money seems to me to be a highly overrated commodity."

"I agree," said Mel, "but it's always nice to have it. There's an old Yiddish saying my grandfather used to tell me: 'With money in your pocket, you're wise and you're handsome—and you sing well, too.' "

"Well," said Flo bluntly, "you seem to sing pretty well to me."

# CHAPTER SEVENTEEN

THE NEXT DAY AFTER LUNCH, HY PROPOSED CHEERFULLY, "WHAT do you say we keep this lively group going and play a hand or two?" Flo and Mel were among some six or seven people who had been at his table, most of whom seemed pleased enough to recess to the card room near the pool. Mel, however, hung back, clearly looking to Flo for his cue.

"Count me out," she said briskly, "I don't play."

"You don't play cards?" Mel seemed surprised.

"I'm afraid not. My husband did. It was the occupation he had in mind for his declining years."

"I'm sorry," said Mel.

"Don't be. Cards are a leisurely game—something Eddie wasn't. He liked to rush off to meetings, yell on the phone, and have four secretaries running around looking for the sheet of paper that he just put down. In my dreams, I still hear the phone ringing."

"It sounds like a hectic life."

"It was. Fortunately, I spent my working day in the library. It was my chance for peace and quiet. Our tastes in that respect were very different, but we got along."

"I suppose you complemented each other."

"Yes. He was the noisy lawyer; I was the mousy librarian."

"Mousy, no."

"All right, not mousy; say 'cranky.' "

"I wouldn't say that, either. I'd say 'feisty.' "

"That's what Eddie used to say." Flo's voice grew wistful—
for Flo.

"You must miss him terribly."

"I do miss him," said Flo, regaining her matter-of-fact tone,
"but not terribly. I don't miss anything terribly. I take life as it
comes."

" 'Life is a dream,' as the Spanish philosopher said."

"Oh, I think it's real, but it's a reality we get on loan, and
we need to remember that. My Eddie had a good life. He did
everything he ever wanted."

"Except play enough cards," noted Mel.

"Except play enough cards. But as I say, I don't know that he
would have wanted to play more."

"You're a wise woman."

"I'm a realist."

"Whatever you call yourself," concluded Mel, "I like it. I'll
tell you what, I'll play hooky from the card game, if you'll let
me walk you back to your condo."

"I will," agreed Flo, "but be prepared to get the once-over
from everyone between here and pod nine. Walking along the
road in Boca Festa is like strolling the grand boulevards in Paris
in the nineteenth century. You'll be seen and you'll be talked
about."

"So much the better," said Mel gallantly. "I can't think of
anyone I'd rather stroll the grand boulevards with than you."

# CHAPTER EIGHTEEN

Toward the end of the week, Flo asked Mel if he was interested in going to see the documentary about New York intellectuals being shown at the Jewish Y downtown. Flo was secretly pleased that May and Lila had begged off. The film was just the sort of thing she thought Mel would enjoy, and it would give them a chance to be alone away from the familiar scenery of Boca Festa.

She asked him when she saw him at breakfast that morning. He had taken to having all his meals at the club and had let drop that he was seriously considering a spacious two-bedroom in pod 9 of Eastgate, not far from Flo.

"They say it contains fascinating interview footage with Daniel Bell, Irving Howe, Irving Kristol, that whole City College crowd," Flo explained of the documentary.

"I'd love to come," said Mel. "I remember reading the review in *The New Yorker* and wanting to see it. I'm impressed that the film got here so fast. Sometimes I think that Boca may be a suburb of New York City. The restaurants are almost on a par, and you get the good movies right away. It's gratifying to know that, living here, I won't feel culturally deprived." Flo said nothing, but was pleased by the implication that Mel had decided to make the move.


When they arrived at the Y that night, the place was packed. Flo was reminded, as she often was, of the intellectual vitality that characterized so many of the area's residents. Even the uneducated ones, who had spent years doing back-breaking, quasimenial work, managed to keep abreast of events and to entertain ideas. The number of film festivals and lecture series going on in Boca at any given time supported Mel's observation that it was a far-flung borough of New York City. And if perchance there happened to be a Jewish theme or character involved in the entertainment, interest was likely to reach a fever pitch. Famous in this regard was the screening at a Boca theater some years back of *Schindler's List* when the film broke midway through. The audience, many with walkers and some with oxygen tanks, had been so incensed by the disruption that a small riot had ensued and the police had to be called in to calm things down. Such passionate involvement was a hallmark of the Boca population. Flo felt, all things considered, proud to be associated with people capable of such enthusiasm, who were determined to remain culturally "in the swim" despite age and illness.

She and Mel had arrived at the Y on the late side and were among the last to get tickets. As they entered the auditorium and walked to the back of the room where a few empty seats remained, Flo saw Stan Jacobs, Norman Grafstein, and a woman seated near the aisle in one of the rows. She stopped to say hello, introducing Mel to Norman, who shook hands amiably. But when she turned to repeat the introduction to Stan Jacobs, he nodded without offering his hand. Mel, though uncomfortable with the situation, continued to stand by her side and maintain a smile.

"Stan dragged us here," declared Norman. "Usually I like to stay in on Sunday night." Flo noted that he spoke louder than usual, as though covering his embarrassment at not having asked May to come. "Stan insisted, though," he continued, blusteringly, "so I dropped everything. He says the New York intellectuals are the Jewish founding fathers. They drew the map for— what is it?—cultural achievement in the second half of the twentieth century." He turned to Stan for verification on this, and Stan nodded stiffly.

"Oh, by the way," Norman added, as though suddenly remembering, "this is Nina Ratner." He gestured sheepishly to the woman next to him.

"Rivkin," corrected the woman.

"My mistake, Rivkin," said Norman. "Nina's a friend of a friend," he explained. "I take it May wasn't up for this kind of thing."

"No," said Flo, "she was tired and wanted to spend the evening at home."

"I understand completely." Norman nodded. "I generally find documentaries to be very boring. Except that one they showed here a while back on Hank Greenberg. Now, that was first-rate. I could see that again."

Flo, who had missed the documentary on Hank Greenberg, said that she had heard it praised by the men in Boca Festa, who always succumbed to a dreamy reverie in speaking about it. Hank Greenberg was every older Jewish man's idol. Forget Bellow, forget Brandeis, forget even Einstein. If these men had a choice as to who, from among their people, they would most want to be, it would be Hank Greenberg every time.

"Flo, we better find our seats," said Mel. It was clear that the program was about to begin. The master of ceremonies, an intense, dwarfish man who ruled special events at the Y with autocratic zeal, had scuttled to the front and was raising his hand for attention. He was now giving background on the New York intellectuals in a voice in which the accents of Brooklyn had been seamlessly blended with the intonations of an Oxford don.

"We have a special treat for you this evening," expounded the man with relish. "This film will give you an inside look at what was going on at *Partisan Review,* at *The Nation,* at *Commentary* during those turbulent years of intense creativity that we've all heard so much about. There was a lot of thinking going on then, and a lot of fighting—two things, if I may say so, that we Jews do very well." There was laughter and a general nodding of heads as the proper *haimisha* tone was established.

"That Stan Jacobs is insufferable," Mel whispered as they sat down.

"Do you know him? Is there a problem between you two?" asked Flo, genuinely eager to hear.

"Who knows? A rivalry, mostly in his head." Mel paused. "When I was down here last, we knew people in common. He always seemed to resent my influence with them. He couldn't stand having his word challenged."

"I've seen that side of him," acknowledged Flo.

"Although I have no proof," continued Mel, "I suspect that he worked behind the scenes to deprive me of a plum job—a chaired position in journalism at Florida Atlantic that would have been a nice way to ease into retirement."

"That's horrible!" exclaimed Flo.

"Yes, it's why I left the area a few years ago. I went right up to Washington and did some consulting for a PR firm there; put my nose to the grindstone, made some money for a rainy day. Then, a few months ago, I said to myself, 'Enough! Now's the rainy day. I'm tired, worn out; I want sun; I want poolside. The hell with Stan Jacobs,' I said to myself. 'Boca isn't all Stan Jacobs.' "

"But Norman Grafstein's such a sweet man; how could he be devoted to someone like that?"

"That's the thing. Jacobs has a powerful personality. He can be quite charming when he wants to be and, to his credit, fiercely loyal to his friends, so long as they kowtow to him. I can't say I know Norman Grafstein; he seems like a nice enough fellow. But some people, weak people, feel flattered that Jacobs gives them attention, and develop a kind of slavish devotion."

"I knew he was arrogant, but I didn't think he was that narcissistic!" exclaimed Flo.

"I can't say I know what to call it," said Mel. "I only know that he's not a man I like to see, though he's the one who has reason to dread the encounter. It's *his* conscience that should suffer. It's certainly not going to get in the way of my happiness." He looked into Flo's eyes for a moment and then, as if not wanting to expose his feelings too fully, turned abruptly to the screen, where the documentary had gotten under way.

Flo also turned to watch the film. Diana Trilling was talking about how she and Lionel had broken ranks with the New York intellectuals over Stalin. It was a topic that would normally have held her interest, but now she could only think of Mel's appreciative look, and of what he had told her about Stan Jacobs's malevolent plotting.

# CHAPTER NINETEEN

FLO FELT IT WAS IMPERATIVE TO TELL MAY WHAT MEL HAD SAID about Stan. She had no wish to cast aspersions on Norman, but she thought the story had indirect bearing on him and thus was something May should know. She was further troubled, though she didn't mention this to her friend, by Norman's appearance at the Y with another woman. Albeit a casual date, it indicated to Flo that Norman was still playing the field.

"I can't believe it," said May when Flo told her Mel's story. May had developed a true liking for Stan and often conversed with him about gardening, a passion they shared.

"So what are you saying—Mel is lying?" demanded Flo.

"No," said May, who liked Mel, too, "I think there's probably been a misunderstanding and that each one has gotten the wrong impression about the other."

"Oh, May," said Flo with some exasperation, "you need to take mean lessons. You couldn't see bad in a person if they rubbed your nose in it."

May shrugged. In fact, she couldn't begin to imagine how anyone she knew could be bad. "Bad" was what you saw in the movies; real people, if they weren't good, were good enough. She put the best construction that she could on everyone's be-havior—or simply failed to notice if they treated her shabbily.

"Stop telling me to be nice," Flo responded irritably when May urged her to take a kinder view of others. "It's not in my nature. It's one thing to appreciate you, another to be like you.

I can appreciate a good meal, but I can't cook one—and if I can get you to do it for me, why should I?"

May told Flo that she was nicer than she thought (which was what nice people always said), and continued looking through her drawers for a good recipe for borscht. Flo had received an e-mail the day before from her great-niece Amy with the succinct demand, "Send recipe for borscht ASAP." From anyone else, such a message would have seemed bizarre, but knowing her great-niece as she did—which is to say, knowing that she could as easily be competing in an Eastern European cooking class as trying to impress a Russian boyfriend—Flo simply went about fulfilling the request, assuming that she'd get the background in subsequent e-mails. She herself had never made borscht in her life, but tracking down information was her stock and trade, a fact that Amy had long understood and taken advantage of. In this case, May Newman was the obvious place to go for what was needed, and Flo now stood waiting while her friend riffled through a stack of possible recipes.

"Just pick one!" Flo ordered in exasperation while May considered the relative merits of this one and that one. "We're not writing a dissertation here."

"Be patient. I don't tell you how to do your work," responded May with a certain defiance. "Here." She handed a recipe card to Flo. It was, she declared proudly, the simplest and most dependable borscht recipe to be found anywhere; Amy couldn't go wrong with it.

Flo took the card, squeezed her friend's hand, and sighed. She had gotten the recipe for her niece, but she had not been as successful with the other part of her errand. She had not managed to prepare May for possible disappointment from Norman Grafstein. May was simply too nice to take a hint.

# CHAPTER TWENTY

A FEW DAYS AFTER THEIR Y OUTING, FLO WAS AWAKENED BY A very early phone call.

"What are you doing today?" It was Mel Shirmer.

"Let's see," responded Flo. "I was going to work a bit on my novel, perfect my cure for cancer, and then, possibly, whip up a gourmet meal for fifty."

"Good. Then you'll have time to come with me to the casbah."

"Well," ruminated Flo, "I do like Charles Boyer. . . ."

"Then you *will* come with me to the casbah?"

"It depends where the casbah is," said Flo warily. "There are places I definitely won't go. If the casbah is Disney World, for example, count me out. I don't do cute with anyone over six."

"I assure you, my *liebchen,* that the casbah is not Disney World," said Mel. "More than that, I will not say."

"Should I take a bathing suit, oh mysterious guide?"

"Of course, and a little overnight case as well, in the event we should want to linger. The casbah, you see, has many attractions."

Flo was a bit nonplussed by the prospect of an overnight stay, but she put a toothbrush and an extra pair of underwear into the bag with her bathing suit and towel—just in case, as she put it smirkingly to herself. She was old enough to find her own tricks of self-deception amusing.

———

It was a beautiful day when Mel pulled up in his Corvette convertible. Flo considered the Corvette a ridiculous car, and she believed a convertible of any sort was dangerous and should be kept out of the hands of people over sixty. But with Mel, somehow, she made an exception. He had the romance of the maverick about him, and the car did not seem like an affectation so much as a natural extension of his personality. Had he shown up on a motorcycle, no doubt she would have accepted this, too, and climbed on behind him without giving it a thought.

"I feel like I'm seventeen, being whisked away to play hooky by the high-school quarterback," said Flo, looking at Mel's handsome profile as they sped off.

"Not football, I'm afraid, swimming—the Jewish contact sport. I wanted to play football, only my mother wouldn't let me. I was too precious, she said. She held my price very high, you see, which spoiled me for hard labor."

"The standard recipe for the Jewish prince," observed Flo. "But you seem to have accomplished a great deal, all things considered, and turned out better than most."

"I don't know about that," laughed Mel. "I've certainly done what I liked, though whether I've done well is another story. And if I've turned out better than most, it depends on 'the most' you're talking about."

"Well, Stan Jacobs, for one. He seems to me your antithesis. Perhaps his mother didn't dote on him enough."

"It's possible. But his wife did," said Mel, frowning. "She worshiped the ground he walked on, and expected others to do the same. It was a trial being around them: self-love bolstered by hero worship."

"It sounds intolerable. Why did his friends stand for it?"

"The power of self-promotion, what can I say? And the appeal of fraternizing with a professor—a role he played to the hilt, let me tell you. You're right about one thing. You couldn't find two more different people than Stan Jacobs and me. Have you seen him since our unfortunate encounter?"

"No," said Flo, "though I expect I will. I drive May when she meets Norman at Broken Arrow, and Stan tends to show up."

"He'll probably try to bad-mouth me. Promise you won't be swayed."

"I won't," said Flo. "I have a mind of my own."

Mel turned his head and smiled admiringly at her, then changed the subject: "I've been looking seriously at a place in Boca Festa, as you know. I like the club and your friends, but I would have thought someone like you might seek more—how shall I say?—'elevated' company."

"They're not highbrow, if that's what you mean," laughed Flo. "I find I can get enough highbrow from reading good books."

"I'm not talking education, so much," said Mel, "but—well—style, class, if you will. The folks at Boca Festa are burghers, simple shopkeepers; plain people."

"As opposed to, what, fancy people?"

"Not fancy, sophisticated. People with some worldliness, some experience and savoir faire."

"Rich people?" asked Flo. "Boca Festa isn't the Polo Club, if that's what you mean, though I thought you found those people snobby. Some Boca Festa residents are very comfortable; you'd be surprised."

"I'm sure I would. And I'm not pushing the Polo Club. I know the place, as I said. It's really no different, though there's more posturing. It's that I imagine you in a more refined environment. When I see you with Hy Marcus, I want to laugh."

"Hy's a fool, I grant you, but a sweet fool."

"That's the question: At our stage in life, do we want to mix with fools, sweet or otherwise?"

"You think we should be more discriminating at 'our stage in life'?"

"I do. You know what the poet says: 'And at my back I always hear time's winged chariot hurrying near.' I hear it, all right, and it's starting to make quite a racket. Times's running out for us, my darling. We need to use what we have left with—yes, to be blunt about it—discrimination; not waste our time with fools." Mel's voice had taken on resonance as though he had tapped into a deep well of private conviction. "I want my last years to be like a well-edited story or a fine, short poem," he continued. "No fat, no excess; just pure, undiluted quality. That, my *liebchen,* is why I like you."

Though his tone had grown lighter again, Flo felt the force of his words and was silent.

They were heading west on Alligator Alley, and Flo deduced they were on their way to the exclusive towns on Florida's west coast. Once off-limits to Jews, these enclaves had recently been stormed by those looking to reduplicate the habits of earlier inhabitants and escape undue proximity to their peers. The west coast was also the site of some breathtaking scenery. Flo had visited several times, the last with Amy, who at twenty-one was finally too old for Disney World. Amy was partial to nice landscape and to the spectacle of what she called "a good stretch house"—that oversized habitation that was the house equivalent of a stretch limousine.

"Mom and Dad are thinking of taking a place out here," Amy explained when they drove past the mansions in Naples during an outing last spring. "Daddy wants to lord it over his old Newark buddies, and this is the way to do it: It's the latest wall to be scaled. You know how he likes marauding into the old Wasp bastions and staking his claim or spilling his seed—ergo, *moi,* product of his union with my Mayflower mom. I'm encouraging him to buy something, preferably beachfront with lots of bedrooms so I can bring my friends for long, debauched parties when Mom and Dad are in Europe. But you have to promise me you won't move out of Boca. I wouldn't trade the shopping and the prime rib with baked potato at the club for all the cathedral ceilings and unspoiled landscape in the world."

Flo assured Amy that she shouldn't worry; she had no intention of leaving Boca Festa.

Now that the traffic had thinned and the Everglades had begun, Mel drove with one hand on the wheel, whistling. "I love it out here," he said. "It's unspoiled, it's open, it makes me think *possibility*. You know I'm itching to get myself settled down so that I can do some serious writing. It's been my dream to put on paper some of the experiences I've had."

"Your memoirs?" asked Flo, remembering Lila's having mentioned this.

"Well, possibly, but lately I'm thinking more fiction than fact. I'd draw on my own experiences, of course, but I like the freedom of being able to invent and embroider. I have an outline in a drawer and even a draft of some of the chapters. People I know in publishing have expressed interest. But it's a matter of getting the time and the space to sit down and write. I've been hoping that soon I will. But writing's a lonely business, and I like company." He glanced meaningfully over at Flo.

"I'm sure you could find company enough," laughed Flo nervously.

"Oh, but I mean the right company," said Mel. And when Flo didn't answer: "I'm thinking an intellectual soul mate as well as a companion. Someone who can act as my editor—and my muse." Flo still said nothing, but she felt the compliment, and turned to look out the window so as not to show that she was blushing.


The drive was a long one—almost four hours—and at one point, Mel pulled over and took a bottle of wine, a baguette, and a slab of cheese from a bag in the backseat. They took turns taking swigs from the bottle of wine, which made Flo feel as though they were teenagers, stealing off with their parents' car for the day.

"Simple fare, I'm afraid. But it's not easy getting to the casbah," said Mel.

Flo said she liked simple fare. "You're an adventurer," she said, then rephrased: "You like adventure."

"I do. I've never been satisfied with the humdrum and the ordinary. Life has so many pleasures, and we only go through once. It's a matter of taking some risks, making some far-flung calculations. There are things I'd do differently, but overall, I accept who I am. You can't teach an old dog."

"Not such an old dog," said Flo. It was hot, and Mel had taken off his jacket and unbuttoned the top bottons of his shirt as they sat by the side of the road. She was struck once again by what a good-looking man he was.

He gave her a deep look. "You don't think so? That pleases me." He leaned closer, so Flo could smell his aftershave as it mixed with the sweat that came with being outdoors in the Florida Everglades in the middle of the day. She stayed still for a moment, their faces close to each other, then she drew back.

"It's hot," she said, "and if we're going to the west coast, which I've deduced is the location of the casbah, we better get moving." She put out of her mind the difficulty of covering so much distance for the return that night.


When they approached Naples, Mel slowed, took a sheet of directions out of his pocket, then drove on for a few miles, finally pulling into a long driveway. It led to a sprawling postmodern castle with a wraparound porch on the second floor. He gave two short honks on his horn, and a portly man with a pompadour bounded out to greet them.

"Mel Shirmer, as I live and breathe, what a surprise. I was hoping you'd be coming this way one of these days to take a look at our fair digs. And you've brought a lovely lady, I see. Scouting for the honeymoon, perhaps?"

Flo shrank at the man's crudeness, but Mel seemed amused. "No, no, Sid, just a joyride. I told her that I knew some of the prettiest scenery in Florida, and thought she might want to take a look at the homes you're showing. She's nicely settled in Boca Festa, so there's no prospect of a sale. And no, Sid, we are two mature adults enjoying each other's company, nothing more." He winked at Flo.

"Well, let me show you two around, just for the hell of it," said Sid cheerfully, putting his arm on Flo's to steer her in the right direction. Flo instinctively moved away, and Mel, sensing her discomfort, stepped forward and took her hand. "You never know what you ladies might fall in love with," gushed Sid, "ladies being unpredictable that way. One thing I can tell you, I love house-sitting this place; it'll be hard to get me out, eh, Mel? We both have a taste for luxury, though we can't always afford it."

Mel laughed, and looked over at Flo, as if to say, Let's indulge the man and take a look around.

"This place is a dream," continued Sid, "though it's on a smaller scale than most around here. Just sold one up the road to a surgeon—the one who put back the hand on that girl pushed under the subway a few years ago; it was all over the *Post*. Big practice, very high-toned. Wanted something out of the way, private. They've got a home on the Riviera, and the one on Park Avenue, but this is their favorite. They love the seclusion. The sunsets. If you're poetic—and I can see, Mel, that this is one poetic lady—the sunsets will really do it for you."

Flo said that, actually, she could take or leave sunsets.

"But it's the structure that's the thing here," Sid continued, unfazed. "Best materials, latest design; the Flettermans did it—

they're the big developers for West Florida. Top of the line. This one here's a tad smaller, but the idea's the same, nothing spared in the way of amenities. They'll tear out the bathrooms for you, if you like, and do them to your specification."

Flo, who had begun to take a certain pleasure in thwarting the man's assumptions about her taste, murmured that bathrooms were not very important to her.

"You don't say? Well, you're an exception. But Mel was always one for exceptional ladies. Most of them, though, like a good bathroom. And I can understand it. Living room is important; kitchen, yes. But bathroom. That's where you're going to spend the most time, when you get right down to it, and from my experience, ladies like bathrooms. But you're exceptional."

Flo agreed that she must be. Mel laughed and squeezed her hand.

"We have four bedrooms in this model," Sid continued. "Can't go with less than four around here. They say you need less space when you're older, but that's all wrong. The opposite is true. You need more—that is, if you can afford it. One for each of you—at our age, forget the romance, we need our own rooms. Then, there's one for the children; one for the grandchildren—when you have a house like this, believe me, they visit—and, bam, you're full up. Now, in Mel's case, you might consider a larger model since you'd probably need to turn one of the bedrooms into a study. You don't want to stop those creative juices. One thing I always said about Mel, he's got plenty of creative juice." Sid slapped Mel on the back, who laughed indulgently.

"Sid, I already told you," said Mel with mock exasperation, "we're not looking for ourselves. Just taking a ride."

"Mel and I go way back, so I know his tastes," interrupted Sid, speaking directly to Flo. "Mel's modest. He doesn't like to say things so direct. I'm Jerry Lewis; he's Dean Martin, the cool one. It's always been that way. I accept it."


As they drove away, Mel was apologetic. "I've known Sid forever, so you'll have to excuse his style. We both grew up in the Bronx, and he, I'm afraid, never got very far beyond his roots. Couldn't buckle down in school, never did very well in business. This real-estate gig is a big step up for him, and though he's crude, I admit, I have affection for him. I'm loyal to my friends, you see, and I try not to judge them."

Flo said that she admired the trait.

Mel had pulled into a stretch of beach and told her that he'd been here before on his own to admire the scenery. "I like this spot. I visit when I feel the need to put things in perspective. It helped during that Stan Jacobs thing. Grounded me; calmed me down." He paused and then took Flo's hand, looking at her as he recited, " 'Ah love, let us be true to one another, for in this world that seems to lie before us like a land of dreams, there is really neither joy, nor love, nor light, nor certitude, nor peace, nor help for pain—' "

" 'Dover Beach,' " said Flo. "It's one of my favorite poems."

"I read it in college, and it stayed with me. It seemed to speak the truth."

"I don't know about that," objected Flo. "I used to think so when I was younger and liked to indulge the tragic perspective. But now, with life mostly behind me, I'm less pessimistic."

"You're lucky. My experience has reinforced what the poem says." Mel spoke softly, but his voice had grown gruff with emotion. "I don't have a very elevated view of human nature, you see. Comes with the territory, I guess. I've encountered some ugly things in my line of work"—he paused and looked out to sea—"and I've been lonely."

"I'm sorry," said Flo.

"But I don't feel lonely now." He turned and looked deeply into her eyes. "I'd like never to be lonely again." Then he leaned forward and kissed her. It was a strange feeling. She knew that at some point he was probably going to kiss her, but, even so, she wasn't prepared. She felt his lips on hers and wanted to respond, but drew back. Part of her was resistant.

"I like you," said Mel. "I don't want to spoil things."

"I appreciate that."

They drove to a small seafood restaurant nearby, where the owner seemed to know Mel and gave them a table toward the back.

"There's a hotel down the road," said Mel. "I was hoping we could stay over and drive back tomorrow. Take our time."

Flo felt tempted, as she had guessed she might be, but again she resisted. "No, I'd like to get back, if you don't mind," she said. "It's far, I know, and I'll share the driving, but I have an appointment with the club pro in the morning, and I promised May I'd go with her to look for a dress for the Valentine's Day dance. She's been hocking me about it for a week."

"No problem," said Mel. He was trying not to look disappointed.

"I hope you'll come to the dance. It's Boca Festa's gala event. From a strictly anthropological point of view, it's worth seeing."

"Of course I'll come," said Mel, his voice deep with emotion. "If you ask me, I'll go anywhere." Then, regaining his more ebullient tone: "It'll be something of an expedition in itself digging into my closet and dusting off the tux. It used to be an old friend: wore it almost every week, what with the diplomatic parties, the press club affairs, and so forth. But it's been a while. It may be a little snug under the arms. Are you good enough with a needle to let it out?"

"I'm afraid the needle and I have never hit it off," said Flo, "but May's a wonder when it comes to sewing. I know she won't mind. She really loves to do things like that."

"Such a sweet woman," Mel mused.

"Norman Grafstein also, I'm convinced, is a genuinely good person," added Flo. "Maybe a bit under the spell of his friend, but with the judgment and sense to make decisions on his own in a pinch."

"I hope so," said Mel. "But I'd keep an eye out if I were you. Norman may seem nice, but he's got a powerful influence in Stan Jacobs. And you never know what people's motives really are."

# CHAPTER TWENTY-ONE

VALENTINE'S DAY WAS THE BIG ANNUAL EVENT AT BOCA FESTA.
Other clubs went all out for New Year's or for the spring gala
that marked the end of the season for the "snow birds," those
who lived only half a year in Boca and flew north to children
and grandchildren during the late spring and summer months.
But Boca Festa had developed a unique affinity with Valentine's
Day ever since the wedding ten years ago of Phyllis Dickstein
and Morris Kornfeld.

The Dickstein-Kornfeld romance was legendary at Boca
Festa. Phyllis and Morris had each been married to beloved
spouses for almost fifty years, and had been widowed for several
more before meeting each other. They shared the same mix of
reverence for the past and joy in the present, which made their
companionship seem a pleasing coda to two wonderful lives. In
the ceremony marking their union, staged in the Boca Festa
dining room, children and grandchildren on both sides had been
present to give testimonials. Morris and Phyllis had spoken at
length about their departed spouses, explaining to the assembled
company that though they loved and admired each other, no
one would ever hope to replace the lost loved one at the center
of their affections. The entire ceremony was deemed "classy beyond words," and when it was topped by an extravagant bequest
for a yearly Valentine's Day celebration, the couple entered the
pantheon of Boca Festa Greats that included the millionaire de-
veloper who had endowed the poolside cabanas and the bestselling author of *Keeping Slim Over Sixty*, who had given money

to keep the Boca Festa salad bar stocked with tofu ("the secret," she said, "of feeling full without blowing up like a balloon").

Morris Kornfeld had worked on Madison Avenue and, ad man that he was, had not been content to bankroll the Valentine's Day event; he had also stipulated certain rituals. These were simple: He wanted the club, as he put it, "to bond" during the festivities, and mandated that a period after the main course and before the dessert be set aside for interested guests to stand and pay tribute to important relationships in their lives, past or present. He conceived of the testimonials as proceeding in the manner of a Quaker meeting, until someone pointed out that Quakers were supposedly anti-Semitic at some point in their history, and the analogy was dropped. In any case, it became a source of delight and pride on the part of many Boca Festa residents to take part in the Valentine's Day event, using it to wax nostalgic about dead spouses, to celebrate friendships, to boast about the engagements of children and grandchildren, and, most popular, if rarer, to announce the engagements of residents themselves.

The Valentine's Day dinner-dance was, owing to its generous budget, the most lavish of the many lavish affairs at Boca Festa. Decor, food, and clothes were important features of any Boca Raton event. The gold standard was the Long Island bar mitzvah and, given that the inhabitants of Boca Festa had been to many of these, every effort was made to imitate such affairs to mark the seasonal passage of time and the principal secular holidays throughout the year. Religious holidays were never formally celebrated at the club. Most of the inhabitants were Jewish, but there was a tacit understanding that the festivities be maintained on a purely secular level. There were several reasons for this. For one, religious holidays were conventionally spent up north with the children and grandchildren, who, it was believed, were likely to lapse into total nonobservance were their elders not present to make them feel guilty about it. And what would the holidays be, after all, without at least one substantial fight that both sides could stew over for months afterward and make the subject of lengthy long-distance phone calls?

Another reason why the club steered away from religious observance was because there was considerable disparity in the piety of the residents. Some had not attended synagogue for years; others remained dutifully attached to the major rites and rituals; there was even a small contingent that observed kosher dietary practices—perhaps five percent, for whom special meals were provided—though they were impossible to differentiate on the golf course from their more secular peers. Overall, it was the unspoken view that the club was a social community rather than a religious one: The members were bound together less by faith and ceremony than by similar life experiences in the New York boroughs and suburbs, by a shared sense of humor and taste in food, and by resemblances in the education and accomplishments of their children, whose lifestyles they could all boast about and disapprove of in the same basic proportion.

The Valentine's Day event was always a subject of intense speculation. The menu for the affair was widely discussed. Filet mignon was a given. Morris Kornfled had decreed it—he was one of that generation of men who were fond of pronouncing that "nothing beats a good steak and baked potato." But there were always at least three more main dishes, not to mention the endless number of side dishes, salad combinations, and famous desserts. The presentation was as eagerly awaited as the food. Who could predict what the club president, in consultation with the assistant manager (a woman who had once served as a store decorator at Neiman Marcus), would come up with in the way of positioning tables, designing centerpieces, and coordinating tablecloths, napkins, plates, and cutlery?

With the approach of the event, May had confided to Flo that she had asked Norman Grafstein and he had enthusiastically agreed to attend. Norman had called May soon after Flo's encounter with him at the Y, and they had gone to the movies and dinner several times since. Their last date had been a very fancy dinner-movie combination at Boca's famed Muvico complex, which featured a gourmet restaurant alongside a deluxe movie theater that charged fifteen dollars a ticket (*after* the senior discount). For the ticket price you got seats like armchairs and all the free popcorn you could eat. May had reported the extravagant evening to her friends.

"What's so special about free popcorn when we can make it in the microwave at home?" asked Flo.

But Lila, attuned to the pleasures that her lack of money denied her, explained succinctly: "It's the whole package. You go; you feel like a queen."

May admitted that she had certainly felt like one, though it was more the presence of Norman Grafstein by her side than the plush carpeting and chairs to be credited for that.

"With Norman, we have enough for a table—almost," said Lila now as she mulled over arrangements for the Valentine's Day dance. "There's Hy and myself, May and Norman, and you," said Lila, motioning toward Flo. "I assume Mel will be coming? Did you ask him?" Lila knew that Flo was capable of forgetting to do this.

"Yes," said Flo, "I asked him, and he's coming."

"Good," said Lila, as though pleased to see that everything was as it should be. Then, triumphantly: "Do you realize that this is the first time that we'll all have dates for the Valentine's Day dance?"

"With that accomplished, we might as well die now," commented Flo drily.

"Norman said that he'd like to bring along Stan Jacobs," added May in a tentative voice. It suddenly appeared to her that this might throw off the symmetry of the group. Plus, she knew Flo's feelings about Stan.

"Absolutely not," said Flo, "he's been awful to Mel, and they hate each other."

"Well, I'll tell Stan that Mel will be there. Maybe he won't want to come," said May meekly. "But I can't very well disinvite him, can I?" She seemed genuinely upset.

"It's inappropriate," added Flo with surprising vehemence. "It makes for an extra man."

"And since when are we against an extra man?" said Lila. "I'd say it's a nice change of pace."

"It's true," said May, gaining some confidence and taking a new tack. "Since when are you into couples, Flo?"

"You're right there," Flo acknowledged grudgingly. "I'm not saying it's because we all have to have dates. I'm just saying that it will make things uncomfortable."

"And since when are you against uncomfortable?" May prodded again. "You always like to stir things up." Then, moving to a more heartfelt argument: "You're much too hard on Stan. I know Mel doesn't like him, but I'm sure he's mistaken. He's really a very nice man. Norman told me how he suffered during his wife's illness, and how devastated he was by her death last year. It's been difficult for him."

"And not for us all?" snapped Flo.

"We all handle loss differently," persisted May, "and for men, what with their difficulty expressing emotion, it must be much harder."

"May, I'll say it again: We have to give you mean lessons."

"I just want you to be tolerant," said May. "Besides, Stan's a knowledgeable man; you can talk to him about books. And maybe you could play peacemaker between him and Mel."

May had a point, thought Flo. Perhaps this was a way to get to the root of the matter. She had an interest in Mel, she admitted to herself, but she wasn't in love with him—yet. It would be interesting to see the two men interact and judge for herself. And there was the additional incentive, as May mentioned, of talking books with Stan. The idea of having two literate men around her for the evening seemed like a veritable feast to her starved intellect. Perhaps they would do battle over the chance to converse with her. Where other women might have fantasies involving push-up bras and stiletto heels, Flo's involved good conversations about books. She let herself go: She'd have them discuss the latest Philip Roth she was reading. Time had certainly brought about a change in her fellow Jews' response to this once-despised author—he had received a standing ovation last month when he spoke at Boca West. Flo was probably alone among her peers in thinking *Portnoy's Complaint* a very funny book, the high point of Roth's career, but she was eager to hear what the English professor Stan Jacobs and the cosmopolitan Mel Shirmer had to say on the subject.

"Let him come," she conceded, shrugging, "but I won't promise to be civil."

"You may not be civil"—May smiled, in another one of her flashes of spontaneous insight—"but you'll be smart, and with a man like Stan Jacobs, smart is better."

# CHAPTER TWENTY-TWO

"I wonder what Chef has up his sleeve for the Valentine's Day dinner?" Lila raised the question at lunch the next day. She had returned to the table with her plate heaped with salad. ("No club has fresher greens," Hy Marcus liked to boast, "or a better variety of fixings.") But the existence of the food before her had obviously not suppressed her interest in food at some prospective date.

"It's supposed to be a secret," said May, who was highly cognizant of club rules and regulations.

"All the more reason to want to know," said Flo. "Last year, as I recall, Pixie Solomon got into the kitchen, found the list of ingredients, and pieced together the menu. It made quite a scandal."

"One thing about Pixie," said Lila, "she has initiative."

Mel arrived at the table at this point, and everyone shifted so that he could pull a chair in next to Flo. "Are we talking about the upcoming dance?" asked Mel. "I hear it's the social event of the season. But I feel like Cinderella without a gown. May, Flo tells me you're a wizard with the needle and wouldn't mind letting my tux out under the arms. I don't have the build I had when I was thirty-five—that's when I first bought that monkey suit, and it's held up pretty well, I must say, given some hard wear and tear in between."

May said she'd be delighted to let out Mel's tux.

"I'll bring it over tomorrow, if you'll allow me," continued Mel cheerfully. "I don't mind saying that I'm looking forward to getting out my dancing shoes and twirling this lovely lady on the dance floor." He looked over at Flo, who lowered her eyes. She hadn't danced for almost ten years. Eddie had been a good dancer, but the first stroke had put an end to the dancing. The second stroke had put an end to him.

"Speaking of the dance," said May, clearing her throat and taking a leap that went against her timid nature, "I wanted to let you know, since I'm responsible, that Stan Jacobs will be attending. I know you two don't get along," she added hurriedly, glancing at Mel, "but I'm sure you can clear things up with a nice talk." She looked plaintively over at Flo. "I told Norman last night to let Stan know that Mel would be there, thinking he might not want to come. But Norman called this morning to say that Stan didn't seem to care. Maybe," she said hopefully, "he wants to bury the hatchet."

Flo noticed that during this speech, Mel's face had lost its smile. Now he appeared to regain his composure and said lightly, "Why should I mind if Stan Jacobs chooses to inflict himself on me? I'll have the loveliest lady on my arm, and it wouldn't bother me if the devil himself sat at our table." Then he leaned over and kissed Flo on the cheek.

Lila gave Hy a look, and Hy twirled his finger in the air. "L'amour, l'amour," he said, and dug into his salad.

# CHAPTER TWENTY-THREE

FOR THE VALENTINE'S DAY DINNER-DANCE, THE ACTIVITIES COM-
mittee of Boca Festa had gone all out. The dining room had
been festooned in swathes of red velveteen drapery, and lumi-
nescent red and pink plastic hearts hung from the chandeliers,
themselves newly installed when the clubhouse had a face-lift a
few months earlier. They now cast a romantic luster on the
freshly painted faux-marble pink walls. The tablecloths were red
embroidered with gold sequins, producing the illusion that each
table was actually in the shape of a giant heart. The buffet table
was awash in roses and baby's breath.

The three women had taken pains to look their best for the
occasion, each according to her taste. May wore a pink chiffon
sheath, empire style with a high neck that she had been assured
by the saleswoman was both elegant and slimming. Her hair had
been swept back by Lila's stylist into an elaborate twist—she
usually wore it clipped up more casually—and she put on the
amethyst-and-diamond earrings and brooch that had been Irving's one gift of fine jewelry in commemoration of their fiftieth
wedding anniversary, their last, for he had had a heart attack six
months later and survived only a month beyond that. The gift,
which she sensed had not been without the involvement of her
daughter-in-law, had struck her at the time as too extravagant.
Tonight, however, the purple stones went well with the pink
dress, though most becoming was her expression of luminous
happiness, which, Flo thought, gave her friend the appearance
of an aging madonna.

Lila had always been more glitzy than her two friends, and she had for this occasion a kind of nervous enthusiasm that was reflected in her choice of attire. She wore a red dress plunging immodestly low—or so Flo thought, since breasts, beyond the age of forty-five, she took to be assets best kept under cover. Flo was distinctly in the minority among her peers in Boca Raton, however, where cleavage was as common as Bermuda shorts and often worn with them. Lila's unusually extensive cleavage on this evening might have been explained by the hefty gold necklace that dominated her throat and upper chest—and that her friends, who knew one another's wardrobes by heart, had never seen before.

"It's amazing!" said May, gazing at the large knucklelike links that looked heavy and were therefore likely to be real.

Lila patted her chest complacently. "Just some baubles," she said, laughing, "that happened to come my way."

"Lila is being mysterious," said Flo. "Tell me, Lila, did you rob a bank, or did your long-lost grandfather leave you some money?"

Lila laughed. "It's from Hy," she said, looking at both women somewhat accusingly, as though expecting them to say something and warning them against it. "It's a token of his affection."

May kissed her; Flo said nothing. Lila's involvement with Hy Marcus struck her as distasteful, and yet she also couldn't help feeling that her reaction was an injustice toward her friend, and maybe even toward Hy. After all, she had never had to count pennies like Lila. And what did she know of Hy, besides the few encounters in which he had rattled on about his children, their possessions and accomplishments? A man had the right to be proud, as Lila said, and it was unfair to jump to conclusions based on so little evidence.

Flo had tried to share her friends' enthusiasm in preparing for the dance, but she had to admit that the affair had lost some of its luster when Mel called that morning to say that he wouldn't be able to attend. He was under the weather—more than under the weather: temperature of 102, throbbing headache, nausea, diarrhea, and a hacking cough.

"I wouldn't inflict myself on a dog, no less a woman I care a lot about," he said gallantly between spasms of coughing. "It must be a bug I picked up in the hotel." Mel had been staying in one of the area motels for the past few weeks as he scouted Boca Festa. "You saw that special on *20/20* on hotels and how they use the same rag to wash the toilet as they do the telephone—" Mel broke off with another spasm.

"Don't speak," said Flo. "Rest yourself. I could care less about the Valentine's Day dinner-dance."

"I'm sorry," said Mel. "I wanted to twirl you across the dance floor."

"There'll be other occasions," said Flo. "Just get well. I wouldn't want you to pass away before we had a chance to twirl."

Mel laughed. "You're the woman of my dreams, you know," he said softly. "Good common sense, not a prima donna, fun to talk to."

"Quite a résumé you've got for me," laughed Flo. "But remember, I can't cook or sew."

"You can always hire someone to do that. Anyway, I didn't say you were perfect, just the woman of my dreams—" He was cut short by another fit of coughing.

"You better get off the phone," said Flo. "I wouldn't want you to rupture something talking to the woman of your dreams."

"Okay," said Mel, "but think kindly of me in my misery while you're at the dance. Think more than kindly, if you can."

# CHAPTER TWENTY-FOUR

WITH THE PROSPECT OF BEING DATELESS AND, WORSE, FETTERED to Stan Jacobs for the evening, Flo looked at herself in the mirror without much interest. Even so, she had to admit, she looked about as good as her age and natural endowments would permit. She wore, as she always did for Boca Festa events, her long black dress, bought years ago during a trip to New York City when Eddie, who was forever trying to convince her to buy expensive things after he made partner, had pushed her in the door of Martha's, then the chicest of Madison Avenue boutiques, and insisted that she choose something for the University Ball. It was the year she was being honored, along with about twenty others, for "her service to the intellectual life of the academy." The prospect of the award had embarrassed her. As a mere librarian, she hardly thought she merited special consideration in an institution in which the likes of Saul Bellow and Allan Bloom had taught the great books for decades. As it turned out, however, the event had been the highlight of her life when Bellow himself had stepped to the podium and personally thanked her for helping him with his research on *Mr. Sammler's Planet*. She was at a loss as to what he meant, unless it was the brief conversation they'd had in the library one day about the quality of New York versus Chicago delis. For a novelist, she supposed, that probably did count as research.

She and Bellow had, over subsequent years, developed a friendship of sorts, since whenever he came into the library he looked for her to chat. He seemed to appreciate her brand of wit, and they had traded quips on such topics as the eccentricities of the Jewish people, the war between the sexes, and the trials of being no longer young. He sometimes sent her an announcement about a new book or a reading he was going to give somewhere in town, always with a scribbled personal note. She had saved these notes, not above the awareness that in time they would come to be worth something. He was, she thought, a good writer ("great" she reserved for Tolstoy and Henry James) but also a fairly typical Jewish man of his generation. She had recently read in the paper about his becoming a father, again, at age eighty (no personal note to her on this accomplishment!). The news made her glad that she no longer risked running into him; she might have ended forever his appreciation of her wit by letting loose on the subject of an eighty-year old man having a baby.

The black dress from Martha's still managed to evoke that auspicious moment when she had stood at the podium next to Bellow. And given its durability and its simple stylishness, she acknowledged that it had been worth its exorbitant price. It lay with the sureness of its pedigree, following the lines of her large-boned body without being clingy, which her figure could not have carried off. The neckline, likewise, had a stylish diplomacy: It was modest without being Legion of Decency. Best of all, the dress was comfortable, which for Flo was a prerequisite for anything she put in her closet. She liked to feel that, if she had to, she could play tennis in whatever she wore. For shoes, she had on a pair of two-inch Ferragamo heels, bought on sale at Saks two years ago. For jewelry, she wore the diamond studs that her son had given her during one of their periods of truce and the gold chain with the peace-sign pendant that had been a birthday present from Amy. Her hair, she left alone. It was short and, unlike her friends', aggressively gray. Thirty years ago, finding herself graying at the temples, instead of "going blond" like so many women she knew, she had taken an unusual but characteristic step and gone the other way. With the help of a product called True Gray, she had dyed her whole head that much maligned color and never turned back. Being gray at forty, she liked to say, had made her distinguished before her time. In fact, it softened, in a way ash blond never would have, her rather hard and angular features, and gave a sheen to her hair that made it glow silver. For those discerning enough to tell, it was highly becoming. For Flo, it afforded the satisfaction of going against the grain of her peers, something which, reverse snob that she was (and she admitted this freely to her friends), she enjoyed.

"I like the novelty of gray in a land of red and gold," she explained, "and who knows, but it might catch on: like the success they had bringing back corn flakes."

Flo usually looked forward to Boca Festa events and, even without Mel's presence, would have been inclined to have a good time were it not for the prospect of Stan Jacobs being a wet blanket and judging them all. Thinking about him made her angry, and she determined then and there to resist his spoiling her fun—even if it killed her.

As the three women made their way up the steps of the clubhouse into the lounge area that preceded the main dining room, they saw Hy Marcus waiting expectantly by the door. Hy was sporting what in Boca circles was termed "a look." All affairs at Boca Festa were black-tie optional, but most of the married men, at the promptings of their wives, and even the few single men, tended to opt for the tuxedo. They enjoyed dressing up as much as the women. As Norman Grafstein had said, the lure of the English aristocrat always beckoned. At clubs like Broken Arrow, there were even dining rooms in which black tie was favored on a regular basis, as though the members had decided to bodily transplant themselves to nineteenth-century England and play at being, if not the Duke of Windsor, then at least Queen Victoria's favorite counselor, that charming Jewish prime minister, Benjamin Disraeli.

There were, however, always those who preferred the flashier version of black tie—more Las Vegas than Hampton Court. Hy was of this school and had chosen to deck himself in a lime-green cummerbund and matching lime-and-yellow bow tie. Carol, thought May, would have approved. She was always nagging Alan to liven up his attire. Hy was definitely lively, his good cheer manifesting itself in a veritable avalanche of anecdotes about his children and grandchildren. In between, he chose to comment appreciatively on the women's appearance. Lila's red dress pleased him exceedingly, but he also took admiring notice of May, whose relationship with Norman Grafstein he had decided should proceed at the same pace as his with Lila.

"May Newman is certainly looking fancy," he exclaimed now. "Looks to me like she's after a big fish."

May blushed and looked down, but Hy was undeterred. "I can see that Norman Grafstein had better watch himself or he's going to be walking down the aisle sooner than he thinks."

"Hy, enough," pleaded Lila, who could see that her friend was embarrassed and that the remarks were in bad taste.

"And what's so bad about congratulating a lovely lady on making a good catch?" asked Hy gleefully. "A woman gets dressed up—a few curves don't hurt"—he patted Lila's hip—"and before you know it, it's wedding bells." He leaned forward to kiss Lila's cheek and peer appreciatively at her exposed neckline, the sight of which fortunately seemed to distract him from postulating further on May's marriage plans.

The four had deposited themselves on one of the sofas in the lounge to await the remaining members of their party, and while Hy chattered and Lila dutifully nodded, May and Flo watched with interest as the members of Boca Festa paraded by in their finery. Among the more notable was a woman in a red-and-gold floor-length sheath with what looked like a bustle, and a silver sequined headdress with a feather.

"I'd say we have here a cross between the races at Ascot and a popular New Orleans bordello during Mardi Gras," Flo whispered to May. "For a woman closing in on seventy-five, that outfit takes more than chutzpah—it takes stamina."

Mixing among the throng was Rudy Salzburg, president of the club, a dapper impresario of a man with a massive mane of gray hair and an exaggeratedly continental manner. Rudy, a former concert-level violinist in his native Hungary, had survived Auschwitz and gone on to found a chain of lucrative soft ice cream stores in New York and Connecticut. He was a man of enormous joie de vivre and know-how, and it was said that his indefatigable spirit and capacity for organizing had saved many during the direst times in the camps. An Olympic kibbitzer, he wielded his genial authority over all aspects of the life of the club, raising money for this and that, planning, gossiping, and schmoozing. It was Rudy who had spearheaded the famous father-son golf tournaments, in which members played against each other with the help of their sons, hot-shot New York lawyers and brokers. It was an opportunity for father-son bonding as well as a networking opportunity for the children (the Viacom merger was rumored to have had its beginnings at this event). Rudy was also responsible for bringing Jackie Mason to the club last year. He had been loyal to Mason during the comedian's down years, when he had hired him to do the Ice Cream Association of America banquets, and Mason, as word had it, owed him big-time. It was also said that Rudy had engineered the Dickstein-Kornfeld bequest, though it was not beyond Rudy to take credit even if he hadn't.

Now he wended his way toward Flo, saying a word to this one and that one as he went, finally arriving to emote that mixture of schmaltz and old-world elegance that he was known for.

"Flo Kliman, your beauty is breathtaking," he pronounced with his thick Hungarian accent, kissing her hand and placing his other hand on his breast.

"As dapper as ever, Rudy. I see another success," said Flo,

casting her eyes around the room. There was no denying that Rudy had a talent for making a large and festive statement. He had hired Ellen Rabinowitz (the Neiman Marcus decorator), and he was not above adding a few touches of his own. The hearts from the chandeliers, for example, were pure Rudy. At some point in the evening, he would undoubtedly take out his violin and play the old favorites with the throbbing glissando that put the native New Yorkers in mind of that Lower East Side culinary bastion, Moskowitz and Lupowitz—now, sadly, like so much else, gone.

Rudy's special attendance on Flo was owing to the little-known fact that she, too, was a benefactor of Boca Festa. Soon after moving down, she and her husband had donated ten thousand dollars for renovation of the card room. Eddie Kliman intended, in retirement, to spend a large portion of his time playing pinochle and gin rummy, the games of his halcyon childhood years in Brooklyn. With a hefty sum accumulated from a lucrative career in real-estate law, he had decided to make the Boca Festa card room, a shabby corner off the club dining room with a sixties-era shag rug and no windows, into a bright and airy breezeport where card-playing could be pursued in style. It was just like Eddie to put money into something so essentially frivolous and fanciful, and Flo had thoroughly supported the idea, especially since a larger sum had been donated to the University of Chicago library in her name.

Eddie had died before the renovation was complete, though not before a few ill-timed investments had deprived him of the larger part of his fortune. His last regret, before succumbing to the stroke that finally killed him, was that he'd been seduced by the bull market when he should have known better.

"It's a lesson," he said, his voice slurred from the stroke. "I was greedy."

Flo assured him that he was the least greedy man she knew

and that she had more than enough to live on, what with the bonds, the remaining good investments, and her pension. "Besides," she said, "I'm grateful not to be rolling in dough since I'm saved the trouble of figuring out how to spend it." It helped Eddie in his final hours that he believed her. She had never had a talent for spending money.

Still, the card room gave Flo pleasure in its tribute to the whimsical side of Eddie's nature and to those earlier days when they could afford such openhandedness. Flo never played cards herself, but when she missed Eddie, she liked to wander into the room and contemplate the scene there. Invariably, the men sat congregated together at one table, the women at another, each group engrossed in play. The gender demarcation was mysterious. All other pastimes in Boca Festa were entirely gender-integrated, but cards held to some deeper, more atavistic tendency, reminiscent of old-world davening. The room was perhaps a vestigial remnant of the Orthodox shul in which men and women were kept apart. This may have been why Eddie had never pressured Flo to play: His pleasure had been in a man's game where he and his friends could escape, if only briefly, from the vise of their wives' control.

A small gold plaque near the door noted discreetly that the room was "the generous gift of Florence and Edward Kliman." Few noticed the plaque, and Flo certainly never pointed it out, but Rudy knew and, in the manner of all impresarios, was not one to forget. He had the solid, European sense to believe that where once money had come, more might follow. Flo was not about to disabuse him of the notion. She liked the special attention he paid her because of it, and the room had been worth the last gasp of their disposable income, as far as she was concerned.

# CHAPTER TWENTY-FIVE

As Flo and May sat waiting for Norman and Stan, Dorothy and Herb Meltzer paused to chat. His barrel-chested, lilliputian frame was stuffed into a tuxedo, making clear to those who might not have understood it the mechanism behind the lightning-flash transformation of Clark Kent into Superman. Had Herb suddenly flexed his chest and broken through the outer garments to reveal a skintight body stocking beneath, it would hardly have seemed surprising given his aura of barely contained energy. Though he was pushing eighty, one could still see why Herb, former owner of a successful moving business on the Lower East Side, had been rumored to be able to carry a piano single-handedly up four flights of stairs.

If Herb put one in mind of a well-known cartoon figure, Dorothy evoked one less familiar. Her complexion, the color of aged mahogany, stood in violent contrast to an aggressively white gown. She was one of those women for whom sunbathing remained an unalterable rite that no amount of basal-cell skin cancer and no barrage of *60 Minutes* specials on "The Sun: A Killer" would ever cause her to forsake. It did not faze her in the least that her skin had the consistency of rawhide. She had always been tan, she would continue to be tan. Like Sadie Litman in pod 5 (Fairways), who, despite the extensive no-smoking restrictions recently instituted at the club, continued unapologetically to smoke like a chimney, Dorothy was one of a group of Boca Festa residents who remained blithely confirmed in age-old habits, even as their neighbors shed these habits, clucked disapprovingly, and voiced exaggerated concern for their health.

In truth, Sadie, Dorothy, and their ilk were viewed as courageous, iconoclastic souls and were admired. Deep down, everyone had doubts about the litany of health hazards that seemed to have been devised to whittle down the few pleasures that remained to them during their twilight years. Everyone secretly believed that their gifted and talented children were keeping those coveted ounces of red meat from passing their lips and those golden rays of sun from penetrating their pores in a malign plot to punish them. Inevitably, whenever a Boca senior visited some young doctor (who they knew as sure as they looked at him didn't call his mother half as often as he should) who told them to reduce their salt intake, they followed his advice (especially if he had an Ivy League diploma) but maintained a profound skepticism that such a little *vantz,* hardly as old as their Richie, was doing much more than playing doctor. Of course, in some quarters, the ability to lower one's intake of salt and sugar became a source of pride and achieved the status of a senior competitive sport. But this was mild compensation for the pleasures that had to be bypassed in exchange.

"Isn't it stunning?" pronounced Dorothy, waving a cocktail shrimp the size of a tennis ball in the direction of the red velveteen drapes near the door of the dining room. "Hasn't Rudy outdone himself?"

Lila, May, and Flo agreed, while Hy, squinting at Dorothy's brown-speckled bosom, cracked a joke to Herb about the damage the event was going to do to their yearly dues. Roz Fliegler had also stepped up to the group. "The potato pancakes are exquisite," she said, moving her fork dexterously on the small plate to carve a morsel from the crisp pancake and deposit it gingerly into her mouth without damage to the carefully applied double layer of lipstick pencil and gloss that gave that orifice the appearance of a particularly exotic tropical fish. "But keep away from the chopped liver," she warned in a theatrical whisper. "Too much salt."

It was at that moment that Flo saw Norman and Stan make their appearance at the lounge door.

Norman was dressed impeccably in black tie, his tuxedo fitting his large, imposing body like a glove. Many years ago, in the course of his dealings with quality department stores up and down the East Coast, he had come to an appreciation of the importance of cut and fit in a man's suit. He had always known that he did not possess the most felicitous proportions—with arms and legs too long for his body and a tendency to run to fat toward the midriff. But once he discovered that careful buying in the best men's departments could camouflage these defects and show him to advantage, he made it his business never to scrimp when it came to his wardrobe. He had grown successful in business under the well-known dictum "Dress British, think Yiddish," and over the years had acquired his own salesmen at both Brooks Brothers and J. Press in Manhattan, where his measurements were kept on file and revised yearly. Every other year, he had a suit made to order by Felix, J. Press's veteran tailor, a refugee with an obsessive dedication to perfecting the line of a seam. He had more ties than he could count, and a particular devotion to bow ties that he ordered from the Ben Silver catalog straight from Charleston. He was, in short, a dandy, though a dandy in the best, unobtrusive English style.

Tonight Norman had dusted off his J. Press tuxedo, last worn more than three years ago at a charity fund-raiser in North Jersey that he had attended with his wife. Had he had more time, he would have made the trip to New York City for Felix to make alterations, for he found that with age his body had a tendency to get lumpy in new places. Norman had noted that while women seemed obliged to get face-lifts and liposuction as they aged, men had the advantage of simply making a visit to their tailor to smooth themselves out—another instance, he acknowledged, of the double standard to which his daughter, the feminist, had awakened him. But though he would have liked to have Felix work his magic on the jacket, it still, all things considered, fit him nicely. He looked, as he saw himself reflected in May's admiring gaze, very well indeed.

Stan Jacobs, by contrast, was hardly a clotheshorse. He had never owned a tuxedo in his life, and never intended to buy one. Tonight he had on a simple gray suit, which, though almost twenty years old, was hardly worn. As an English professor, he had had very little use for one, especially since a large part of his career had been spent during the heyday of a more relaxed academic era, when blue jeans and flannel shirts were the norm for professors as well as students. Since his daughter had married Mark Grafstein in an elegantly informal ceremony on Martha's Vineyard, even that auspicious occasion had required him only to wear white duck pants and a sports jacket. Flo would have liked to have found Stan's gray suit, oxford shirt, and rep tie objectionable, and she did sense in them a certain condescension toward the festivities at hand. But she had never been a fan of male formal attire. A tuxedo, she felt, had a tendency to make every man, with the exceptions of Fred Astaire and Sean Connery, look like a headwaiter. It was hard for her to admit, but the person whom she liked least was dressed more to her taste than anyone else at the dance.

The two men approached the group, and Roz, Herb, and Dorothy parted like the Red Sea to make way for them. Roz gave Norman a very thorough once-over and emitted a regal "Excuse me" as he passed her. During the introductions, she reached out a hand, diva style, and pronounced, "Charmed, I'm sure," in an accent that vaguely recalled the forties Hollywood ingenue. Though born in the Bronx and generally sporting a very flat, nasal articulation, Roz sometimes affected a different style of speech, one part Claudette Colbert and two parts Barbara Stanwyck. Lunch with friends might garner a simple "Pass the budda," with a kind of bellyflop at the end, but when she was with strangers whom she wanted to impress or a man with possibilities, it suddenly became "Would you kindly pass the buhtah"—with a lilting consonant in the middle and a kind of mock-British vocable at the end.

The accent had come out in force tonight with the appearance of Norman Grafstein. As she presented her hand gingerly, her long nails arched forward like a friendly cougar proffering a paw, she cast a glance down at Norman's left hand to note the appearance of the wedding ring. The continued wearing of the ring during widowhood was seen by most Boca Raton women as a sign of sensitivity, and men earned extra points for it—assuming, that is, that the old ring could eventually be pried off and replaced by a new one.

Last widowed three years ago, Roz was between boyfriends at the moment and was what Flo liked to call "on the prowl." Though she was talked about for her predatory style, Roz was also much envied among the widows of Boca, who never ceased to wonder at her ability to land men. That she had been left a fortune by her first husband, the laudromat king, was discreetly ignored in discussions of her romantic success. She had been married twice and engaged again, a sudden fatal illness canceling the third wedding even as the caterer had begun to draw up the menu. No doubt she would soon find another prospect, though she liked to say she was in no rush and could afford to be picky: "I want a tall man, and I like a full head of hair," she was known to announce, even in the presence of her son (who was five-three and as bald as a cue ball).

In the Boca Festa locker room, after her tennis and before her massage, Roz was in the habit of expounding on her romantic conquests to anyone interested in hearing (and there were women who got out of the sauna to listen):

"First, I'm not shy," she explained. "It's a plus to be outgoing, especially since most men are shy and need you to draw them out. Second, I laugh at their jokes. Some aren't so funny, but I laugh anyway. I learned this from my mother. She said, 'Laughter is the best aphrodisiac'—and she was right. Third, I have a good nose." She pointed to the rather amorphous appendage at the center of her face. "A Jewish girl must never underestimate the importance of a good nose. As I told my daughter-in-law on the subject of my granddaughter, if you're not born with one, I don't care what it costs—get one." The women in the locker room nodded at this advice. It seemed to make sense.

But Norman showed no particular inclination to get on better terms with Roz's nose. Instead, he turned his attention to May, who was sitting demurely, asking Stan about his plans for a garden this year. Stan's interest in the subject gave his face an uncharacteristically gentle appearance.

"I wouldn't recommend irises; there's been too much rain," counseled May. "I was testing the soil the other day and it seemed a little too acidic for the delicate plants." Gardening was one area where May, usually tentative, showed conviction and authority. It amused Flo and Lila to accompany her to the Boca nursery, where she would scrutinize seedlings and minutely question the manager about watering schedules and feeding regimens. Stan was one of the few people she knew who shared her passion, and the two had developed a tendency to confer on the subject whenever they could. Had Flo not been so thoroughly put off by Stan Jacobs in other respects, she might have been charmed by the sight of these tête-à-têtes. May, for her part, was not to be shaken in her belief that a man with such a feel for flowers and shrubs must have a good heart.

"I would advise that you plant more pansies and impatiens," she counseled him now. "If I had a garden," she added wistfully, "it's what I'd do."

"That's just what I was thinking," said Stan. "I don't want to go overboard, but I think doubling the impatiens would be a good gamble this year, especially if it continues to be so wet."

Norman interrupted. "Enough with weather and flowers. I didn't come here to talk topsoil. Let's let the nonexperts into the conversation." He gave May his good-natured smile. "You, my dear," he said, "are a vision of loveliness. Jennifer Jones in *Love Letters*." May blushed. "And you, Flo, look like Rosalind Russell in *His Girl Friday*, smart and sophisticated. Don't you think, Stan, that there's something of Rosalind Russell about her?"

"I can't say I see it," said Stan. "I don't think she looks quite like anyone."

"A high compliment from my friend," exclaimed Norman. "He only likes originals. He scorns the paintings on the walls of Broken Arrow for being reproductions of old masters."

"Well, better reproductions of great art than original bad art," noted Flo, glad to divert the subject from herself, especially as she sensed that Stan might not have meant his response in the complimentary way that Norman suggested. Following her gaze now, Stan looked at the large canvas near the bar and said nothing. It was an abstract piece in pink and yellow with a turquoise border, not unlike the one that Carol had commandeered for May's living room.

Their foray into art criticism was cut short, however, by the announcement that it was time to move into the main dining room. Flo noticed that Stan had been looking around, obviously preparing himself to meet Mel, and she finally decided to put his mind at rest.

"Mel's not coming, by the way," she said as the group stood together near the door, waiting to be shown to their table. "He's indisposed, I'm afraid."

"Ah!" said Stan, then shut his mouth, as though determined not to say anything further on the subject. The curtness of his response piqued Flo, and she secretly decided to make him speak about her friend later in the evening.

# CHAPTER TWENTY-SIX

THERE WAS A GENERAL BUZZ AND A MURMUR OF OOHS AND AAHS as people appraised the room and the food. A small band, one of Peter Duchin's stock of middle-aged men in shiny tuxedos and comb-overs, was playing "Funny Valentine" in one corner. The chandelier and pink hearts were throwing off strobelike pink and red lights, and a phalanx of buffet tables, each groaning under the weight of ingenious food combinations, scattered the room. At the center table was a massive ice sculpture of two naked cupids entwined around a heart. The sculpture was the brainchild of Ellen Rabinowitz. No one had ever seen anything like it.

In best Boca tradition, the meal was a combination buffet and sit-down dinner. A black-tie affair could not, in good conscience, be an all-out buffet: It wasn't done. But no one wanted to bypass the luxury of display and sampling that a buffet afforded, and so (again, under Morris Kornfeld's clever directive) appetizers and desserts were buffet, while the main course was served by waiters, fitted for the occasion in red shirts and pink vests.

As expected, the buffet spread was spectacular. One table was entirely salads, many of the garnishes dyed red and pink. There was lettuce of every variety, from the standard iceberg to the more refined arugula, bibb, and endive mix, as well as cold salads of fish, shrimp, calamari, and sliced beef; potato salads (at least three varieties); cucumber salads (two); tomatoes (with, respectively, mozzarella, avocado, and Vidalia onion); eggs (deviled);

carrots; celery; artichokes (hearts, stuffed, whole); and so on—
and this was just the salads. There were two other tables with
appetizers, and a Viennese table of desserts along the back wall
that defied any attempt to do it justice in words.

The main course options included beef Wellington, lobster
thermidor, Chilean sea bass, and veal française. A small card at
the center of each table listed the choices in elegant gold script
and was the object of intense scrutiny for the first ten minutes
of seating—the women invariably torn between the veal and the
sea bass, and the men between the beef and the lobster (with
the beef, in line with Morris Kornfeld's preference, winning out
two to one).

As the guests settled themselves noisily and debated such decisions, Rudy took the microphone. In his capacity as impresario
he bore a striking resemblance to Joel Grey in *Cabaret,* except
that he might well have been the original upon which Grey's
role was based. He welcomed everyone to the Tenth Annual
Valentine's Day Dinner-Dance, recalled Morris Kornfeld's un-
timely passing on the tennis courts two years ago, and read Phyllis Dickstein Kornfeld's message from her North Jersey nursing
home. He reminded everyone that formal testimonials were
scheduled to begin at ten P.M., after the main course, but that
the Viennese table—the best display of desserts he'd seen since
his son's bar mitzvah at Leonard's of Great Neck forty years
ago—wouldn't be open until after the testimonials were complete. "So be sure to leave room for dessert. And ladies," Rudy
counseled winkingly, "this is no time to watch the waistline; you
can start the diet tomorrow."

There was a general convergence on the food. The women
tended to take only a smidgen of this and that with the result
that their plates looked like petri dishes decorated with bacterial
samples. The idea was to avoid unnecessary calories without losing the chance to taste everything. Ultimately, of course, a large
accumulation of smidgens is likely to approximate a fairly large-

sized portion. The men were less circumspect in filling their plates and sometimes two plates at once. When the main entrees were served, there was much in-depth discussion as to the relative merit of the lobster versus the beef. Forkfuls were passed back and forth for tasting. At one table a great deal of time was spent speculating on how much lemon had been used in the veal française. At another, an argument broke out as to the propriety of serving shellfish.

"It's not right," said Maurie Gluckman, who prided himself on being a man of principle. "This is a Jewish establishment. It sends the wrong message."

"It's not a Jewish establishment," insisted Sadie Litman. "We're most of us Jews, I'll grant you, but it's not a Jewish establishment."

"Well, I say that if you get enough Jews together, you have a Jewish establishment. And looking at shellfish makes me sick," responded Maurie.

"Then don't look at it," said Dorothy Meltzer, who happened to like lobster and thought that Maurie was trying to spoil her fun.

Rudy, who was making the rounds with his violin, intervened diplomatically to suggest that maybe next year they could keep the lobster and shrimp in the card room, and only those interested would need to face the shellfish directly. The debate eventually died a natural death as the band struck up and dancing began.

The band kept assiduously to popular selections from the thirties and forties, and was complimented for its choice of music and, more important, for not playing too loudly. Not playing too loudly was a primary prerequisite for bands at West Boca affairs. Horror stories abounded of being stuck at functions in which the band made such a racket you couldn't hear yourself think. Roz Fliegler said that the noise had been so bad at her granddaughter's bat mitzvah that she had to stay in the ladies'

125

room the whole time. Pixie Solomon, possessed of the gift of conferring to memory long exchanges of dialogue verbatim and bringing them forth as needed to illustrate her points, told an assembled throng, "My daughter says, 'The kids like it loud,' so I say, 'That's why they're kids. You need to put your foot down.' And she says, 'Mother, you don't understand.' And I say, 'I understand only too well. . . .' "—and so on. Pixie's account of her conversation with her daughter had the quality of a very long tennis rally performed by a single player.

With the rumbas, cha-chas, and merengues, only the serious couples—those with years of Arthur Murray dance lessons under their belts—took to the floor. Dorothy and Herb Meltzer were well known at Boca Festa for their talent in this area. Whenever the notes of a rumba, their specialty, struck up, Herb would give Dorothy the nod and the two would sashay onto the floor, their well-packed posteriors moving purposefully to the Latin beat. Herb held Dorothy's large, undulating hip very low and turned his own body left and right with military precision, maintaining the implacable facial expression favored by the serious dancer.

When the standard waltzes and fox-trots were played, more people got up. Many of the women, being without partners, made up a loose chorus line, snapping their fingers and swaying as though they were backups in an elderly Jewish girl group.

Norman asked May to dance. She said she could do nothing but a slow waltz, though under his competent lead did well in a fast fox-trot and even held up in a swing dance as the music segued into big band. Joining them on the floor were Hy and Lila. Hy was a surprisingly good swing dancer with an antic, simian agility, while Lila, who had always loved to dance (only Mort had never taken her anywhere), looked beatific as she swung under and around Hy's prancing body, her red dress whipping around her short figure, the gold necklace on her ample bosom catching the pink light of the chandeliers. Watching her, Flo thought that perhaps the match was not quite as bad as she had imagined. If Hy could dance, at least that was something, and the faster dancing had the further advantage of making it impossible for him to talk while doing it.

# CHAPTER TWENTY-SEVEN

Flo was left at the table with Stan Jacobs. He had seemed morose on first entering the club, brightening only during the gardening conversation with May. After they settled in the dining room, she had decided to break the silence between them by asking his opinion of *American Pastoral,* the Roth novel she had just finished.

"The book's uneven," Stan pronounced tersely, "but with some fine passages that, in my view, compensate for its flaws." He spoke as though giving the last word on the subject, but Flo, who had looked forward to a discussion, countered energetically:

"I don't see it. I'll grant he did a good job describing old Newark, a subject I know something about, but the rest was a heavy-handed bore."

"Heavy-handed is not a word I'd apply to Roth," responded Stan in what Flo took to be a dismissive tone. "He's a stylist of enormous subtlety and skill."

"When did Roth become such a great stylist?" she demanded. "I remember when people were throwing him out with the trash."

"Well, he grew up and became a great stylist."

"That's the problem, then. It's a book by someone who doesn't like being a grown-up—I know the type, my son suffers from the same disease. Roth wants to shock the way he did when he was young, only now he gets invited to Hadassah luncheons and discussed at B'nai B'rith book clubs instead. He

attacks the 1960s because that's when he could have had a family—but God forbid he should have been so middle-class! The
daughter in the book, Merry, is every parent's worst nightmare
and Roth's way of announcing he was right not to have children.
It's pure sour grapes, as I see it, and, style or no style, it leaves
a bad taste in my mouth."

She had spoken longer than she intended, but she had clari-
fied, at least for herself, what bothered her so much about the
book. She noticed that Stan had listened as she spoke.

"That's an interesting reading," he conceded, and seemed to
be contemplating a reply. Before the discussion could continue,
however, his attention was diverted by something across the
room. Seeming to lose interest in their conversation, he abruptly
excused himself. The next thing Flo knew, he was talking with
a Hispanic waiter stationed near two huge tureens of vichyssoise
and gazpacho. While the guests swirled around them, Stan and
the waiter stood planted in one spot, engaged in earnest conversation for at least ten minutes. Norman was too busy trading
jokes with Hy (while May and Lila looked on) for Flo to ask
him what in the world Stan could be talking about with the
waiter, and by the time he returned, they were all too caught
up in the general mayhem of dispensing with the remains of the
appetizers and receiving the main course for any questions to be
asked. After the feeding frenzy had subsided and the dancing
begun, Stan seemed to withdraw further into himself, and the
moment for clarifying the mystery had passed.

There was certainly no possibility of asking Stan about Mel
Shirmer. Flo considered herself a woman of some courage, and
yet even she felt disinclined to raise the subject given Stan's
brooding, uninviting demeanor. She thought of trying to continue their discussion of Roth or bringing up the latest and,
thankfully, last Joseph Heller novel (what was it with these elderly Jewish novelists, anyway, that kept them writing when they
should have gone off to play cards and golf in Florida?). But Flo

decided against it. She would not succumb to the woman's role of drawing the man out. If he wanted to talk, fine; if not, she had inner resources enough to entertain her.

Yet the prolonged silence began to grate on her nerves. She watched the couples expending various degrees of energy on the dance floor—some of the healthier ones gyrating with show-offy zeal, others maintaining a careful, almost motionless shuffle— as the band struck into a medley of old standards. She and Eddie had cut a solid figure on the dance floor, and she had always found dancing to the tunes of Cole Porter and Gershwin about as pleasant a pastime as she could imagine. Filled with a sudden desire to move to that glorious music, she turned to Stan and asked him if he'd like to dance. The question seemed to wake him from a stupor. He looked at her for a moment with an air of surprise, then turned away, mumbling that he'd rather not.

She had assumed that if he refused her invitation it would be with the familiar excuse that he had two left feet. Flo knew that men feared making fools of themselves on the dance floor, seeing dance in the way they saw baseball or soccer, as a skill to be mastered. She knew they were wrong. Dance was less like sport and more like talk, an art in which chutzpah played a major role. The vast majority of men, failing to understand this, were fated to watch their wives and girlfriends swirl past in the arms of men who were five feet tall and wore their shirts unbuttoned to the navel—men who, for whatever reason, had grown comfortable making fools of themselves.

But Stan hadn't even bothered to give an excuse. His mumbled refusal was only a confirmation of what Flo had already seen of his boorish manners and of the mean-spiritedness Mel had described. Her anger was considerable, and she turned away, determined to have nothing more to do with him. But a moment later, to her surprise, he broached the subject she had been holding in her mind all evening but hadn't had the nerve to mention.

"How long have you known Mel Shirmer?" he asked suddenly.

"Oh, a few weeks now," replied Flo lightly. "I'm told you know him, too—or did."

"I knew him quite well."

"No love lost there, I see."

"None." Stan paused, as if considering what to say next. Then, abruptly: "I'd take care if I were you."

"Really?" exclaimed Flo with mock surprise. "I didn't realize he was dangerous. But perhaps in your lexicon, a polite man with a consideration for a woman's feelings is a threat. It gives the rest of you a bad name. No—from what I gather, you're the one that can be dangerous."

"Perhaps you shouldn't believe everything you hear."

"And what do you mean by that?"

"I mean that you're dealing with a man who's not to be trusted around women. You're a woman—though I'd say you're more intelligent than most—and it surprises me to see you taken in."

"If you're complimenting me, you can save your breath."

"I'm not complimenting you," said Stan, "I'm warning you."

"You needn't warn, then. I can take care of myself."

Stan gave her a long look, and Flo, suddenly uncomfortable and wanting to hear Mel's voice, excused herself and went to the pay phone in the lounge. She dialed his number and let it ring until it was clear that no one was going to answer. No doubt he had unplugged the phone so he could sleep.

# CHAPTER TWENTY-EIGHT

AT TEN P.M., WITH A DECREASE IN ENERGY AND APPETITE BEGIN-
ning to be discernible, Rudy took the floor to emcee the traditional closing act of the Valentine's Day celebration. This was
the presentation of testimonials that Morris Kornfeld had stipulated be included in the event.

Rudy opened the proceedings by inviting "anyone who
wished to share a sentiment in the spirit of the occasion. But,"
he cautioned, "we ask that you keep it short, since the hour
grows late, and, let's face it, we're not teenagers anymore—
though watching some of the ladies on the dance floor, I
wouldn't swear by it." He kissed his fingertips in the direction
of Dorothy Meltzer. Rudy was known to be a great admirer of
the ladies, and, unlike Flo, appreciative of décolletage, no matter
the age of the bosom.

Things got off the ground as in quick succession two women
announced the engagements of their children—Moira Plotnick
of her daughter to an orthodontist in Montclair, New Jersey, and
Selma Stein of her son to an aerobics instructor in Anaheim,
California. At table 2, three women in matching turquoise pant-
suits rose to attest to their friendship and distribute friendship
bracelets.

They were followed by Pixie Solomon, resplendent in gold
mesh, who announced the birth of her grandchild, Hannah Git-
tel Solomon. "Can you believe the names they're choosing nowadays?" she asked, while her neighbors at table 6 shook their
heads in agreement. "You'd think they were back in the *shtetl*

instead of living in a big house in Short Hills with a live-in nanny." Rudy, at this point, saw fit to intervene and explain, politely but firmly, that births weren't technically permitted as testimonials, since if he allowed them, they'd be there all night. Pixie Solomon sat down, miffed; she had wanted to describe her daughter-in-law's difficult pregnancy and recount the baby's birth weight and Apgar score.

Bobbie Tarkoff got up next to remember her dead husband, Milt, and to recall that he never once forgot her birthday or their anniversary—"and I have the jewelry to prove it!" Applause followed.

Two other women invoked dead spouses, with one, Minna Freedman, confessing, "When he was alive, I didn't appreciate him. Now that he's dead, I see he was a jewel"—to which there were murmurs of "So true" and sympathetic clapping.

Zelda and Stephen Freed rose to reaffirm their vows and forty-five years of "bliss." The secret, Zelda confided: "separate beds." Laughter and applause.

Trudy and Dan Lebarque (changed from Lebowitz) also testified to fifty-one glorious years. "No woman could be more wonderful than this one," said Dan. "She lights up my life." There was a murmur of appreciation and extended applause. (Pixie Solomon, who knew Trudy, whispered loudly to her neighbor: "She doesn't deserve him.")

It was after this that, to the surprise of the group, Hy Marcus jumped to his feet and, glass in hand, declared he had a special announcement. "Lila Katz," he said, gesturing to Lila with a self-satisfied flourish, "has consented to be my bride." There was an impressed "Ooh" followed by applause before he continued—for he clearly intended to hold the floor as long as he could.

"I just asked her this morning and was pleased to receive a reply in the affirmative. She didn't know I was going to announce it," he continued complacently, "but I say, why hold back? At our age, there's no point being modest. Lila and I will be leaving next week to spend some time with my children, who are eager to wish us the best: Steven, a gastroenterologist on Central Park West—you wouldn't believe what he charges—and his lovely wife, Candace, who converted and is active in Hadassah, along with my daughter, Sarah, a lawyer, and her husband, a hot-shot corporate raider like out of that movie with Michael Douglas. They'll be taking us out to dinner, and we'll be staying over at Sarah's mansion in Great Neck. I've told Lila that marrying me will put her in clover, and I hope her friends will have the same good luck, with no more money worries and plenty of *naches*. I know one couple at least"—he looked meaningfully over at May and Norman—"that should be following us to the altar soon enough."

There was some laughter and pointing over at May and Norman as Hy sat to applause and murmurs of "Mazel tov." May blushed violently at Hy's words, and Norman, Flo noted, seemed distinctly flustered and shot a glance at Stan, who looked poker-faced—but then, he'd looked that way all evening; he hadn't uttered a word since his speech on Mel Shirmer. Flo saw that Lila was conscious of the crudeness of Hy's remarks and was clutching her napkin and staring straight ahead with a fixed smile on her face. Feeling sorry for her friend, Flo reached over and patted her hand. She did not, however, glance at Stan Jacobs again. There was too much to think about in that quarter, and she preferred, as she put it to herself, to rest her brain for the time being.

# CHAPTER TWENTY-NINE

THE NEXT DAY AT LUNCH, LILA PUT DOWN HER FORK, TOOK A breath, and turned to her two friends. She had summoned them together for a farewell meal before taking off with Hy to meet his much-vaunted family on Long Island. Now, as she began speaking, she looked at May and Flo with an expression that was both plaintive and determined.

"I want you to be attendants at my wedding," she said, "and I don't want you to say no."

"Attendants?" said Flo. "Am I hearing correctly? Could we be talking bridesmaids here?"

"Flo," said Lila, "I knew you would laugh at me, but I'm serious. I want to have a big wedding and I want you two to be there at my side. Call yourself bridesmaids, matrons, attendants, whatever. It's what I want, and I beg you to make an old woman happy and do it."

"But what are you talking about, Lila?" asked Flo. Her friend, who had once seemed reasonable enough, appeared lately to have gone completely off her rocker: first, to encourage Hy Marcus, then to agree to marry him, and now, to contemplate a wedding with bridesmaids. The whole thing convinced Flo again of what she too often forgot: that even the most apparently sane and down-to-earth people were capable of frightening lapses in sense.

"The truth is," said Lila, "I've always had a thing about weddings. I never had one of my own, and it's always bothered me. Do you know that I look at brides' magazines in the supermarket and imagine myself wearing the dresses? Of course you don't. You don't know what it is to have been cheated out of one of life's most important events. Mort and I got married in City Hall. He was cheap, but more to the point, he wanted to escape his mother. She hated me. Even at her eightieth birthday party, she toasted Mort and never mentioned my name. Do you know what she did the last time I saw her? She was dying—she couldn't walk and could hardly breathe—but she looked me up and down like I was a bad cut of meat the butcher was trying to put over on her. She asked me what he saw in me: 'You're not pretty, no education, no family, no money, and as barren as a stone.' That was the thanks I got for taking her good-for-nothing son off her hands."

"Sounds like something out of the Brothers Grimm," said Flo.

"Worse!" Lila exclaimed indignantly, with the clear intention of elaborating further; recalling the injustices of the past had inspired her to new levels of eloquence: "I wore a blue suit to the ceremony—white was too stark, Mort said; we didn't want to advertise too much. And our only witness was his cousin Sam, that louse—he borrowed a hundred dollars to join a swim club and never paid us back. Mort was cheap about everything, but he had to lend his cousin Sam, the biggest lowlife you would ever hope to see, a hundred dollars to join a swim club. For dental work, for life insurance, for the kids' college tuition—that I could understand. But a swim club? And never a thank you. Never even an invitation to the swim club. When I'd mention it to Mort, he'd say I was ungracious. Me, ungracious? When his mother never thanked me once for the *Shabbes* dinner I cooked her every Friday night for forty years. Did anyone ever cook for me? Did anyone throw me a party? I know you think I'm crazy to want a wedding, a woman of my age. But I do. And Hy has no objection; he likes the idea. It gives him a chance to show off his family and pay for a lavish spread. So I want to have a wedding like the kind I should have had when I was twenty-one, and I want you and May to wear long matching dresses and walk down the aisle and carry bouquets. And if you won't do it, I'll never forgive you."

May and Flo were silent. Lila's outburst made Flo's usual quipping impossible, and yet the idea of being bridesmaid to Lila's bride was so patently ridiculous that she tried to find some sensitive but straightforward way of telling her friend that it was out of the question. But before she could gather her thoughts, May had spoken.

"We'd love to be your attendants, Lila," she said. "You're our friend, and anything that would make you happy would give us pleasure."

Lila smiled weakly and reached out her hand to May, who clasped it. But she didn't dare look at Flo, which was just as well.

# CHAPTER THIRTY

FLO AND MAY GAZED AT EACH OTHER IN THE MIRRORS OF LOEH-mann's communal dressing room. They were wearing matching aqua taffeta dresses with mutton sleeves and sequined bodices— "cocktail dresses" was the way Lila had described them. She had picked them out herself from Loehmann's Back Room before she left with Hy for Long Island, and had them held for her friends.

"I think the idea of matching bridesmaid's dresses at our age is obscene," said Flo. She had hardly recovered from the shock of Lila's idea; now here she was helping to implement it.

That they were doing so at Loehmann's was hardly surprising. There is a great deal of shopping in Boca Raton—a plethora of department stores and boutiques, outdoor and indoor malls, and flea markets and bazaars specializing in all manner of clothing and accessories. Yet despite the array of shopping opportunity, it is Loehmann's where women invariably find themselves when they want to buy something "for an occasion" or, for that matter, for everyday. Here are racks and racks of remaindered Calvin Klein and Ralph Lauren jackets, of Sonia Rykiel dresses and Oleg Cassini tops. Zones of the store are designated for hand-bags, shoes, jewelry, belts, and scarves, and in the Back Room, a cordoned area of spacious proportions, are the more exotic designer pieces. Everything is drastically reduced.

Loehmann's draws the cream of West Boca. Jags and Mercedes line up for weekly, often daily, pilgrimages, their owners running in for a quick survey of the merchandise in the hard-to-fill time before doctors' appointments (the "truck," the cognoscenti know, arrives daily with new stock). Indeed, a visit to Loehmann's is said to lower blood pressure and boost performance on a stress test (this owing perhaps to the vigorous arm exercise necessary to move garments speedily across the rack in advance of the woman behind you).

Loehmann's merchandise runs the gamut. It can supply a drop-dead outfit for a swanky affair just as it can provide the proper selection of stretch pants and chic embroidered T-shirts for the daily trek from pool to clubhouse to Early Bird Special to movies. Although the store is aggressively wholesale, no one in Boca sees herself as above Loehmann's. It is an enduring landmark, a city shrine, known and frequented by all. A nice piece at Loehmann's is, after all, as nice as you could get elsewhere, so why go elsewhere? Common poolside banter is the proclamation "See this? Twenty dollars at Loehmann's." When an outfit is complimented, even at the most elegant affair, the owner will think nothing of responding with pride, "A hundred and twenty reduced from four-fifty at Loehmann's."

Once a Loehmann's shopper has amassed a suitably unwieldy pile of promising merchandise, she will recess to the dressing room, a large communal changing area, lined with mirrors, located at the back of the store. Individual changing rooms were installed in Loehmann's years ago in a concession to the possible modesty of customers, but no one uses them. Part of the Loehmann's mystique lies in the brazen openness of the changing area. It seems to insist that its customers bare their bodies in order to earn the right to purchase at such a discount.

There is something of the group therapy session about the Loehmann's communal changing room—with women in nothing but bras and panties loudly bemoaning to other women, perfect strangers, their problems with saddlebag thighs. The atmosphere can also be compared to the creative writing workshop favored in small liberal arts colleges, in which a participant's poem or story is passed around and critiqued by selected members of a peer group. At Loehmann's, the work in progress is the draped body, and the peer group a collection of like-minded shoppers. Thus, it is not uncommon for a number of women to engage in a close reading of the fit of a skirt on a less-than-svelte line from waist to hip.

"I think you can get away with it," one ample matron observes.

"It's cute, but I wouldn't risk it," another volunteers, her opinion no doubt informed by her own skeletal slimness.

"I disagree," the ample one proposes more vehemently, sensing a personal affront in the other woman's critique and directing her response to her. "She likes it, *kayn-aynhoreh,* She should wear it. Who is she, Cindy Crawford?"

"I'm only saying she might feel self-conscious with the bulges showing," the anorexic replies testily.

Meanwhile, the object of scrutiny will be turning this way and that and, depending upon which of her advisers she feels the more kinship with, will buy the skirt or leave it on the center rack—though if she leaves it, a thinner or more confident woman across the room, who has been watching like a hawk for this to happen, is sure to dart over to grab it.

There is always a certain bravado that reigns in the Loehmann's dressing room. No garment is too outlandish, too tight, or too short, at least to try on. Everywhere, half-naked women stand appraising themselves in the harsh fluorescent light, a piece of cut-rate designer apparel stretched across hips or bosom. Flo liked to say that the varicose veins and cellulite on display in the Loehmann's dressing room could keep an army of cosmetic surgeons busy for a decade. Of course, in Boca, many Loehmann's shoppers have already visited those surgeons, some more than once, a fact that can be gleaned by the shiny, overstretched look of the septuagenarians wearing G-strings. The fluorescent lights spare no one. Indeed, it is another rule of thumb: Nothing ever looks good under the lights of the Loehmann's changing room. One has to read the label and the price and take it on faith that the thing will look much better at home.

Lila had hyped the dresses as lovely and capable of being worn again.

"Wear this again?" said Flo, looking at herself with amazed repugnance. "When, to my bat mitzvah?"

"They'll look good in the ceremony," said May. "Lila is wearing the same color."

"What are we, fairy godmothers in a Disney movie?"

"Flo, they're not so bad," said May. "They're . . . festive."

"At our age, festive is the last thing a wedding should be. It should be discreet, if done at all. All participants should wear gray and look morose, like the rehearsal dinner for a funeral."

"Lila is happy."

"How could she be happy with that nincompoop?"

"Perhaps it's a matter of what she's had to compare him with. He's not a bad man. She needs the security."

"But I can't comprehend how a woman could turn herself over to a—a moron."

"I think," said May, losing her temper, "that it's time that you stopped the name-calling." The words and the commanding tone as they issued from her mouth surprised even May herself. She could not remember speaking with such authority since her Alan was a little boy. "It's her choice," she added more tentatively. "She's not asking you to marry him."

"May, I've never seen you so . . . forceful."

"Well . . ." May stammered. "I'm only asking you to be nice." She couldn't believe that she had had the courage to criticize Flo Kliman. But Flo was not offended.

"Of course you're right," Flo responded in a softer tone. "I'll try to restrain myself. But you must let me ventilate once in a while. Unless I get the bad vapors out, I might poison myself. You're lucky that I can't say a bad word about Norman. He has the good fortune of a sense of humor—he even laughs at himself sometimes. I can't laugh at someone who laughs at himself. I'm deprived of the advantage of getting there first."

"Flo, you're terrible!"

"You always say I'm terrible, but you don't really think it. You know that I have a heart of gold." Flo smirked at this idea of herself. "Okay—let's say I'm not as bad as I seem. Men, of course, don't realize this. They take me literally and leave it at that. My husband used to say that if he weren't married to me, he would probably loathe me. I sometimes thought he was trying to tell me something. But then, I told him frankly that I loathed him sixty percent of the time."

"I'm sorry," said May.

"Don't be. Forty percent nonloathing is an excellent percentage for me. When I realized that the odds of breaking forty percent with any man were slim at best, I decided to marry him. It was not a bad marriage, all things considered."

"I think I would say the same about mine," May mused.

"Perhaps next time we'll break forty percent," said Flo, and began tugging at the zipper of her dress. "I hate to say this, but I think I need a girdle with this thing. If I have to wear a girdle, Lila Katz is going to owe me big-time."

May laughed. "We should buy them."

"You think we have to?"

"Yes," said May.

"Okay," said Flo, "and we'll pick up the wands and tinsel on the way home."

# CHAPTER THIRTY-ONE

"I UNPLUGGED THE PHONE AND SLEPT LIKE A LOG FOR FIFTEEN hours," explained Mel when he saw Flo at the clubhouse two days after the dance. "It was short and rough, which is more or less the way I like to take being sick, though not, I should add, other things in life."

"I'm glad you're recovered," said Flo. "You missed a true Boca extravaganza."

"I'm sure I did. And I'm even more sorry I had to leave you at the mercy of Stan Jacobs. Forgive me. That must have been an ordeal."

"It was," admitted Flo, "but also interesting, in its way."

Mel raised an eyebrow but said nothing. Then, taking a jocular tone: "Well, I was thinking that maybe tonight we could do something quiet. I wouldn't want to court a relapse. I say we rent a movie and hunker down, if you're agreeable. I know you're a movie buff like me."

"An old movie buff, I am—and I'm referring to the age of the movies and not my age, though obviously they go together. My tolerance decreases, I'm afraid, as we pass 1960. I favor black and white."

"My feelings entirely. The world was better in black and white."

"It's a going topic around here that the old black-and-white films get no respect. The grandchildren won't watch them. As soon as they see the credits in black and white, they start to bawl."

"It's the decline of Western civilization," agreed Mel.

"But there's hope. My great-niece, who's studying film at NYU, says there's a whole new breed that want to work in it. They watch the old movies in their film appreciation courses and think: 'That's pretty good, I'll try that.' "

"It's the contrary nature of youth. They'll go against the grain, if they can. Make color the norm, they rediscover black and white."

"My hope is that by watching the oldies, something will rub off about how to write good characters and good dialogue. Black and white just happened to be the form available; it's hardly the point."

"You put your finger on it. It's form over content that they're after nowadays."

"I'm not sure if that's it," mused Flo. "I tend to think that every era keeps to the same basic proportion of form and content. It just depends on getting the balance right at a given moment. But maybe I'm clinging to the illusion that there's still hope for getting it right."

"I like your optimism," said Mel appreciatively. "It's attractive. So—you're on for a film classic? I'll pick something up from the video store and throw in a pizza while I'm at it."

Flo considered. "I rented *Shadow of a Doubt* yesterday and was planning on watching it tonight: Hitchcock, 1943, black and white—you can't do better. Joseph Cotten as Uncle Charlie to Teresa Wright's young Charlie. She adores him, but discovers that he's really a serial killer who preys on rich widows. Come to think of it, I'm surprised they haven't massacred that one in a remake. Or maybe they have, and I thankfully missed it."

"I wouldn't know, but I've seen the original a million times," said Mel dismissively. "What we need is a light romantic comedy. Let me do the choosing; something with Kate Hepburn—who, by the way, looks a little like you."

"I'm flattered," said Flo. "The other day, it was Rosalind Rus-

sell; today, Katharine Hepburn. At this rate, I'll be able to pop-
ulate an entire senior residence for the stars. Too bad the
resemblances weren't so marked fifty years ago."

"I suspect you were a real man-killer in your day." Mel gave
her another admiring look. "And after all, you certainly landed
a big one."

"A big one?"

"Your husband. So I'll pick up the pizza and the movie and
be over around six?"

"I'm afraid you're going to have to get two pizzas. I've promised Lila and May a movie tonight, and I'm too old to ditch my
girlfriends for a man."

"I understand entirely," said Mel, his voice losing some of its
cheerfulness. "I won't say I'm not disappointed, but I admire
your loyalty. It's a rare attribute nowadays. But do you think
your friends will mind me butting in on the girls' pajama party?"

"No," said Flo, considering, "they like you."

"And I like them. But I like you best. I was hoping for some
private time with you. Maybe a repeat of the casbah—or better.
Maybe later in the week?"

"I'd say that's a definite possibility. So long as I don't have to
cook."

"Never. A woman like you doesn't need to cook."

"Elucidate, please."

"Let's say your attractions lie elsewhere."

# CHAPTER THIRTY-TWO

"NICE PIZZA PARTY." MEL APPEARED IN THE LOUNGE THE NEXT morning, earlier than usual. He generally came by at noon to join them for lunch, but it was now only ten-thirty. Flo had been reading the paper and sipping a cup of coffee. The four of them had been up late. Mel had brought *The Philadelphia Story* (Lila and May agreed gamely that Flo bore a definite resemblance to Katharine Hepburn), as well as two pizzas and two bottles of red wine. They'd eaten the pizza and drunk one bottle of wine, and when the movie was over, Mel was still hungry, so May whipped up an omelet, which, though no one else really had an appetite, they ate anyway and drank the second bottle of wine. There was a good deal of laughter, and Mel, Flo admitted to herself, was marvelous company. He made them all feel beautiful and interesting, and Lila said that she hadn't had so much fun since her junior prom.

And now here he was again, obviously looking for her, perhaps intending to plan that private evening together that he had mentioned the other day. It had become increasingly clear that he was serious, and Flo, though not sure how serious she was, knew at least that she was flattered by the attention.

He had deposited himself on the sofa beside her, putting the large book he was holding under his arm on the coffee table in front of them. "Finding you here at this hour is more than I hoped," he said, taking her hand. "I decided to come by early to wait, in the manner of the chivalric knight of old." He bent forward and lightly kissed her hand. Then he laughed and stretched back on the sofa with obvious satisfaction, gesturing to the book on the table in front of him as he continued, "I'm looking forward to doing some serious reading once I settle down. It's hard when your life is up in the air. I've been carrying around this doorstop by Tom Wolfe, *A Man in Full,* hoping to get to it, especially since the last time I saw Tom, I promised him I'd read it."

"You know Tom Wolfe?" asked Flo.

"We worked together years ago, when the New Journalism was just taking off, and I saw him again after the Boca debacle I told you about, when I went to do consulting in New York."

"I thought you went to Washington when you left Boca?"

"Oh, yes, well, I split my time really between Washington and New York. There were two PR firms that wanted my humble services, and since I have friends in both places, it was easy to move back and forth. Each, I must say, had its enticements— Washington has the Smithsonian and the National Gallery, and New York has the Met and the Mets."

It was at this point that Rudy Salzburg approached. He'd been prowling the lounge, stopping here and there to chat and schmooze as was his fashion, though he seemed to have a particular eye on Flo, waiting for a lull in her conversation to dart in and kiss her hand.

" 'She sits in beauty,' " he said now, clicking his heels and leaning forward obsequiously.

"Rudy, you dazzle me," declared Flo.

"We're thinking of refurbishing the porch restaurant," Rudy explained, cutting to the chase now that the ritual amenities were out of the way. He was referring to the screen-enclosed area near the pool where lunch was served to those unwilling to go back to their apartments and change into "proper" clubhouse attire. "I've been looking at drapes and upholstery, and it occurs to me that, with a little help, we could make it very ritzy. I've been polling our benefactors to see if there's interest."

Flo promised to give it some thought, as she always did, and Rudy went off to approach Roz Fliegler, who was lying by the pool with Dorothy Meltzer, working on her tan. Roz had underwritten the potted plants in the dining room for the reason, as she put it, that "plant life makes for healthier air"—a fact of particular importance to her since she suffered from emphysema. Rudy had enthusiastically agreed that the plants were as good as oxygen tanks.

"I suppose you get asked to contribute quite a bit," said Mel, "a woman of your means."

"Only Rudy," said Flo. "He doesn't realize that Eddie lost the bulk of our play money in a bear market before he died. He thinks I have deep pockets, and I can't say I mind him thinking it. It makes him so pleasant."

"Ah," said Mel reflectively. "A shame about the money. You must have been upset."

"Not really," said Flo. "Eddie was, but not me. I have what I need. I'm not a diamonds-and-pearls sort of girl, as you can see."

"I can," said Mel slowly. "You're certainly not an ostentatious person."

"It's just that my pleasures happen to be cheap ones. I was never into clothes or jewelry, as I say, and I like to read. I'll read a book as soon as travel around the world. There, you see, we differ."

"Yes," said Mel, leaning back on the sofa again, his face taking on a dreamy, distracted look, "I suppose we do."

# CHAPTER THIRTY-THREE

TIME PASSES DIFFERENTLY FOR BOCA RETIREES THAN IT DOES FOR other people. Gone are the familiar rhythms of school and work. Days swim by, the demarcation of weekday and weekend eroded by the ebb and flow of golf games and long hours at bridge. Some days, a gastric ulcer flares and the sufferer may rise at six, walk the lush grounds of the complex, meeting others with similar complaints, then return for a leisurely breakfast, a game of cards, and a long nap, only to rise again for an early dinner and movie, then back to sleep, not rising until eleven or twelve the next day. Days and nights take on an uncharted, unpredictable aspect. Time moves either fast or slow depending upon the state of one's muscles and the offerings at the multiplex.

For May, the days since the Valentine's Day dinner-dance had passed slowly, though for the life of her she could not recall what she had done with herself since that Saturday night. She had expected Norman Grafstein to call—if not the next day, given that Sundays were often sacred, do-nothing days for many seniors (the result of the enduring habits of shopkeepers for whom Sunday had been the sole day when the bakery or restaurant or dry-goods store was closed), then certainly the next. On Monday, she had gone to lunch with Flo and Lila (the "bridesmaids lunch," as Flo referred to it) and expected a message on her machine when she returned. There had been no message. On Tuesday, she had remained around the house, reading the *Sun-Sentinel* more thoroughly than usual and thumbing through the Judith Krantz novel that Carol had left behind, possibly as inspiration to May (it was the kind of touch Carol was capable of). She had written a letter to her grandson, taken down the hem of a dress, and baked a kugel with cinnamon and raisins, which she recalled that Norman had expressed a fondness for. But no one had called that day either, outside of Flo to arrange for their Loehmann's trip the next day. Now, Wednesday afternoon, having returned with the dress, she had hurried into the condo, relieved to hear the clicking that indicated a message on her machine, only to discover that it was Carol ordering her to "call and fill me in on every detail of the dance." It was at this moment that May felt the pall settle over her, the kind of throat-choking, stomach-aching disappointment that she hadn't felt since high school nearly sixty years ago.

The next morning when Flo called to ask about her plans for lunch, May could hardly keep her voice steady.

"What's wrong?" demanded Flo, who immediately registered the tremor behind her friend's words. "Aren't you feeling well?"

"It's nothing," said May. "Only a headache. I'll lie down for a while and be fine."

"I'm coming right over," said Flo. "You sound awful."

When Flo arrived, May was sitting on the little balcony off the living room, staring out at the golf course. She was still in her housecoat, and as she turned, Flo saw that her eyes were red. "He's decided he doesn't like me anymore," May said, stretching out her hand to Flo, who, for all that her heart went out to her friend, couldn't help thinking that she had been privy lately to more emotional immaturity than she had a taste for. May, for the life of her, looked like a love-sick teenager.

"What are you talking about?" said Flo, taking her friend's hand and contemplating the irony that seven decades of life had done nothing to alter this age-old scenario.

"It's Norman," said May. "I hadn't heard from him since the dance, so finally I called and left a message. I asked him to brunch tomorrow. I made the kugel he likes." She gestured weakly toward the kitchen. "He called back at six—he knows I go to dinner around six, we all do, so he must have wanted to miss me. Here, listen."

She walked over to the phone machine on the coffee table, rewound the tape, and pressed the button to play (she had clearly replayed the tape many times already). Norman Grafstein's loud, genial voice, more tentative and halting than Flo had ever heard it, filled the room.

"May," he said, then paused for a few seconds and cleared his throat. "I got your kind invitation and am afraid I'll have to decline. Stan and I are off to North Jersey today for"—he cleared his throat again—"an indefinite stay. Stephanie—that's Stan's daughter, my daughter-in-law, you know—is expecting, and we, uh"—again a pause, as he seemed to lose his train of thought— "we haven't seen Ben, that's the three-year-old, in a while. It was Stan's idea"—Norman at this point seemed to get a burst of energy and continued in a rush—"he says club life makes for selfish grandparents and we need to get up there and hone our skills. Well, that means a break from Boca for a while, and I'm afraid no brunch, though I appreciate the thought, especially of the kugel. I haven't had that in a million years." There was a pause again, this time a longer one. It was the logical place to sign off, but Norman seemed to find it hard to hang up the phone. "Well, I just want to say that I've very much enjoyed our time together and that I look forward"—he cleared his throat again—"to, maybe, soon—someday—having that brunch." At this point, he seemed to think he had spoken too long and was determined to get himself off the phone immediately. "That's about the gist of it, then. Take care of yourself, May." He hung up.

Flo sat for a second, saying nothing. Then she looked at May whose face was streaked with tears. "I can't say I'm entirely surprised," said Flo, shaking her head. "I think Norman got scared, and I think his friend, Stan Jacobs, egged him on. Stan, from what I can guess, has a way of influencing people based on his own prejudices and preconceptions. He probably thought that because he's not ready to settle down, then Norman shouldn't be, either. And it's not as though Norman hasn't enjoyed his popularity with the ladies. It didn't help when Hy made the point about finding a man for financial security. It could only have fed his paranoia about being trapped. It's the male fear of commitment that they write all the books about, and Norman, I suspect, was susceptible."

"So you think he's not going to call me again?" asked May, sadly.

"I wouldn't say that," said Flo. "I think Norman genuinely liked you—more than liked you—and if he has the decency and feeling that I think he has, he can't help but eventually want to get back in touch. You can tell from the tape that he's speaking against his will, like someone has a gun to his head, as they say. But men are weak creatures, May, and at this age, their memories aren't good. I'm not trying to be pessimistic. I think Norman was happy with you—in fact, I know it. But there are distractions to get in the way, not to mention the possibility that he might drop dead of a heart attack tomorrow."

"Oh, Flo," said May, laughing weakly in spite of herself, "don't say such things."

"I say them because they're true," said Flo, "and because I don't want you to pine away. At seventy-two, you don't have time for such things. I'm going to have to keep you busy. I may even have to bring in a professional—your daughter-in-law—to make sure that you're properly distracted."

"You wouldn't," said May. "You wouldn't call Carol."

"I don't want to," said Flo with mock sternness. "It's stiff medicine, I know, but if you mope, I'll be forced to. So don't push me. Now get dressed. We're going to lunch, then we'll pop over to Royal Palm for a little shopping, and then maybe to the dinner-theater in Ft. Lauderdale. They're doing *Meet Me in St. Louis* with a Judy Garland look-alike, rumored to be a man. A soppy, badly produced musical comedy is just the tonic you need."

# CHAPTER THIRTY-FOUR

The wedding of Lila Katz and Hy Marcus was held in the large activities room of the Boca Festa clubhouse, with guests repairing to the dining room for the subsequent wedding brunch. The couple had invited a hundred guests, making it an unusually large wedding for people of their age, who had already been married over eighty years between them. It was no secret that some of the guests disapproved of the fanfare, but the immediate family appeared to be tolerant. Hy's brother, who still worked in the family hat business outside of New Haven, had observed philosophically, "He was a fool all his life—so why should he change?"

Hy's children were also surprisingly accepting, having learned years ago to ignore their father and do whatever they pleased. He had been an indulgent parent, proud of them and generous to a fault, and as they grew to maturity and came to modulate their earlier mortification at his boastful chatter, they treated him with irritable affection. Steven, the doctor in Manhattan, had been initially concerned that a marriage on such a scale was an insult to their mother, and that so much hoopla was undignified. His sister, Sarah, however, had set his mind at rest. She had pointed out that thinking about the effect on the dead was unprofitable, their mother not being around to be offended. As for the question of dignity, such were the privileges of being in one's dotage. If anything, their father's age had finally caught up with his mentality, making behavior that had been inappropriate all his life—most notably, at school graduations and recitals—entirely forgivable and even charming. She reminded her brother, moreover, that the marriage was a godsend, relieving them of responsibility for their father's care and allying him with a woman whom they could actually like. For Lila appeared to them to have unusual common sense and personal attractiveness. Wasn't it a wonder, Steven confided to his sister, that such a woman would choose their father for the companion of her declining years? Hy was not a wealthy man, after all, though he was quite comfortable, and he was far from an intellectual heavyweight (the word "fool" always hovered in the air in any conversation regarding Hy Marcus). To this, Sarah, always with the greater abundance of insight, pointed out that Lila, without children, might be fearing the solitude of old age as well as the financial obligations. All in all, both concluded, after many phone conversations in which they congratulated each other on their mutual wisdom, the match had much in its favor, and they applauded it. If their father wanted a wedding that resembled the bar mitzvahs they were currently throwing for their children, then so be it.

Now, as the guests took their seats, Flo and May were asked to position themselves on one side of a large, ornately decorated *chuppa,* while a young woman in a black evening gown plucked the wedding march on a harp beside them. Flo was trying to hide her bouquet in the folds of her dress. The bouquet, she thought, struck a particularly ridiculous note, making her feel like one of those dogs wearing embroidered jackets that are a common sight around Boca, where many dog owners feel their pets should be entitled to enjoy an accessory now and then.

There was a low hum of voices as the last guests seated themselves and whispered to their neighbors, trying to get a handle on what was going on. Suddenly a hush fell over the assemblage, the back doors of the activity room opened, and the bride entered to a surprised murmur. Lila's aqua gown trailed slightly on the floor (she had stopped short of a train, though the idea had occurred to her). She had enlisted the services of a professional makeup artist, and her face appeared smooth and glossy in the manner of Loretta Young in her later years. Flo thought the look smacked of the mortuary but could hear whispers of admiration from some of the throng.

As for Hy, who stood opposite Flo and May on the other side of the *chuppa,* he had a strangely formal appearance—almost as though he were impersonating someone else. Owing no doubt to Lila's intervention, he had abandoned the lime-green cummerbund and tie, and was wearing a conventional cutaway. Holding himself stiffly, his chest pushed forward, his head held high in deference to the occasion, he looked deceptively dignified. He might have been a foreign diplomat or the maître d' of a luxury restaurant. It was amazing, thought Flo, what the help of a tailor and the absence of speech could do for a man. The couple had taken on the look of one of those shimmery senior couples out of a made-for-TV movie or an episode of *The Golden Girls.*

Presiding was a young rabbi, formerly a junior rabbi in a temple in Livingston, New Jersey, who had just taken over the congregation of the Reform temple in West Boca. His predecessor, who had been greatly admired, had decided to leave the rabbinate to devote himself full-time to his real-estate interests. This new rabbi had an air of audacious greenness about him. He was a very with-it rabbi, according to those in the know, and was in the habit of playing his guitar at Shabbat services. Today he had been asked to leave his guitar at home, and seemed at a loss for what to do with his hands. He was the kind of young Jewish man whose youth seems his most marked characteristic— one still saw the loose-lipped face of the bar-mitzvah boy and JIFTY regional leader. One wondered whether such an elderly couple could indeed be legally married by one so young; did the striking disparity in age invalidate the vows? Yet the rabbi had a loud, aggressive confidence, as if daring anyone to challenge his grasp of the prayers or his handling of the prayer book, which he carried with a cavalier recklessness that made some of the guests fear he might suddenly throw it to someone across the room. His yarmulke, heavily embroidered in blue-and-gold thread, sat jauntily, slightly to one side, on his bushy black hair. He chanted loudly in Hebrew, overemphasizing words here and there rather like a Hebraic newscaster. Finally he paused and gazed at the couple as though drinking in the pleasure their particular union afforded him.

"We have here two people," he said in the familiar rabbinical singsong that seems to become more pronounced the closer one gets to Unitarianism. "We have here two people who have had the good fortune to find each other at a time of life so often marked by loneliness, financial burden, and dependence. When many must see their physical capacities diminished and their accomplishments dismissed by a young, uncaring world, these two can cleave to each other. Here are a man and a woman who have found love again even when other loves have been sundered from them. Here are two people who have not been afraid to seek fulfillment at a time when so often fulfillment is deemed complete, the book closed on that chapter of life's experience. Mark the fruit of that search: a handsome couple, the pride of their children and grandchildren. May their marriage be a time of ripening friendship, even as the throes of passion fade and dissipate—a new beginning when so much has been concluded already, a last walk down the passage before the door closes forever. Let this aging Romeo and Juliet light up the world with their love."

"Did he really say what I thought he said," whispered Flo, "or has my Alzheimer's finally set in?"

"Shh . . ." said May, trying not to laugh. "No one is listening to what he's saying. It's the tone they're after."

"The tone, of course. We must soak it in, before the door closes forever. . . ."

May and Flo had been placed at the Boca table. Since most of the guests were relatives or representatives of an earlier life, the number from Boca could be relegated to one table. They sat with two widowers, card-playing friends of Hy's, who kept saying over and over that they hoped this wouldn't spoil their Sunday games. Also at the table were Lila's upstairs neighbor and her husband, who seemed obsessively focused on putting a claim on the centerpiece, and her Tuesday golf partner, a woman who seemed composed of bones barely covered with darkly tanned and wrinkled skin, who kept sending platters back to the kitchen to have the dressing, butter, and sauce removed. "I want," she said to the harried waitress, "a plain piece of fish with nothing on it. Do you understand? Nothing!"

There was also a younger woman—in her forties—who had supervised Lila's stint as a volunteer floral arranger for the Jewish Federation banquet. Known by the Boca set as a genius with flowers, she had built a lucrative career as a floral consultant for Boca charities, where she helped a bevy of artistic matrons construct the centerpieces for important affairs. She was dressed in high Boca style—an elaborate gold-and-silver tie-dyed evening T-shirt and multilayered, sequined silk skirt carefully mismatched with the top. Her nails were very long and very purple, and her face was made up in strong earth tones. She was judged to be stunning and carefully scrutinized by the female guests, who could recall her outfits at previous occasions. She had done Lila's flowers gratis, a fact that had been disseminated widely, and she was busy talking to the couple interested in the centerpiece on how they might best care for it to assure maximum longevity.

Lila and Hy were making rounds while a photographer snapped their picture. When they arrived at Flo and May's table, the flower arranger began to applaud and the rest of the table entered in, all except Flo, who pretended to be fishing for her napkin under the table. Lila grabbed her friends by their arms and pulled them off into a corner.

"Finally I can relax," she sighed.

"It's beautiful," said May, "just what you wanted."

"It is," said Lila. "I know Flo disapproves, but I needed to get it out of my system. You don't know what it's like to have been married to a miser all your life. Hy is a generous man. I can excuse a lot in exchange for generosity."

"Mazel tov," said Flo—she could never dislike Lila for long.

"Nothing will change with us," Lila assured them. "Hy wants our lives to continue just as before. We'll have our separate schedules. Did I tell you we're moving into the three-bedroom next to Hy's old place? He says now that there are two of us, we need more room. He has no objection to my having my own bedroom or my going out with the girls, as he says, whenever I want. I'm even planning to take that literature course with you in the spring. The only difference is that now I can relax. And guess what? I even like his children. They have a surprising amount of sense considering"—she laughed—"their father. I can't complain."

With that, she was off to pay her respects to the next table. May and Flo looked at each other.

"To each her own," said Flo, lifting her glass of champagne with the strawberry fastened to its side, and sloshing some on the sleeve of her taffeta cocktail dress. "What the hell, I'll never wear this thing again," she said. "To the fairy godmothers!" She clicked May's glass.

"To us," said May wistfully.

# CHAPTER THIRTY-FIVE

FOLLOWING THE WEDDING, LILA AND HY LEFT FOR A TEN-DAY honeymoon trip to Italy. It was a Club ABC Tour. Club ABC, headquartered in Bloomfield, New Jersey, is a popular tour operator for the North Jersey set. Since West Boca residents tend to hail from that region, it continues to do a brisk business with a Florida clientele. Billed as a club because of its nominal membership fee, it offers trips to a variety of foreign destinations and boasts a lot of bang for the buck: Airfare, high-quality hotels, and breakfasts are always included. Available on arrival at the destination are personable local guides trained to lead expeditions to local synagogues and discount stores and to generally tolerate the demands of Jewish seniors. To "go ABC" (jocularly said to be an acronym for "All But Christians"), whether to Italy, England, Greece, or Turkey, means that one's needs will be attended to in style and one won't have to pay an arm and a leg in the process. Thus, it is common to hear of an octogenarian with a walker on a strict low-salt diet talking about his trip to the cisterns in Istanbul with ABC, or praising the expertise of ABC's Georgio in getting a special price on gold chains on the Via Veneto. Dear friends have been made on ABC trips, made all the dearer when it is discovered that the individuals involved live only two pods away from each other in the same retirement complex.

Lila and Hy had chosen the three-city deluxe Italian package, which upgrades the four-star hotels offered in the standard package to five stars. Lila had never been abroad and, heady with her newfound monetary security, was intent on going whole hog. But this was no mere sybaritic holiday. Starved as she was for the life she had missed, she was serious about gathering knowledge and worshiping at the shrine of culture.

To this end, she read voraciously in preparation for the trip, clipping articles and assiduously marking guidebooks. Once arrived at their destination—after inspecting the hotel room to ascertain that room size and amenities were as promised—she went to work. She proceeded to see the sights with fierce and concentrated energy. While Hy and the other men sat in outdoor cafés, smoking cigars and talking about the best routes from Boca to New Jersey, Lila and a group of like-minded women spent their days climbing the stone steps of cathedrals and peering at madonnas. All the while, they pelted their long-suffering guides with questions about everything, from the meaning of religious iconography to the fine points of cleaning stained glass.

The energy and inquisitiveness of the elderly Jewish female traveler can be a source of wonder and surprise to the uninitiated. Local guides comment on it all the time, and are known to up their coffee intake and go to bed earlier than usual in preparation for the demands placed upon them by ABC patrons. While a church, a museum, a lunch, and perhaps some light shopping will be fine for another tour group, an ABC group will not be satisfied with such insubstantial fare and will demand at least two more museums and, if possible, a trip up a narrow side street, not generally visited by tourists, to see either an esoteric monument not in the guidebooks or some wizened artisan making rare baubles that can be bought at a discount. Local guides are forever astonished to have a blond-haired seventy-year-old yenta in a sun visor inquiring about a classical frieze that she read was absconded from some Roman temple in the fifth century, brought to a certain local site, and placed in a special crypt, open only between twelve and two during the last two weeks in August—the reason, she will explain, why she booked her trip when she did. Incidents of this kind happen all the time with ABC patrons, and are compounded by a scrupulous attention to the accurate billing and delivery of amenities as promised. What keeps the guides coming back, given the stress such behavior is likely to generate, is the fact that if you perform well, you not only receive a generous tip but are likely to be invited to a grandchild's bar mitzvah or receive yearly mailings of polo shirts, belts, and homemade pound cake on your birthday.

The enormous energy that women like Lila bring to the act of sightseeing might be seen to derive from energy once employed in household management and child-rearing. Yet such an equation fails to make clear the amount of raw power involved. For at the height of domestic exertion, women of this kind tapped into energy storehouses far greater than a given task might seem to warrant. If, for example, one could harness the wattage used in the single feat of shopping for a daughter's bat mitzvah dress (a task whose difficulty is compounded by the fact that the daughter is a carbon copy of the mother, only operating in direct resistance to her), it would no doubt be possible to run a small corporation, map a good portion of the human genome, or supply power for a moderately sized city like Detroit. All of which is to say that Lila was doing a very thorough job getting the three great Italian cities under her belt.

# CHAPTER THIRTY-SIX

FLO WAS VERY DIFFERENTLY ENGAGED IN THE WEEK FOLLOWING the Marcus wedding. After the encounter with Rudy in the club lounge, Mel seemed to have become scarce. She had had a call the next day on her answering machine in which he said he was going to be out of town for a while. He'd been offered a lucrative consulting job in Washington—or was it New York?—that he couldn't afford to turn down. This would force him to put on hold his plans to move to Boca Festa.

Was it a shock? Truth be told, no. Flo felt that she had had intimations, though she'd tried to put them out of her mind. There was no denying that the man had charmed her and that she had enjoyed the attention. But looking back, she realized that the seeds of doubt had been planted quite early, during the trip to the casbah, with its detour to the stretch house in Naples. Mel's friend had not sat well with Flo. She had tried not to see what she had unconsciously known in her heart: that the two men were, as one used to say, "in cahoots." She was thankful that her affections had never really been engaged. The whole incident only served to prove what had long been her maxim: It was better to get your romance between the covers of a book, where you could choose the very best. Anna and Vronsky in *Anna Karenina*—now, there was a relationship worth getting on the edge of your seat for.

A week later, Flo was on her way to meet May at the porch restaurant when she suddenly bumped into Mel near the main pool. He was speaking to Dorothy Meltzer and Roz Fliegler, and excused himself and took her aside. He smiled warmly and showed his usual ingratiating manner, but she discerned a forced note in his voice, and noticed that his eyes traveled over her head as he spoke, as if keeping track of what was going on at the pool nearby.

"I came over to look for you and to apologize for my disappearance. I've been swamped ever since our last talk. Back and forth, up and down. There's the job in Washington, and then some additional work with a small firm here in Boca. Nothing fancy, but it's a favor to a friend. You know how it is when they ask you; you can't turn them down. I must say, I miss our tête-à-têtes." As he spoke, he waved to Roz and Dorothy, as if to say that he'd be joining them again in a moment. "Anyway," he continued in a sprightly tone, "the work in Washington has some perks attached. They want me to put my two cents in on a PR plan they're pitching for Jamaica or Bermuda—one of those vacation spots, it doesn't matter, the stuff we do is pretty boilerplate—and they say, out of appreciation, they'll spring me for a trip over to wherever—St. Croix, St. John's. Now, that's the kind of place I'd like to retire to. The islands, I must say, have it all over the west coast of Florida. Plenty of open beach and solitude. Plenty of space to write." Flo nodded politely, agreeing that the islands would be just the place for him, then excused herself, saying she had an appointment that, delightful as she found his company, she just had to get to. He showed no unwillingness to let her go.

What, she wondered to herself as she hurried off to meet May, had she once seen in this man?

And that was the last, quite literally, that she had seen of him. She hoped it would remain the last. It pleased her to note that she did not miss him. She was now determined to rely on her own resources—to spend her time playing tennis with the club pro, taking meals at the clubhouse with May, and sitting by the pool reading Mary Gordon's latest novel. Flo realized that Gordon's Catholic guilt relaxed her because it made her Jewish guilt seem light-hearted by comparison. It was always nice to think that someone's else's family was crazier than yours.

Flo also found diversion in her ever-lively correspondence with Amy. She had to admit that the computer, on which this correspondence was transacted, had become a necessary adjunct to her life. Blaming computers for killing off books was an accusation that she had long made to her son, the dot-com millionaire. But a computer had arrived, despite her protestations, a year ago as his birthday present to her—a gift, she thought at the time as she extracted the thing from its miles of bubble wrap, that clearly reflected his unconscious hostility. As part of the gift, Jonathan had also sent a personal Internet "trainer," who showed up at the door in a black turtleneck and dark glasses, announcing that he had been instructed to get her up to speed, no matter how long it took. It did not take long. In no time, she was surfing the Web, participating in a nineteenth-century literature chat group, and e-mailing Amy about the latest Eric Rohmer movie and the moral issues surrounding Woody Allen's marriage to his quasi-stepdaughter. Sometimes, when she couldn't sleep, she would sign on to Instant Messenger and find that her great-niece (screen name: womanwarrior) was on-line, too, and it was like wandering into a coffee shop at two A.M. and finding your best friend there. In the end, she humbled herself and admitted to Jonathan that she'd been wrong: The computer was a delightful diversion and a vast, if unsifted, resource for information.

In this way, Flo's days passed pleasantly enough.

For May, however, it was another story. It bothered Flo to see that her friend was depressed, try as she might to hide it. Not being a reader and having no interest in tennis or golf, May had little to occupy her time. This had never been a problem for her before. She had busied herself cooking and cleaning the apartment, taking walks, and going shopping for gifts for her grandchildren. But lately these pastimes had seemed insufficient.

She was by turns restless and lethargic, eager to do something but not interested in doing anything in particular. She was, concluded Flo, unhappy, and when May reported that Carol had invited her to come up for a few days and celebrate Adam's eighth birthday, she urged her friend to go.

"Normally, I would be against your traveling a thousand miles to watch thirty eight-year-old boys squirt water guns at each other. But given your mopey state, I think this might be just the medicine you need."

Carol, who had a preternatural ability to sense indecision and take advantage of it—in the way a predatory animal can sense the vulnerability of its potential prey—continued to call every night with added reasons why May must come to North Jersey.

"I need you to help me with the goody bags for Adam's party," she insisted at one point. "They've become a big thing. No more lollipops and jump ropes. You can turn your child into a social outcast giving things like that. The kids are educated consumers nowadays. Which means it takes work. And, by the way, I had a thought. Since we give *shmendricks* to the children, why not to the mothers? It's a nice gesture, and no one's done it yet. You could make your truffles; they'd make a nice gift."

Carol had already checked the flights for the next two days, and when May failed to refute her suggestion for a Thursday evening departure forcefully enough, the tickets appeared the next morning by FedEx. What could she do? May packed her bags, put her truffle recipe into her purse, kissed Flo good-bye, and went.

# CHAPTER THIRTY-SEVEN

AMY RUNCIE-SLOTKIN WAS THE TWENTY-ONE-YEAR-OLD DAUGHTER
of Flo's brother's son, Philip, and his wife, Meredith. Amy was
a free spirit and the bane of her parents' existence. She had always
acted contrary to expectations, choosing to play the drums instead of the piano, to pierce her nose rather than her ears, and,
subsequently, to go to NYU Film School instead of Yale. Flo
had tried to point out to Amy's parents that their daughter's
rebellion was fairly benign, there being no evidence of drug ad-
diction, pregnancy, or serious eating disorders, and that Amy
seemed a happy young woman with a great deal of enthusiasm
for the things that interested her. But her parents, who had decided when Amy was in preschool that she would become a
lawyer like themselves (though a career in medicine was not to
be ruled out), were endlessly complaining about her perverse
interests and underachievement.

They had asked Flo, whom they knew had leverage in being
eccentric, to speak to Amy before the fateful Yale decision. Flo
had told her great-niece that, personally, she thought being a
filmmaker, even an unsuccessful one, was more potentially gratifying than being a lawyer. This advice had put something of a
pall on Flo's relationship with her nephew and his wife. But it
had earned her Amy's eternal friendship.

Lately, the issue of a documentary film project had been
Amy's overriding preoccupation. She had been e-mailing Flo
almost daily, trying out ideas and picking her great-aunt's always

fertile brain. Topics relating to the homeless, Korean markets, rock bands, and in vitro fertilization had all been raised as possibilities and then quickly dismissed as being trite or done to death. Flo had suggested a piece on New York delicatessens (the subject of her bonding experience with Saul Bellow), but after a bit of research, Amy discovered that the subject had been used last year, and had even won third place at the senior awards festival. Apartment hunting in New York City was also given a bit of consideration, especially since Flo knew a successful East Side real-estate agent, a part-time Boca Festa resident, who would jump at the prospect of being followed around by a camera. But Amy reported that last year's winning film had been about house-hunting in Westchester, and the idea seemed to her too close for comfort.

In the course of their correspondence, Flo had supplied her niece with running commentary on the minutiae of Boca life. It was not an unfamiliar subject to Amy. She had visited what she liked to call "shopper's paradise" over the years with her parents, long before Flo had moved down, and had enjoyed herself immensely.

"I admit it, I love to shop," she confessed when Flo had shown surprise at Amy's desire to spend hours going through racks of leather pants at Mizner Center or poring over about ten thousand pairs of earrings at the Festival flea market. "It's one of the few things my mother and I have in common, though since she's a shiksa and I'm only half of one, I'm better at it than she is."

The day after May left, Flo got an e-mail message from Amy in her characteristically brief and cryptic style: "By George, I've got it! Inspired subject for my film! Will be down tomorrow, arriving West Palm Airport at 5:30. Love and kisses, Amy."

Flo liked to say that Amy used e-mail the way people used telegrams in the old days. "You're not being charged by the word," she often wrote back. But Amy's existence seemed too hectic to allow for elaboration in any medium, even e-mail, where everyone else had a hard time staunching the tide of verbiage. Flo used to try to phone to fill in some of the gaps in their correspondence, but had learned that Amy was never in her apartment. Among her set, going out did not necessarily mean coming back—at least not at any hour when a reasonable person could be expected to be awake. Without thinking too deeply on what her niece planned to do—a docudrama on the endangered Florida alligator or on shopping in the Boca malls?—Flo made sure to be at the airport waiting when Amy's plane came in. Her great-niece was one of her favorite people, and the prospect of spending some time with her, especially with May and Lila gone, was a source of pleasurable expectation.

Amy was nearly the last off the plane—she and two companions, each carrying a large and unwieldy collection of cameras, tripods, lights, microphones, and assorted equipment. With their appearance and their baggage, they made for a distinctive presentation among the passengers in pastel jogging suits.

Amy was wearing very short cutoffs, a black leather halter top, a nose stud, and (this was a new addition) a swatch of pink hair over her left ear. She had Flo's large-boned, lean body and angular features, and she walked with the purposeful air of a woman who, even if she didn't know where she was going, was determined to make where she was going into a destination. With her was a very tall, young black man whose hair was half in cornrows (as though he had lost interest in the idea halfway through) and another young man in a tight half T-shirt and an earring. Amy ran forward to greet her great-aunt with the same delight and abandon that she had displayed at age ten. "Auntie!" she screamed, hugging Flo. "Isn't this the neatest idea? Aren't I a genius?"

"I know you're a genius," said Flo, "but I don't think I've fathomed the idea."

"What do you mean?" asked Amy. "I e-mailed you. We're going to film at your place—what's it called, Boca Festa?—a documentary on senior life in the mecca of Jewish retirement, Boca Raton: the intricacies and vagaries of life in a gated community under the Florida sunshine. 'From *cukalane* to clubhouse'—right, George?"

She turned to her friend with the cornrows who was carrying the camera and tripod.

"What's a *cukalane* again?" asked George.

"Well, it's something to do with Jews taking vacations, though I'm not sure what," said Amy. "It sounds good. Flo can fill us in. She'll have loads of ideas. She always does. And she's a librarian, so she can help us with research."

Flo must have looked confused, because Amy hugged her and took a breath.

"Let me start again; maybe I'm getting ahead of myself. First, I'll introduce you. This is George." She motioned to the half-braided giant with the cameras. "He's my boyfriend, and he'll do most of the shooting. He has a way of getting in anywhere he wants."

George shook Flo's hand and smirked at Amy.

"This is Jordan." She motioned to the earringed young man in the skimpy T-shirt. "He'll handle the mike—he's also a crackerjack editor. Oh, and he's gay. He always likes people to know that up front so they're not surprised later."

"Thank you, Amy," said Jordan sarcastically, "for being so considerate."

"They're really nice guys," continued Amy cheerfully, "and we're doing this advanced DV project together, and we're all really talented, and now, since we have an absolutely awesome idea, we intend to win first prize at the student festival. I promise we won't bother you at all. We'll sleep in the kitchen or the bathroom or something—you won't even know we're around. There's one thing, though. We need to get permission to shoot in the complex. I told George and Jordan that you would handle it, since you're my brilliant, eccentric great-aunt and can handle anything." She gave Flo the look, half stubborn defiance and half little-girl pleading, that Flo remembered her using on everyone since she was five to get whatever she wanted.

The prospect of having Amy and her friends camping out in her living room did not pose a particular problem for Flo, who had never been one to care about the condition of her rugs or to put too much stock on personal space. But she was a bit concerned about how her neighbors would react, and she was uncertain about her ability to finagle permission for the group to film on the grounds of the complex. Normally, such a thing would be impossible. The people at Boca Festa paid for privacy and predictability, and the appearance on the scene of the road show from *Hair* was likely to fluster and intimidate all but the hippest of residents. Fortunately, Flo realized she had a resource that might help in obtaining the permission her niece needed: Rudy would be on her side.

She knew this implicitly for two reasons. One, since she was a club benefactor, he would want, above all, to be of service to her. She was glad that she had let drop the other day her disappointment in the conventional nature of Boca Festa's landscaping. Rudy had explained that the budget did not allow for anything too elaborate, given that the unpredictable climate had a way of killing off more interesting, less hearty plants. "Of course," he had noted, "this is precisely the kind of thing that would be ideal for a bequest," and had leaned over to kiss her hand by way of punctuation. She had said nothing, a response she had learned worked well to fuel expectation without in any way establishing a commitment.

The second reason she counted on Rudy's support was that he was by nature and inclination a performer. The idea of being part of a documentary film, even a student one—and Flo had no doubt that Amy would effectively sell herself as a future Steven Spielberg—would be irresistible to him.

"Don't you see, Aunt Flo, what a good idea this is?" Amy insisted as they walked across the airport parking lot toward the car. "Here we have an enclosed, homogeneous community in which very intricate and elaborate relationships are generated. It's the ideal narrative material with visual appeal for a post-modern age."

"Stop with the metababble," said George. "Cut to the chase: It's cheap; it's doable, and it'll be funny as hell."

In point of fact, the more Flo thought about the idea, the more she saw its possibilities. Boca Festa as the subject of a documentary? Why not?

"I see what you mean," she said, nodding as her niece and her friends trundled toward the car. "It's Jane Austen's 'two or three families in a country setting,' updated and up-aged. And, yes, it could be damned funny."

# CHAPTER THIRTY-EIGHT

MAY WOULD NOT HAVE DREAMED A MONTH AGO THAT SHE would welcome being taken in hand by her daughter-in-law. Generally, she fled from Carol's desire to direct her life with the twitchy alacrity of a frightened rabbit. Yet given her depressed and lethargic state, there was something comforting about turning herself over to Carol's direction and being placed into the jigsaw puzzle of her daughter-in-law's mind-numbingly complicated but highly organized existence.

Carol met May at Newark Airport with the declaration that "there's loads to do and we better get busy." Of course, with Carol, there was a certain paradox attached to her frenetic busyness. She was like a farmer who keeps horses in order to haul away the manure that they generate. She was forever devising complicated chores out of the most seemingly straightforward and simple tasks. One would have thought, given the energy she was expending now, that she was planning the entertainment of an important business colleague or a high-level community official, not the birthday party of an eight-year-old. But the fact that Carol did not draw such distinctions was part of her success. It showed a refusal to give anyone or anything short shrift. Truth be told, it had a disarming effect on those with whom she came into contact. Even as she irritated many people, she also, strangely, endeared herself to them by giving them her complete and undivided attention.

"We have to go pick up the cake," she said as she wove expertly in and out of the heavy traffic leading out of the airport.

"Wait till you see it. I designed it myself and went over it with the baker yesterday to be sure he followed the sketch. I tried to color code, but bakers tend to be color-blind." (These were the sorts of bizarre but often accurate observations that Carol excelled in.)

When they arrived at the bakery, the cake was ready, on display at the counter, and already being admired by a group of women who seemed to find it entrancing. It was in the shape of a baseball field. It had candles in the shape of players and peppermints designating the bases. "All my idea," Carol explained to May. "They say they're going to make it a standard from now on. And I have extras of the mints"—she took a bag from her pocketbook and shook it consolingly—"so each of the boys can have one. You know how they fight about things like that."

Once arrived at the house, while May made the truffles, Carol laid out the materials for the boys' goody bags, carefully checking to be sure that there were an equal number of the requisite items: a yo-yo that played the *Star Wars* theme, a key chain with a miniature catcher's mitt, and sundry erasers, stickers, and whistles, all of which would no doubt be lost or thrown away as soon as the guests got home from the party, but were nonetheless de rigueur as ritualized talismans. Carol had also bought small baskets for the mothers, which she planned to fill with May's truffles along with containers of hand cream and lip gloss. It was clear that with the brainchild of the matriarchal goody bags she had reset the bar for children's birthday parties in the northern New Jersey suburbs. They would be that much more labor-intensive from now on.

The family went out to dinner that night. Carol had deemed cooking impossible in a kitchen in which the counter space had been turned into a miniature assembly line and the table taken over by boxes of paper plates, plastic knives and forks, hats, noisemakers, and the like, all of which held to the baseball theme. At one point, Adam proclaimed that baseball bored him and he wanted to take up hockey. Carol had responded that he was to like baseball for at least one more day, and then they'd talk about it.

The restaurant chosen for dinner was called the Jolly Traveler and had a definite kid-friendly atmosphere. It featured a large-screen TV showing cartoons in the corner and a kids' menu longer than the adults'—just the sort of atmosphere that Boca Festa residents loudly decried. It was a source of ongoing discussion among May's peers that their children were spoiling their grandchildren and creating a new generation capable of God knows what. "I've never seen such a thing," it was observed. "What with the lessons and the special schools and the taking them to Europe as though the Catskills weren't good enough, no wonder the children talk back. We would never have stood for it." The idea that this generation of parents was creating monsters of entitlement by tailoring the world to their needs was one of the few generally agreed upon notions in Boca Festa (no one breathed, of course, that the notorious Jewish American Prince and Princess, not to mention the young Philip Roth, had been the product of *their* generation of child-rearing). They also suspected that what their children were doing was somehow in retaliation for what they had done, and hence they sensed in it a definite accusation. It didn't help, of course, that the whole thing placed them in the double bind of wanting to prove that their children were on the wrong track while at the same time not wishing misery and failure upon their grandchildren.

Whenever the subject of child-rearing was raised, it invariably led to the recounting of the famous Weintraub incident near the Boca Festa pool last year. Tara Weintraub-Kaplan, age six, had told her mother that she would not wear flip-flops to the club-house, "and you can't make me," whereupon her grandmother, Hettie Weintraub, announced to her daughter, Cindy, that she would never have allowed Cindy to speak to her that way.

Cindy, instead of muttering under her breath as she generally did in these cases, was suffering from PMS and reacted violently, throwing the flip-flops at Hettie and screaming that maybe if she had, she wouldn't be taking 150 milligrams of Zoloft a day. The scene, played out in front of at least twenty residents, was talked about for months with that particular brand of schadenfreude reserved for incidents striking very close to the bone. Everyone knew that it could just as well have been their daughter, which of course did not prevent them from shaking their heads over poor Hettie.

At the Jolly Traveler, the children had indeed taken over the establishment, and May found it difficult to digest her salad in a setting in which there was so much shrieking, as sodas spilled, crayons broke, and toddlers were thrust into and pulled out of booster seats. Carol, May noted, appeared to thrive on the mayhem (she had cut not only Adam's meat, but the boy's at the next table), while Alan, in the fashion cultivated from his own childhood, remained unperturbed, his mind occupied elsewhere. It was not relaxing, May thought, but it was lively, and in her droopy state, it had a cheering effect. By the time they got home, the two-year-old was asleep in her car seat and Adam, who had been whining loudly about wanting to take up hockey and buy the needed implements immediately, had also fallen into a weary stupor. May, too, felt tired, and thought finally she would be able to get a good night's rest. She looked forward to climbing into the bed in the guest room, which Carol had decorated in a riot of color and design coordination. The bedspread, sheets, curtains, rug, and even the tissue box holder all shared the same basic motif of black and lavender flowers—a veritable carnival for the eye that had initially made May squint. Tonight, finally, tucked under the dizzyingly colorful sheet and, more important, under her daughter-in-law's wing, she would sleep.

The birthday party was held the next day at a roller-skating rink outside of town. Carol had rented the rink for three hours in the afternoon and had replaced the in-house DJ with one of her own choosing. The regular musical fare, she said, was "too rinky-dink"—an odd criticism, thought May, for the music of a roller-skating rink. Carol had also hired a roller-skating game leader (a rarefied version of the *tummler* May remembered from vacations in the Catskills), who led the thirty boys in various roller-skating tricks and games. Carol had assigned May the task of waiting near the opening of the rink with a box of Band-Aids and tissues, with instructions to minister to injured or otherwise disgruntled boys who sought to exit. No one, as it happened, seemed inclined to do so. The boys remained in a state of frenetic activity within the parameter of the rink, lunging, shouting, attempting with variable success to roller-skate, occasionally kicking and grabbing at each other and having to be torn asunder by the roller-skating game leader. Their mothers sat, huddled and exhausted, at a picnic table in the corner of the room. It was clear, looking at them, why Carol predominated within her circle. She alone appeared energetic and bouncily efficient, her brightness undimmed even by the demands of thirty preadolescent boys. She was wearing black leggings, a long Donna Karan wraparound sweater, and black mules, giving her the look of a high-fashion security guard as she flitted back and forth among the group of mothers; Alan, whom she was directing in the use of the camcorder; the DJ, with whom she had struck up a lively rapport and whose business card she had promised to distribute to her friends; and May, whose well-being she was not above considering. Carol had even found May a comfortable swivel chair in the rink manager's office. Though the manager was sitting on it, she had snatched it out from under him and dragged it over to May with the order that she sit down and relax.

The next morning, Carol directed May to help Adam write his thank-you notes while she fielded calls from the mothers. At some point in each call, she would pause in her conversation to shout out that "Billy's mother wants the recipe for the truffles," only to cover the phone with her hand and mouth in an exaggerated whisper: "Don't give it to her."

It should be noted that among the calls received that morning one was from Carol's friend Sandy, a resident of Scotch Plains, whose son Jeremy was in a play group with little Benjamin Grafstein. Sandy, it must be added, was privy to Stephanie Grafstein's intention to purchase an armchair for the corner of her living room that weekend—a fact to be kept in mind when considering ensuing events of the day.

In the afternoon, it was decided they would go to the Short Hills mall to look for pillows for the den. Carol had already visited several department stores and seen a number that she liked, but she was a fiercely thorough comparative shopper. Every possible version of the item in question had to be inspected, its merits cataloged and weighed, before the idea of purchase could begin to be contemplated.

It was in the mall that May saw him. They had left Bloomingdale's after Carol quickly ascertained the absence of the desired pillows, and May was standing holding Adam's hand as Carol maneuvered the stroller out of Ann Taylor, where she had been looking at the sale sweaters. Norman Grafstein was walking with a tall pregnant woman, also pushing a stroller with a toddler in it; Stan Jacobs was on the woman's other side. Norman must have seen her, too, because she saw him stop for a moment, then lean across and say something to Stan, who looked her way. Before she knew it, they were face-to-face, and May, overcome with emotion, had turned white as a sheet. She felt weak and might have lost her balance had she not had Adam's hand to steady her.

Norman, looking flustered and excited, was the first to speak: "May Newman, as I live and breathe, what a delightful surprise!"

May was too shaken to say anything, but fortunately, Carol, who was never at a loss, jumped in and took over:

"May came up for Adam's birthday," she explained, smoothing her son's hair for emphasis. "Alan and I think it's important that he have his grandma with him on such a special day." She smoothed Adam's hair again, and he pulled away in annoyance, sensing he was being used. She then concentrated her attention on Norman. "It's nice to see you again, Mr. Grafstein. This must be Mark's wife, Stephanie, and this must be little Benjamin." Carol's ability to call forth names mentioned in passing at an earlier date was nothing short of miraculous.

The tall woman acknowledged that she was indeed Stephanie Grafstein, and reintroduced Carol to her father. Stan shook Carol's hand, then turned back to study May. He had registered her paleness and noted that she had not yet spoken.

"These are the Newmans," Norman continued with more confidence now, his eyes focused on May, who had begun to turn from pale to red as she felt herself scrutinized. "Alan, Carol's husband, went to high school with Mark, if you remember my telling you. Carol was kind enough to visit a few months ago. May"—he put his hand on May's arm—"lives in Boca, and has become a good friend."

Carol quickly engaged Stephanie and Stan in conversation about the comparative virtues of shopping in Short Hills, New Jersey, versus Boca Raton. She had understood, with her usual rapidity of deduction, all the particularities of their circumstances, down to the proportion of Jewishness in Stephanie's makeup. It was Carol's gift to be able to take the measure of things very quickly and assume the right tone when the situation demanded. In this case, she knew instinctively to reign herself in so as to give these somewhat aloof, somewhat alien people a chance to orient themselves. During the duration of her conversation with Stan and his daughter, she was not for a moment unaware of the engrossing conversation that was proceeding off to the side between May and Norman Grafstein.

After his original embarrassment, Norman seemed to embrace

the occasion with enthusiasm. The decision to flee commitment had sprung less from his friend's influence than from his own vanity; he had resisted giving up the heady pleasures of geriatric dating. Suddenly he saw things differently. While he had balked at the idea of being hooked, he now asked himself: Had he really enjoyed the dating scene so much? The answer was no. The various women whom he had squired about were hardly recognizable to him as individuals. He could never recall their last names, and he was often allergic to their perfume. It suddenly seemed obvious to him that May was the sweetest woman he had ever met. He would be happy to have her as his date for what remained of his life.

Though it had taken May several minutes to regain her bearings, she soon felt at ease again. Perhaps she had been wrong in her interpretation of his phone message. Clearly he was glad to see her. Her misery was all forgotten, and she felt herself recovering the spontaneity that had marked her manner with him over the past several weeks.

After ten minutes or so, Carol, having assured herself that Norman and May had sufficiently connected and knowing that too much time can be as detrimental as too little in such circumstances, brought the meeting to a close. She announced the necessity of getting Adam to his swimming lesson at the JCC (though the lesson wasn't for an hour). Perhaps they could hook up one of these days, she said to Stephanie; Alan would love catching up with Mark. As for her mother-in-law, Carol explained that May would be returning to Boca directly, where she was sure that Norman and Stan would have occasion to see her.

"And when are *you* going back?" she asked innocently, turning to Norman.

Although he had planned to stay up north for a while, he suddenly felt inclined to shorten his trip. "Soon," said Norman, "sometime next week, if not earlier. I haven't firmed up my plans yet." He looked at May. "But I'll call you. We can have brunch as soon as I get back, and maybe, if I'm good"—he winked—"you'll make me that kugel you promised."

May left the mall holding Adam's hand, but hardly aware of it. She was floating on air.

# CHAPTER THIRTY-NINE

FLO HAD BEEN RIGHT ON THE SUBJECT OF RUDY SALZBURG. HE was perfectly agreeable to the filming, seeing in it the possibility of a starring role for himself. However, he explained, his support was not enough. They still required the approval of the club board.

This was unforeseen. "Going before the board," as the phrase went, was a daunting prospect. The board, Flo knew, was a notoriously contentious body. Its meetings had entered the popular folklore of Boca Festa as occasions for ferocious power struggles and vituperative backbiting. Only last month, there had been an enormous fracas over the issue of relocating the trash bins in the parking lot. A fight had ensued between Pinkus Lotman and Manny Schaeffer, requiring three other board members (one with a heart condition) to separate them. A careful review of the minutes had shown that Pinkus had raised the concern about the bins because his Lincoln had been scratched when someone had pressed up against it in the process of getting from the path to the nearby bin. Though Manny's name was not directly mentioned, Pinkus had already put it out that he suspected him, since he was known to transport large bags of trash from his second-floor apartment and to carry his keys on a chain attached to a belt loop on his Bermuda shorts. Manny flatly denied the charge and resented what he took to be a public accusation. Subsequent meetings had done nothing to clarify whether the bins should indeed be relocated or whether the subject was a personal one, to be resolved between Pinkus and Manny alone.

Such things were standard fare at board meetings and resulted in very few concrete decisions. In the past, Rudy had found it expedient to bypass board approval on minor issues, simply proceeding as he saw fit. He would have most willingly done so in this case, he explained to Flo, only recent events had made this impossible. It all stemmed from a decision he had made two weeks ago abolishing the breadsticks on the table at lunch. It was a cost-saving measure that he had deemed to be uncontroversial. The sticks tended to get stale quickly and were rarely sampled, since guests liked to leave room for more substantial fare. Yet the decision to abolish them had resulted in a storm of protest.

Roz Fliegler had been the first to mention the absence of the breadsticks in a pod meeting. "Where are the breadsticks?" she had asked in a peremptory tone, after which others were quick to second the question, though they hadn't noted their absence until Roz had pointed it out.

Finally, Rudy had been called in to explain. He noted that the breadsticks were rarely eaten and that the chef found himself with more croutons than he knew what to do with.

"That's not the point," noted Roz huffily. "They were decorative. Now the tables look naked."

Others chimed in, with some maintaining that they actually ate the breadsticks.

Ultimately, the point was raised that this was, after all, a board issue. Why had Rudy not gotten the approval of the board before removing the breadsticks?

"It's a matter of democratic process," noted Isadore Waxman, whose interest in history and political theory was well known. "We pay our dues and we expect proper representation. This kind of high-handed decision making"—he waved his hand toward Rudy, who straightened defensively—"does not reflect the principles upon which our club has been duly constituted." The statement drew enthusiastic applause.

The issue had become a firebrand, taken up across the complex, with a special committee assigned to look into recent decisions that Rudy had made without board consultation. It had been, he confessed to Flo, a humiliating ordeal. Eager as he was to facilitate her niece's project, he was obliged to conform to the letter of the law, though he admitted that taking anything before the board, especially now in the wake of the Lotman-Schaeffer dispute, was a gamble.

It was decided that Amy would accompany Flo to the meeting and, with her aunt's help, present her request in person. Flo had convinced her niece to use a cream rinse on her hair, remove her nose stud, and wear a skirt. "There's no point giving them fodder," explained Flo. "We'll have enough on our hands as it is."

The board listened to the case politely.

"What," someone asked, "is the story the film is going to tell?"

Amy responded that this was a difficult question to answer. "We'll try to capture the daily life of the club: how you spend your day, what you like to do and talk about, that sort of thing." A number of members nodded their heads as if rehearsing their day as she spoke. Amy continued, "In time, what happens is that a story emerges; it kind of finds its way into the film—like a lost child." There were further nods and murmurs as they tried to take this image in. "But you have to understand," she concluded, smiling her most ingratiating smile, "with a documentary we can't entirely predict what the story will be in advance. It has to take shape on its own. It's fishing for diamonds, so to speak." There was another murmur and rustle among the audience as they considered this metaphor.

"Personally"—it was Pinkus Lotman, rising slowly with the mannered deliberation of Spencer Tracy in *Inherit the Wind,* a film that had much impressed him—"I'm against it. It's a powder keg. She says she's fishing, and fishing is not what we want here.

She'll start filming and find things that make us look bad. It happens on *60 Minutes* all the time. Bad is always more dramatic, so they make it a smear job."

"It's only bad if you have something to hide," piped up Manny Schaeffer, jumping to his feet. He was a small man with a high, reedy voice that nonetheless carried a great deal of authority (some people said he bore a striking resemblance to that fearsome Hollywood mogul Harry Cohn). "I think it's an excellent idea. It will make us stand out from the other clubs and show us to advantage."

In no time at all the group had polarized along two lines, strangely reminiscent of the breakdown in the trash-bin controversy. There was the Lotman side, which feared an embarrassing exposé, and the Schaeffer side, which saw the opportunity for free publicity. It was clear that a stalemate had been reached and that a creative maneuver was called for to break the impasse. Not by accident had Rudy Salzburg made a fortune in the ice cream business.

"You know," he said, tapping a manicured finger on the table where the refreshments committee had laid out a nice spread, "correct me if I'm wrong, but isn't there an Academy Award given for documentary film?"

There was silence. The board looked expectantly at Amy.

"Well, this happens to be true," she said, nodding to Rudy and smiling at the group before her, "and I might add that NYU has done very well at all the awards. I mean, it's common knowledge that most of the winners in the major festivals nowadays have attended either NYU Film School or USC, and I'd say that recently, NYU has the lead. That's one of the reasons I chose to go. And besides, everyone knows New Yorkers are smarter."

This drew a laugh and a murmur of agreement.

"I have a really talented crew," continued Amy, "and as my aunt mentioned, I'm on a merit-based partial scholarship, and last year my student film won an Olive Branch at the Village

Film Festival, where there were over five hundred entries. I don't want to get your hopes up, of course, but with a subject with this potential interest and visual richness, an Academy Award nomination is not out of the question. And in the event that we were nominated, it stands to reason that we'd want the subjects in the film at the awards ceremony. It's great human interest and publicity value for the film."

Flo was impressed to see that Amy was as good as Rudy at working her audience. Everyone had a question, including what to wear to the Awards. And when it came time for a vote, it was discovered that opposition to the project had evaporated. Permission for filming was unanimously approved.

# CHAPTER FORTY

To HER SURPRISE, FLO FOUND THAT AMY AND HER FRIENDS AS-
similated with relative ease into the life of Boca Festa. The cameras, initially feared by many of the women concerned about
cellulite on their thighs and hair in need of a touch-up, were
soon forgotten.

Amy used the analogy of science fiction genre films to explain
this to a puzzled Flo. "Once the society accepts the alien visitors," she said, "nobody ever notices them much. They lose their
shock value and everybody just goes back to business as usual."

The analogy, Flo thought, was apt in other ways as well. Amy
and her friends were so different in appearance from the general
run of club members that their cameras seemed like just another
piece of physical exotica, like Amy's nose stud or George's cornrows—or, to use Amy's analogy, like the third eye on an alien
visitor.

There was also the kibbitzing factor that soon wore away any
sense that the filmmakers were aliens. The population of Boca
Festa was by temperament curious and inclined to engage. They
liked to question, probe, and commiserate, and they held to the
steadfast assumption that everyone, however superficially different from themselves, was at heart really exactly like them. Amy
and her friends were therefore continually peered at in a penetrating though not entirely unpleasant way, as though those scrutinizing them had seen them somewhere before—perhaps at
their daughter's wedding—and were trying to place them.

It helped as well that the filmmakers were an easygoing and

appreciative lot. Amy knew Boca from her numerous visits during childhood, when her parents, during rough spots in their marriage, had taken short jaunts there to unwind. Later she had been shipped down to Eddie and Flo (an exposure that her parents now thought far less benign than they had imagined at the time). But even George and Jordan, for whom Boca was an entirely new experience, quickly developed a taste for the pastimes and personalities of the place. George took to playing cards with some of the men in the evening and was judged an above-average pinochle player, while Jordan was known to spend time at the pool putting suntan lotion on the women's backs and admiring their jewelry. The manicured grounds, the leisure activities, and the pleasant weather were all seductive, the group agreed. They were particularly taken by the quality and quantity of the food, not only at Boca Festa but everywhere in West Boca.

"Everything tastes good," remarked George, taking a large forkful of smoked sturgeon and eating it with his bagel with schmear. "It's like they've discovered some miracle seasoning that gives everything maximum flavor."

"Maybe we're in heaven," noted Jordan.

"Or in that place in the Albert Brooks film, where everybody goes after they die and waits to be assigned their ultimate fate," added George.

"*Defending Your Life.*"

"That's it. Remember how the food was really good there, too? Is Albert Brooks Jewish?" He turned to Amy. "Maybe his parents live in Boca."

It wasn't long before the group had become extremely sought after by a certain segment of the Boca Festa population who enjoyed debating topics like affirmative action, rap music, and body piercing. These debates sometimes grew loud and intense, and the group soon learned to take comments made in the heat of argument in stride. Arguing, for Boca Festa residents, was not necessarily a sign of dislike—on the contrary, fifty-year marriages had been sustained on this foundation alone. Vigorous debate was even said to have health benefits, getting the blood circulating better than a good game of tennis.

The group had spent the first days of their stay collecting general background footage that could be used to add atmosphere and provide filler once the structure of the film was in place. There were panning shots of elderly men moving in procession in their golf carts like generals surveying a battlefield, and of jaunty septuagenarian tennis players in pleated skirts who appeared not to generate anything in the way of sweat despite hours of play. Amy told Flo that she had never seen tennis played so slowly, the ball moving back and forth as though underwater, or out of a scene from *Elvira Madigan*.

Some of the best footage involved the kind of spontaneous interchange that was likely to arise when one resident began expounding on a subject to the camera in a public place. The possibility for accumulating commentary was amazing, as talk grew with the rapid, combustible energy of brushfire. It was simply impossible for someone to say something without arousing the need for someone nearby to say something else. Nor was any question in itself a guarantee of the direction the conversation would take. The material emerging from any single question held to a very high level of improbability, as though the principle of chaos theory (that one interference would, over time, cause an outcome very far afield from the original direction of events) was that much greater than normal when the variables involved were elderly Jews with the leisure to indulge in a free play of mind.

At lunch on the Friday of the first week of filming, the group had positioned itself in what seemed to be relative seclusion at the end of the buffet table. George was holding the camera and Jordan the boom mike, and Amy had gotten hold of a man in pink Bermuda shorts and asked him to speak a little about his interests.

"Interests? What interests?" exclaimed the man irritably, as though he had been asked to discuss his bank account or his sex life. The group had learned not to take explosive reactions to seemingly innocuous questions too seriously. In the minds of the respondents the questions might harbor unforeseen depths and implications, or might simply serve as a convenient pretext to vent on a favorite subject.

"How can I have interests? Once Leona passed away, my interests were kaput." The man snapped his fingers and continued in a less irritable tone. "We had interests together. We were best friends." He sighed resignedly. "It's like having your arm cut off. Not here"—he indicated the elbow—"but here"—he pointed to his shoulder. "It's walking around without an arm."

"Don't I know," noted a woman in a sequined jogging suit who had sidled into the conversation while getting herself more potato salad. "Jack and I did everything together. But you make do. The children are always asking: How do you spend your time? I tell them that I find occupation."

"They're running around getting degrees, networking," continued the man, taking up from the jogger's point about children. "I tell them: Find someone, settle down, you'll be happier."

"Marriage today is not such a big thing as it was," explained the jogger philosophically. "Look at *The New York Times*. They're all marrying in their thirties after running corporations; then they get tired and want to be artificially inseminated. It's a gamble. Maybe it works, maybe not."

"We did things the natural way." The man nodded.

"And who says natural is better?" noted a tiny woman in a visor who had been waiting impatiently for a chance to enter the conversation. She had a reputation for stirring things up.

"Natural is nature. Nature is better," spelled out the man.

"You're not saying anything," said the woman with the visor. "You're speaking in circles."

"You're the one with a circle," noted the man angrily. "Your brain"—he made a circle with his fingers to indicate a round, empty space—"is a circle."

"Do you have a boyfriend?" asked the jogger, turning to Amy in an effort to cut short what seemed to be escalating into a nasty confrontation. Amy indicated George. The group paused and contemplated this a moment.

"Modern," said the man doubtfully. But after George had said a few words and been judged "not one of the angry ones," there was a palpable warming of opinion toward him.

"He's a nice boy," the jogger whispered to Amy. "Maybe he'll convert."

"And who's to say he's not Jewish?" said the man in the pink shorts. "There are Ethiopian Jews, you know. Are you, by any chance"—he turned to George inquiringly—"an Ethiopian Jew?"

George said that he was afraid he wasn't, and the man patted him on the back as though giving him credit for trying.

"And you?" The woman with the visor peered up at Jordan, her eyes taking particular note of the earring.

"I'm gay," said Jordan, smiling down at her.

There was another moment of contemplative silence.

"My brother-in-law's son is gay," noted the man in the shorts. "You'd never know looking at him."

"I'm just saying," continued the jogger, returning to her point, "that marriage now is different. It used to be early, now it's late; it used to be a nice Jewish girl or boy, now it's gay or Ethiopian. I'm not saying it's bad," she noted, nodding at George and Jordan, "just different."

"It's the children who suffer," noted the man.

"I don't know," continued the woman with the visor. "Too much yelling and screaming in a house—it's better the parents divorce."

"Leona and I never raised our voices," protested the man.

"Better you should have," said the visored woman. "It gets things out in the open. I knew a woman, never yelled, died of a stroke from bottling it up."

"Ridiculous," said the man. "Leona never yelled. But she smoked like a chimney. That's what killed her."

"Cut!" said Amy. "I think that'll do." She patted the Bermuda-shorted man on the back and nodded to the jogger. "Great stuff," she called after them as they began to disperse, with the exception of the visored woman, who had cornered Jordan and was asking him about what she called "the gay scene."

"We've got lots of material," Amy told Flo later. "I mean, everyone talks and the visuals are really awesome. But we don't have a structure. There's no emotional center for the film, nothing to hang things on. I need something dramatic, something with narrative potential."

They were sitting near the main clubhouse pool where a group of women with hair in various sculptural configurations were wading carefully into the water.

"It looks like the Normandy Invasion," observed Flo to her niece. "You should get it on film. They come in together and then they begin to drop down slowly, until they're up to their necks. But I don't think I've ever seen one get her head wet."

On the other side of the pool a couple had appeared: A pleasantly zaftig woman in her seventies wearing a pink sundress was looking up beatifically at a man dressed nattily in white pants and a striped, short-sleeved shirt. Flo noted with surprise that it was May and Norman Grafstein. She had not expected May's return until next week, and she certainly had not expected to see her on the arm of Norman Grafstein. Clearly, something had happened during the time in North Jersey that had brought the couple together. It was evident, even at this distance, that the two were very happy and that the machinations of Stan Jacobs had been thwarted.

"Here comes my friend May," said Flo to her niece, who had also turned to watch the handsome couple as they made their way in their direction. "I'll introduce you."

# CHAPTER FORTY-ONE

LESS THAN AN HOUR AFTER CAROL AND MAY HAD RETURNED from their outing to the mall, Norman Grafstein had called the Newman home. There are those who might believe that the entire train of events leading up to this call had in some bizarre way been orchestrated by Carol—that she had lured May up to Morristown, knowing (though May had not mentioned it and Carol, uncharacteristically, had not asked) of the stalled relationship; that while planning and hosting the child's birthday party, Carol's minions had been busy tracking down the whereabouts and plans of Norman Grafstein, drawing up a map that charted his progress through the diversionary pastimes of northern New Jersey until finally determining on the relative probability of his coming out of the Domain Furniture Store at the Short Hills mall at just the moment when May would be standing outside of Ann Taylor. Such people might be accused of an overly rich imagination and a tendency to embrace the conspiracy theories circulating in the cultural folklore. But Carol was, it must be noted, an Olympic-level planner, a woman for whom organizing the Home and School pancake breakfast in the morning and the 150-person sit-down kosher dinner for B'nai B'rith the same evening, while managing to chauffeur the kids to swimming, piano, and karate in between, was a piece of cake. In this context, the idea that she may have strategized the meeting of two elderly people, both known to be visiting within a space of twenty miles of each other, no longer seems quite so outlandish. It must also be noted that the Short Hills mall is the shopping mecca of North Jersey—Japanese tourists are said to be flown in on special luxury junkets twice a year—and strolling through the mall on a blustery Sunday afternoon might be compared to strolling the grand boulevards of Paris in the nineteenth century at the height of the fashionable season. Indeed, upon further thought, it would have been more surprising if May and Norman had *not* run into each other in the Short Hills mall that day.

When Norman called the Newman home and asked to speak to May, Carol told him she was napping. It was a lie. Her mother-in-law was actually in the other room watching *Wishbone* with Adam, but Carol's orchestrating mind had jumped very far ahead of the situation. In the tradition of the great political machinators, from Machiavelli to Lenin, she was not above engaging in dubious means to produce larger, more beneficent ends.

"Can I give her a message?" she asked Norman innocently.

"Well, I was just curious to know when she'll be returning to Boca," he said.

"Oh, she's planning to go back tomorrow," proffered Carol (in fact, she had originally planned for May to stay through next week). "I was going to call in for the tickets right now. Would you like me to order one for you?" she asked with the mixture of insouciance and pointedness that she had perfected over the years. Carol had learned that it was always better to jump right in and ask something if you wanted to know it, but that there was an art to asking the question as though you weren't aware of its significance and didn't care about the answer as much as you really did. She had never understood the problem that some women had getting dates, for example, since she had always been able to ask men out in such a way that they thought they had asked her. With Alan, it had worked pretty much this way up through the marriage proposal.

"Well, I hadn't really . . ." Norman stumbled.

"If you like," Carol suggested in an offhand but gracious tone,

"I could reserve one for you, too, while I'm at it. I have a travel agent discount and can get twenty percent off on the ticket."

"Well," said Norman, "it's a thought . . ." He appeared to be pondering the issue and turning over the possible deterrents. Stan Jacobs, for example, would no doubt disapprove.

"Just an offer," said Carol, as if she were about to change the subject, then added causally: "That way, of course, you and May would be able to sit together, which is always nice, especially this time of year, when the flights are crowded."

"You know, you're absolutely right," responded Norman with more certainty as he remembered his discomfort on the flights back to Boca. He had often considered going first class for the legroom, but even though he could afford it, he couldn't bring himself to do it. There were some things that a Brooklyn boyhood rendered impossible. The prospect of sitting next to May now struck him as a way of easing the strain of the flight, precisely as Carol intended. "Why don't you go ahead and order me a ticket. I'll mail you a check, and the twenty percent savings is a nice bonus. I appreciate the gesture."

"Think nothing of it," said Carol. Hanging up the phone, she went to inform her mother-in-law and become, once and for all, in May Newman's eyes, the incarnation of a good fairy in the guise of a suburban yenta.

# CHAPTER FORTY-TWO

"MAY, MY DEAR, I DIDN'T EXPECT YOU BACK SO SOON," exclaimed Flo, hugging her friend as May and Norman approached the table where she and Amy were sitting. "And you've brought a companion, I see—the delightful Norman Grafstein, without his less delightful sidekick."

"Oh," laughed Norman, "you mean Stan. Don't be hard on him. He's just a bit overprotective. Stan's a cynic by nature, you know. He's read too many books for his own good."

"Sounds like you, Aunt Flo," laughed Amy, who was watching the encounter with interest. "I'm Flo's great-niece, Amy Runcie-Slotkin." She put out her hand to Norman and May. "And don't laugh at the name. It's really an accurate reflection of who I am; a real point-counterpoint sort of thing: My father's a Jew who wants to be a Wasp and my mother's a Wasp who wants to be a Jew. It's the perfect marriage—they sort of cancel each other out—but it's left me a little confused; hyphenated, you might say. Fortunately, I have Aunt Flo to keep me on the right track."

"Not according to your parents," said Flo. "They think I'm a corrupter of youth. If they had their way, they'd have given me hemlock years ago."

"Well, thank God they didn't," said Amy, "or I'd never have found this great subject for my documentary, which I know your friends will want to be in so they, too, can go to the Academy Awards."

"What's this?" asked Norman. "You want to get us on film

and take us to the Academy Awards?" May looked nervous.

"That's the gist of it," said Amy, "although the Oscars are kind of hypothetical at this point. We're projecting ahead in case you need a lot of lead time to get your wardrobe together. But, seriously, will you do it?" She used her best wheedling tone. "It's just a school project, really. I'd want to follow you around for a few hours every day, me and my crew. We'd be very unobtrusive. Just getting you in characteristic settings, doing some of the things you'd normally do, with some interview footage in between."

"But why do you want to film us?" asked May suspiciously.

"Because you're in love," pronounced Amy.

Norman laughed and May looked taken aback. Even Flo was a bit shocked by her niece's pronouncement.

"What makes you say that?" asked Norman, smiling.

"Well, it's nothing in particular. It's just obvious. I don't know how long you've been married or if you're married at all. That's not the point. It's the feeling I'm after. I want this film to be kind of heartwarming—not soppy, but uplifting in a way. I know my aunt Flo secretly wants me to do a send-up of the place—a kind of Frederick Wiseman in a retirement community—but, I hate to break it to her, I really dig the people here. You're all really adorable. I want the film to show what I think is so neat about this place: that relationships are alive, that they continue to be preserved and renewed even as people grow older and their longtime loves die. I want to show the zest for life that I see here."

Flo never ceased to be amazed at Amy's unique ability to combine sincere emotion with schmaltzy promotional savvy. No one could disarm people like Amy in order to get what she wanted. But it was her sincerity and her generous vision that were the key to her success.

"What a lovely way of putting things," said May, who was moved by Amy's words, though still embarrassed to have her relationship with Norman made the object of public display.

"I agree," said Norman, who didn't seem in the least embarrassed. "I've always wanted to go to the Academy Awards, and I'm vain enough to let you film me all you want. I'm not sure about May, though." He turned to her. "How do you feel about having our budding romance recorded for posterity?"

"I don't know," said May shyly. "Is it a budding romance?"

"You better believe it," said Norman. He put his arm around May and looked down at her. "And if you don't like it, you better get away fast, because once it's on film, it'll be a lot harder. I haven't been this happy in a long time, and I don't intend to let anyone or anything stop it. So you better have dinner with me tonight and tomorrow night, and you better make me that kugel you promised." Norman turned to Amy: "And you can get that on film, if you like."

# CHAPTER FORTY-THREE

THE RESUMPTION OF NORMAN GRAFSTEIN AND MAY NEWMAN'S romance put Flo back into the role of May's chauffeur whenever there was a call for her friend to visit Broken Arrow. Although they spent more of their time at Boca Festa, given the greater convenience for May, there were the special evenings when Norman wanted May to visit him (though not, given the propriety of both parties, to stay overnight). Flo was always willing to provide her services as a driver. She liked being around Norman and May, and while this often brought her into contact with Stan Jacobs, this no longer troubled her. Seeing Stan so often (he sometimes accompanied Norman to Boca Festa as well) had turned what was once a source of discomfort into something more routine. He was always quietly polite when they were together. Although she thought that he looked at her too much, as though hoping to find fault, he was easy enough to ignore. They had never broached the topic of Mel Shirmer again. Flo continued to suspect that Stan had treated Mel shabbily, but her realization that Mel was no paragon had softened her outrage on this score.

She had also become aware of surprising moments of humanity that went against the grain of Stan's general demeanor. He clearly liked and admired May and spoke to her with genuine warmth, even animation. And then there was the time when she had received a call from Norman on the day before May's birthday.

"We came up with just the thing in the way of a gift," announced Norman proudly. "I'm not even going to tell you what it is, because you might give it away in a moment of weakness. It was really Stan's idea, to give credit where it's due, and he's supplying the materials, so to speak. But I'm doing my share. Boy, it's a doozy of a present, if I may say so, but we need you to do some legwork for us."

Flo said she would be delighted. "My guess is that it's one of those elaborate gag gifts. Do you want me to bring May to a certain spot in the Florida Everglades so she can see an airplane writing her name in the sky?"

"No," said Norman slowly, "though that's a good idea, too, come to think of it. I must say that I have some very creative-minded friends."

"If it's not skywriting, then I'm out of ideas." Flo laughed. "Now, what do you want me to do?"

"Here's the way it works." Norman's voice took on a conspiratorial tone. "We need you to drive May to Stan's house tomorrow morning. Make it around ten—no, ten-fifteen, to play it safe. I want to be sure everything is ready. We'll be there waiting with the surprise. I'll e-mail you the directions. Every traffic light. Don't worry. I wouldn't want you to get lost."

"No need to give every traffic light," Flo reassured him. "I can read a map."

"No, no, I want to be sure you have the directions just right. I'll e-mail you." Norman was of the school that believed women needed minute directions to go anywhere. "Meanwhile, not a word to May. Don't even tell her where you're going. It makes for more drama."

"You can count on me," said Flo. "I'll be as quiet as the grave."

The next morning, Flo bustled May into her car with the prospect of a surprise planned by Norman Grafstein. May was in a tizzy. Where could they be going? What should she wear? Should she bring a change of clothes or a bathing suit—or maybe a baking dish or a pie plate? Flo said not to worry, that she wouldn't have to do anything but be surprised. This appeared to be something that May would be able to do very well.

The trip to Stan's house was relatively simple, though Norman had sent Flo three pages of directions. In less than half an hour they had pulled up to a modest, neatly kept ranch house. It was painted a light green and had white shutters. There was a brick walk leading from the front door and a white picket fence around the yard.

"It looks like Stan Jacobs is trying to make South Florida look like New England," noted Flo. "The poor man thinks he's something out of a Nathanial Hawthorne novel—one of those grim, obsessed characters trudging through the Boston snow."

"I think the house is charming," said May, dismissing the entire arc of the metaphor.

They knocked, but with no answer, turned the knob and walked inside. There was a small foyer with a polished wood floor and a worn Oriental rug. To the right was a modestly furnished living room and, to the left, what would have been a den had been turned into a combination library and study, though really it seemed more like a warehouse for books. They were everywhere, as Norman had once said. The shelves along the walls were entirely filled, and there were stacks on the floor. In the center of the room was a large partners' desk with a lamp and a blotter, but it, too, was partially covered with books and magazines. May seemed horrified at the clutter, but Flo secretly found the room very inviting. They walked through it, with difficulty, into the kitchen, again a neat, modestly furnished space with a small table and chairs, behind which was a door leading to the backyard.

"Girls, is that you?" It was Norman's voice coming from outside. "We're back here. Come on out!"

May and Flo opened the door and faced a yard, perhaps three quarters of an acre in size. Half the space was beautifully cultivated with flowers and plants, as well as with a small vegetable garden, neatly hedged. The other half of the space contained nothing but a stretch of turned-over soil. Stuck in the center of this portion of the yard was a large stick with a sign affixed to the top that read (in computerized Gothic print surrounded by an assortment of clip-art renderings of daisies, roses, and daffodils): MAY'S GARDEN.

"What's this?" said May, looking stunned.

"It's your birthday present!" announced Norman. He was standing in the center of the empty area, and reached over to push the sign more securely into the soil. Stan was off to the side of the yard, trying to appear innocuous. "As I told Flo, it was Stan's idea," Norman continued gleefuly, "but I did all the hard labor. Making the sign, turning over the topsoil. And you know how I don't like to get my hands dirty." It was true. Norman's nails were always impeccably manicured, and the thought of him with his hands in the dirt made Flo smile.

"But I don't understand," said May. "There's nothing planted here."

"That's the point," declared Norman. "It's your space. Plant what you please. You can come here whenever you like. Stan says so: open invitation." He looked over at his friend, who nodded and smiled at May. "And since I wouldn't want to impose upon Flo, the driving's on me. Either I'll come to get you or—and this, I must say, was my own brainstorm—I've opened an account for you at Golden Cabs. They're on call to take you, and you're not to think twice. I made money to spend it on things like this. If you make a fuss, it'll spoil it for me, so promise you'll jump into a cab anytime you feel like planting a shrub or whatever it is you and Stan are so crazy about."

Tears were running down May's cheeks as she walked over to Norman and put her arms around him. "It's the best birthday present I ever had," she exclaimed softly. Then, not forgetting Stan, who'd put his head down so as not to intrude on their intimacy, she dragged Norman over to him and took both of their hands. "Such friends," she murmured. "Thank you both." Flo turned away from this too-heartwarming scene and went inside.

"I suppose I need to put some of these in order." Stan had entered the room where Flo had been browsing for some time among the heaps of books. She was on her knees now, looking at the bindings.

"I'll agree, it's not neat," said Flo, "but it certainly is plentiful."

"I get carried away when it comes to books. I buy too many."

"I'm not going to criticize you there," said Flo. "I've always felt you could never have too many books. It's like the feeling I have about those twenty-four-hour diners. I like to know they're there, in case I get hungry at three in the morning. With books, it's the same: I like to know that I'll have something to read at three in the morning."

"As you see, I have plenty to read at three in the morning, which is when, in fact, I often find myself here. I suffer from chronic insomnia." Flo looked sharply at Stan, as if to say, The fruits of a bad conscience, but was diverted from her speculation on this point by the sight of a particularly tattered volume. "My God—Carlyle's *French Revolution*. I haven't seen that one on somebody's shelf for a long time."

"As you can see, it's not on the shelf," noted Stan.

Flo was bending over another stack. "Wait—is this Hazlitt, *Table Talk*? I used to read that to get to bed at night when I was in college. There's one essay in here, 'On the Disadvantages of Intellectual Superiority.' I remember being amused—and humbled. That was a period when I thought I knew things."

"I haven't read it," said Stan, "but it sounds like it's worth looking into. Maybe at three in the morning."

Flo stood up and began examining the shelves. "How many editions of Jane Austen do you have?"

"Some were my wife's." Stan's voice grew muffled. "Together we must have about half a dozen. It's like having multiple Torahs in the ark. You don't need so many, but it's nice to have them there, just in case."

"Here's a pretty volume." Flo had turned to the desk and picked up a small book with a worn leather cover inlaid with a silver pattern. She opened it. "It looks like love poetry: Christina Rosetti, Edna St. Vincent Millay, Elizabeth Barrett Browning . . ." She was thumbing briskly through when Stan leaned forward and swiftly took the volume from her hand. "That one's not for browsing," he said softly, and left the room.

# CHAPTER FORTY-FOUR

LILA MARCUS (THE NAME WOULD TAKE SOME GETTING USED TO, she conceded) returned from Italy with twenty rolls of film, which, when developed, she compiled into a comprehensive album of her trip. Flo helped with the labels, and even put together some short histories of the three cities, which Lila, with sacramental care, pasted on the opening page of each section.

"So much beauty," she sighed, looking through the album wistfully. "I can't tell you how it affected me."

Seeing her friend's response, Flo admitted to May that Lila had gained something from her marriage to Hy Marcus. "She would never have had the chance to go otherwise, I realize that," Flo acknowledged. "I suppose Italy compensates to some extent for marrying a fool."

Lila and Hy had settled into their new three-bedroom condominium, and Lila had renewed her old routine with her friends. Hy seemed more than content to let her do what she liked so long as she was available to sit with him at dinner. Lila confided to May and Flo that the other aspect of marriage ("sex," she whispered distastefully), had fortunately ceased to be an issue. Hy had attempted it a few times but had been unsuccessful. This, she intimated, was just as well. Such things had never appealed to her particularly, and Hy was not likely to change her mind on the subject. Flo, for her part, breathed a sigh of relief. If Lila had been obliged to accommodate Hy Marcus in that department, as she had initially feared, then even Italy might have been small compensation. She was glad that she no longer had to envision her friend as a septuagenarian prostitute.

One day over brunch, however, Lila looked worried. "I want to strangle that Bob Dole," she said.

"Dole?" Flo asked. "You're behind in your elections. I'm afraid his career is over, though he'll make sure, in typical male fashion, that his wife's is, too."

"I'm not talking elections," said Lila with irritation. "I'm talking about that old commercial. It's the sex pill he used to push. Viagra. Hy says he wants to try some."

"My God!" groaned Flo. "Heaven preserve us!"

"Preserve *me*!" corrected Lila grimly.

"I'm told they gain the stamina of twenty-year-olds," said May, who could at times exhibit a certain disingenuous malignity.

"Oh my God," groaned Flo, "all you need is a twenty-year-old Hy Marcus."

Lila looked stricken. "It might not work."

"A ninety percent success rate," said Flo. "It's documented."

"He *is* your husband," proffered May.

Lila and Flo just looked at her.

"What will you do?" asked Flo.

"What can I do? I'll live one day at a time and hope for the best. But one thing I can tell you. I know now why I never voted for that Bob Dole."

# CHAPTER FORTY-FIVE

THE SOUND OF THE AMBULANCE SIREN IS A FAMILIAR ONE TO Boca Festa residents. There are nights when the sound is a continuous grating whine; others when it erupts in a counterpoint chorus, with the lights of the ambulances, like grotesque fireflies, flitting this way and that across the club grounds. No sooner has an elderly insomniac finally fallen into a fitful slumber than the siren blasts him awake again, and there goes not only another night's sleep but another bridge partner.

It stands to reason that in a community of fifteen hundred, in which the average age is seventy-three, illness and death would be frequent visitors. The response to these visitations, however, varies considerably on the part of residents. Some maintain an unruffled detachment—an attitude helped if one lived for some period in New York City, where sirens are as common as crickets in the country, or if one has the option of turning down a hearing aid for an undisturbed night's sleep. But the ability to ignore death is less of an auditory and more of a conceptual feat. After all, death is constantly referred to in the newspapers and on TV, and everyone knows that as the product of a lineage, the people who came before one have died. In Boca Festa, the only difference is that the parameters in which death happens have shrunk. The reported incidents are closer to home and affect people one is more likely to know. Still, the premise is the same. So long as it is not oneself who is dead, then it remains possible to put the topic out of one's mind.

Yet if a willed inattention to the arrival of the Grim Reaper is favored by some residents of Boca Festa, others, far from ignoring the fact, are hyperaware and hypervigilant. This group can pick up the sound of an ambulance from miles away and are likely to speculate on who it is coming for. "Mrs. Schatz in pod eight didn't look too well yesterday," one might say, or "Call Sam and see if he hasn't keeled over." Those who react this way are not necessarily morbid personalities. They simply want to keep tabs on what's going on. If anything, they feel that by being alert as their friends and neighbors drop around them, they may succeed at catching themselves should they be inclined to drop, too.

Both unawareness and hypervigilance with respect to death are possible in the context of Boca Festa. Just as the club buffet table offers dishes to suit all palates, so does the community support numerous viewpoints on the subject. Since the fragility of human life is everywhere on display in the form of walkers, hearing aids, and an abundance of wrinkles, one can think about mortality all the time, if one is so inclined. By the same token, a certain smooth, airbrushed quality characterizes club life, making it possible to ignore death just as completely if that happens to be one's preference. It helps that there are always new residents to replace the old. Friendships are severed—Mrs. Schatz no longer inhabits pod 8—but Mr. Cohen, who owned a shoe store in Queens where you remember once buying a pair of sandals, moves into her apartment and is an excellent companion.

Flo Kliman was of a philosophical turn of mind, and had thought about the fact of death at some length. She had lost many people in her life—her parents, her brother and sister, her husband, and more friends than she could count—and though sometimes she would fall into a musing, wistful state, a kind of dreamy sadness in thinking about the many people whom she loved who had died, her tendency by and large was not to dwell on them. Doing so depressed her, not only in making her miss these people whom she could not see again but also in reminding her that she, too, would die someday, probably sooner rather than later. She had concluded that no one could live with the sense of mortality constantly in mind, and that it was necessary to forget oneself, as much as possible, in living. Flo liked to quote Voltaire's remark that "we are all condemned to death, but with a sort of indefinite reprieve," and, in more serious moods, to refer to Hamlet's famous declaration: "If it be not now, yet it will come, if it be now, 'tis not to come; if it be not to come, it will be now, if it be not now, yet it will come." She had quoted this to Lila once, who, irritated at what she took to be Flo's pretentious side, had given a succinct translation without knowing it. "Hamlet, shamlet, we're all going to die sometime, so we might as well accept it."

Flo was a confirmed atheist, and she had no patience with the way some of her friends, no more pious than she was, gingerly skirted the issue, calling themselves agnostics. The euphemisms for death—references to "passing away," "passing over," "having gone to a better place," and so forth, also favored among Boca Festa residents—struck her as annoying efforts to evade or prettify what she saw as a simple passage from being to nothingness. When confronted with death, her tendency in general was to laugh. "It's not death in itself I find funny," she explained to May and Lila, who often took her to task for her attitude, "but the circumstances around it." She had taken pleasure, for example, in hearing that Clara Zucker had kicked the bucket while leaning over the Chanel counter in Bloomingdale's. And she had delighted in the irony that Yael Levy, who had suffered from emphysema for years, succumbed after exposure to smoke at a barbecue. Life, Flo thought, was absurd, and death was likely to reflect this. She had once told May that she had come up with a spin-off of Clue, the popular murder-mystery board game. "In my game," said Flo, "we deduce who died through knowledge of the pod number and the activity in which the individual was occupied at the time of death: cards, golf, shopping, eating, and so forth." May said she found nothing funny about Flo's idea.

If Flo Kliman had looked for a tale of death fitted to her particular taste in humor, she could not have done better than that of Hy Marcus. She learned about it on a Friday morning. She had arranged to meet May and Norman in the clubhouse lounge at eleven, where Amy and her friends were scheduled to continue their filming. Separate interviews with May and Norman had already been done, in which each had given personal background on themselves and described how they felt about each other. Amy had a gift for drawing out her subjects. She took a gossipy, confiding tone that Flo said made her sound like a young Barbara Walters, albeit with a pierced nose. Flo was looking forward to seeing Amy draw Norman and May out further, and to watching the coy responses of the couple, who were enjoying their time on camera as it paralleled their developing feelings for each other.

Flo had been sitting at the kitchen table with a cup of coffee and the *Times,* whiling away the hour until she had to meet her friends, when Lila walked in. Lila had never been known to walk in without knocking before.

"What's wrong?" said Flo as her friend lowered herself shakily into the chair opposite. "You look terrible."

"Oh, Flo," wailed Lila, "you're not going to believe this."

"Try me," said Flo. "I'll believe it."

"Well, first, I should tell you . . ." She eyed Flo nervously. "Hy is dead."

"No!" said Flo. It was hard to know what to say. "That's terrible!" was certainly too strong and would have seemed disingenuous. On the other hand, "That's good!" would not have been right, either. Though there was no denying that Flo was glad to think that Lila was no longer attached to Hy Marcus, death seemed an extreme way of severing the connection. Hy, after all, had never done anything to her, short of irritating her exceedingly over dinner.

"It's true!" said Lila. "It happened last night. It was . . ." She paused. "Sudden."

"What do you mean?" said Flo, for whom a good story was always welcome. "How did he die?"

"Well, I'll tell you." Lila paused again. "I count on you to be discreet, but you can tell May if you want to." She shifted a bit in the chair, and Flo leaned forward expectantly.

"We had come back from the clubhouse," said Lila carefully. "Hy had had a large meal: two servings of roast beef, baked potato with butter and sour cream, then dessert. It was make-your-own sundae, with the hot fudge and the butterscotch—too much, if you ask me, but that's neither here nor there."

"It isn't?" said Flo.

"No," said Lila, "it's not really relevant to the story. So we go back to the apartment and I notice that he's not acting tired but he's not talking either, which is unusual for Hy. If he's not tired, he's usually talking, and if he's not talking, he's usually tired."

Flo nodded. This seemed an accurate description of Hy Marcus.

"So we go in and I start to go to my room, and he says, 'Not so fast, you sexy thing, you.' That's what he said. I remember perfectly because, as you can imagine, it gave me a shock. He started unbuttoning his shirt and he said, 'I have a surprise for you, you sexy thing.' "

"Oh God," groaned Flo. But Lila was not about to be interrupted now that the morbid trajectory of her story was under way.

"So he says to me, 'Take off those clothes, we're going to do it.' I say, using a reasonable tone, 'Hy, please, it hasn't worked in the past.' But he says, 'Now is different; I took the pill.' "

"Oh God!" said Flo again, putting her head in her hands.

"So what could I do?" continued Lila. "I told him that I thought perhaps we should wait. It was late, he'd had a big meal,

I was tired. But he was jumping around like a monkey. He said it was my wifely duty and so forth, and got very insistent. So I thought, Better to get it over with"—she took a breath—"so I get into bed and he takes his clothes off. His *shlong* was, well—surprising—"

"Lila!" exclaimed Flo.

"I just want to give you a sense," said Lila. "So he starts in very vigorously. *Very* vigorously. The shaking was"—she searched for a metaphor—"like high speed on the blender."

Flo groaned.

"And then it stopped. Like you'd pressed 'off.' Still; nothing. I thought maybe he'd fallen asleep. It's not unheard of, you know. Mort was always very fast, and fell asleep in a snap. But," said Lila meaningfully, "he wasn't asleep."

"I see," said Flo.

"He was dead."

"So I gathered," said Flo.

Lila sighed. "So that's the story. I've called his kids; they're coming down. He wanted to be buried down here. His son is taking care of everything." She paused, then added, "Steven told me about the will. I'm nicely taken care of. I should be relieved."

Flo nodded expectantly. Lila seemed to have more to say.

"It's not like we were married for fifty years," she continued. "It hasn't even been two months. And it's no secret that I married to be comfortable." She paused. "It was a marriage of convenience."

Flo waited.

"And to tell the truth, he was an annoying man. He got on my nerves. He got on everyone's nerves."

"He was," agreed Flo, "annoying."

"But he wasn't a bad man," Lila shot back, as though Flo had missed the point. "He wasn't Prince Charming, I'll grant you, but he wasn't bad. There are a lot worse."

"That's true," agreed Flo, trying to keep up with her friend's reasoning. "There are certainly worse."

"And he had a lot of life. He had what they call joie de vivre: joy in living. It's a quality that you don't always see. Mort, for example, didn't have it. Mort might as well have been underground for all the life he had. Hy had life—and he gave me the chance to live." Her voice had become soft, wistful. "It's hard to imagine him dead."

Flo thought of Hy Marcus. It was indeed hard to imagine that antic and voluble man eliminated from the game of life.

"And to tell you the truth," sighed Lila, a tear rolling slowly down her powdered cheek, "I miss him."

# CHAPTER FORTY-SIX

HY MARCUS'S FUNERAL WAS NOT UNLIKE MANY FUNERALS THAT occur on a regular basis in West Boca. There were a nice number of people: the son and daughter and their families, dressed in black suits and linen dresses from Saks; a few old friends; and a showing from Boca Festa that included Hy's card partners and a few who had known Hy from casual encounters in the dining room or on the grounds. There were also the standard number of funeral "regulars." This group made a point of attending funerals to get a feel for the proceedings much in the way prospective brides look in on other people's weddings to get ideas for their own. There are limits to this analogy, of course. Although some of the regulars were seen to take notes on casket presentation, flower arrangements, testimonial speeches, and so forth, for the most part, the choice to attend the funerals of relative strangers must be put down to the desire to bask in the certainty that one was not being buried oneself.

May, Flo, and Lila sat together near the front of the room where Hy's casket, thankfully closed, gave a far more dignified and imposing presentation than Hy had ever done in life. May and Flo had decided that they would sit with Lila to give her moral support. She still appeared confused and shaken by how quickly she had gone from newlywed to widow.

The young rabbi, the same one who had presided over Lila and Hy's wedding, had once again been commandeered to perform. He appeared no less young than before, though buoyed by the fact that he could claim an earlier connection with the deceased. It gave him a sense of continuity that he lacked in most of the events at which he officiated.

"I married him," said the rabbi sonorously, "I bury him. So is the cycle of life. We live, we joy, we prosper, we wither, we die. The cycle cannot be evaded, neither can it be avoided."

"Neither evaded nor avoided?" Flo couldn't help whispering, though May gave her a look.

"It is with a special sadness, then," continued the rabbi, "having so recently seen joy kindled anew on the face of Hy Marcus, to now be saying farewell. Yet I do so, with the steadfast conviction that Hy Marcus is now on a long and blessed journey, his soul winging its way to be one with *Adonai*."

The rabbi continued with more of the same for quite a while. When he was done, Hy's son spoke about how his father had always encouraged him and his sister to pursue their dreams and never stinted in supporting them, either psychologically or financially. He spoke briefly. Before sitting down, he noted that his father's oldest friend was present and wanted to say a few words.

An old man came forward. He had a cane and he looked something like Hy. He stood for a moment and peered out at the assembled mourners.

"I met Hy," he said, "when I was ten years old. We used to play together, stickball after school. Hy was an excellent stickball player. I also recall that we played marbles. I won all of Hy's marbles. He was a good loser and never complained. Later, in high school, we were still friends, and after that, we continued to keep in touch. Hy went into the hat business with his father and his brother, Michael. He worked hard to support his family. He was a devoted and loving husband to Minna—married for forty-six years—and when he met Lila"—the old man nodded to Lila where she sat between her friends—"he felt he had gotten a new lease. Hy was proud of his children and his grandchildren," the man continued. "I don't think I ever met a man who was so proud of his children." Hy's children bowed their heads. They felt the full force of their father's pride, and were moved by it now that they didn't need to cringe under it. "He thought they were worth a million," continued the man, "and he used to say they should be—he put a million into their education." There was relieved laughter—everyone appreciated a glimpse of Hy as they remembered him, and the chance to escape the feeling, which the speech had so far engendered, that they had not done him justice. "Hy was a good man, Hy was a decent man," intoned the speaker. "He worked hard all his life to provide for his family, and he never, to my knowledge, denied them anything. He enjoyed life and was grateful for the gifts of life. He was my oldest friend," the man concluded quietly. "I'm sad he's gone."

There wasn't a dry eye in the house.

# CHAPTER FORTY-SEVEN

"YOU'RE NOT GOING TO BELIEVE THIS," ANNOUNCED LILA A FEW days after Hy's funeral. For the second time in a week, she had opened Flo's door and walked in without knocking. Something, thought Flo, must have happened on the dramatic order of Hy's death to have precipitated this second instance of passionate trespassing. "Sit down," said Lila, "you're going to be shocked."

"I'm already sitting," said Flo. She was in fact sitting on her couch reading *Daniel Deronda,* George Eliot's "Jewish" novel, a book that she liked so much that she had told Lila and May that she was prepared to read every one of its thousand pages aloud to them.

"Put the book down," said Lila, "and prepare yourself. It's about Mel Shirmer. He's moved into Boca Festa. Pod seven, Eastgate. Not by himself. He's married—to Roz Fliegler."

Flo, not easily surprised, was surprised.

"I know it must be a blow," continued Lila, "so I wanted to be the first to break it to you. I didn't want you finding out through gossip in the dining room or, worse, seeing them there together."

Flo assured her that though she was surprised, she was not stricken. Her feelings for Mel, if she had ever had any, had long since dissipated into indifference—if not distaste. What interested her, however, was how the union had been effected. She had not seen Mel for some time. She had assumed that he had gone back to Washington (or New York) and given up on the idea of settling in Florida.

"It seems he's been courting her on the sly," said Lila disgustedly. "He obviously was embarrassed showing up here since everyone assumed that you two were a couple. It seems they met at the JCC—in the biblical prophets course; it's always the most popular—and she made a beeline for him. He was, they say, very receptive. She's quite well off, you know," said Lila meaningfully. "No doubt that had something to do with it."

"No doubt," said Flo.

"But the nerve of them settling here!" exclaimed Lila. "With you only two pods away!"

"A pod can be an ocean," said Flo. "It's reasonable that they would settle here. Roz has lived here for years."

"Yes. They stayed in the same pod but moved to a bigger condo," noted Lila. "Mel said he needed an extra bedroom to use as his study—for his writing." Lila seemed to have temporarily forgotten her outrage and moved into her strictly reportorial mode. "They were married quietly, but she says she wants to have a big party to celebrate in the fall. She's renting the clubhouse and planning the decorations with Rudy—the sky's the limit. I don't suppose we'll be invited." Lila seemed a bit crestfallen at the prospect of missing such a gala event, but quickly recalled her feelings for her friend. "So you're not upset? Even if you don't feel anything for him, you must admit that it's . . . disrespectful."

"Well, I couldn't expect him not to marry the woman of his dreams out of respect for me," said Flo.

"Roz Fliegler—the woman of his dreams? Feh!" declared Lila.

"Lila! Since when have you gotten to be so discriminating? Mel was not rich. In fact, he didn't have much money at all, from what I could tell. Roz has plenty and is a very lively personality. I don't think you should be one to judge."

"You have a point," admitted Lila, who had the virtue of acknowledging a reasonable argument. "It's just that he led you on."

"He didn't," said Flo. "He may have tried for a while, but he didn't succeed. Now, stop making such a big deal about it. Let's go to lunch. Maybe I'll see them there and can offer my heartfelt congratulations."

# CHAPTER FORTY-EIGHT

THERE WERE TWO OCCASIONS IN THE COURSE OF THE YEAR WHEN the atmosphere of West Boca underwent a dramatic transformation: the week between Christmas and New Year's, and the week following Easter Sunday. These were the public schools' official extended holidays when grandchildren, freed from academic constraints, were shipped down to grandparents who, it was thought, were dying to see them. During these periods, children ranging in age from five to seventeen made their appearance in the Boca clubs.

Boca Festa made special arrangements in anticipation of this deluge. A variety of programs were implemented that included games and contests, barbecues and picnics. Special clinics in golf and tennis were organized, straining the stamina and versatility of the club pros, who now had to adjust their instruction to ten-year-olds who had been taken off their Ritalin. More important than the lessons, of course, were the debriefing sessions that followed with the children's grandfathers, when it was necessary to give assurances that the youngsters had the makings of first-class players if only they could perfect their forehands, backhands, and serves.

Normally, Boca Festa was a quiet place, aside from the skirmishes at the board meetings and the occasional arguments at lunch or in the card room as to whether Bill Clinton was a *shanda* or the best president the country has had since FDR (there appeared to be only two positions on this issue). Another bone of contention was the Bush-Gore election. As residents of Palm

Beach County, many club residents had come face-to-face with the notorious "butterfly ballot," and continued to be indignant on the subject. Some blamed the stupidity of the ballot and others the stupidity of their peers (drawings of the ballot on tablecloths had upped the club dry-cleaning bill by 30 percent). Yet while these topics produced raised voices and slammed fists from time to time, club life tended to be sedate and calm overall. Everyone was cognizant of the dangers of high blood pressure.

The exception was during those two vacation weeks. At those times, toddlers in sodden diapers were seen running across the clubhouse lounge followed by youngish women in high-heeled mules, and there was so much splashing in the pool that the matrons in beehive hairdos had to move their chairs back a good six inches. There were lines for the Stairmasters and hardly room to accommodate the influx of younger women in the aerobics classes. Daughters-in-law were booked for massages with Tiffany, the club masseuse, who was minutely questioned afterward by mothers-in-law desperate for a handle on what their sons were thinking. ("The breasts are definitely not real," Tiffany confided to Mrs. Ruderman.) Candy wrappers were found on the golf course, despite regular announcements at pod meetings to pay particular attention to the disposal of trash. Most under pressure were the culinary staff, who found themselves fielding special requests of a highly esoteric sort: "Leave a few lumps in the potatoes, but not too many, then add parmesan and butter, with a smidgen of salt and a dash of paprika," the chef was told by one woman who explained that her grandson, a picky eater, had gone mad for this recipe when she was visiting him last summer. The staff was finally obliged to post a notice near the entry to the dining hall: THE KITCHEN MUST REFUSE ALL SPECIAL REQUESTS FOR DISHES DURING WINTER AND SPRING VISITING WEEKS OWING TO TIME AND BUDGETARY LIMITATIONS. This, of course, did not prevent many grandparents from slipping the chef fifty dollars along with a scribbled recipe for *matzo brie* with peanut butter.

Carol, sensing that her presence might be distracting at this point in May's relationship with Norman Grafstein, shipped Adam down by himself during the spring vacation week. She had mobilized the entire ground staff of Continental Airlines in the service of his care, and had interviewed all the attendants on the flight, finally choosing a perky young woman named Susie as his personal companion for the trip. He was equipped with a suitcase of games and puzzles, though he had found the barf bags and the cotton eye covers that the plane distributed to its passengers more entertaining than the manifold materials that Carol had carefully selected from the Store of Knowledge in the mall.

May was initially nervous at the prospect of hosting Adam without his parents. She was afraid that a child used to such an energetic support system might feel bored in the face of her limited stamina and capacity for creative play. Alan had never required entertainment, having spent most of his spare time in his room with the television on.

"You can get Norman to help you entertain him," Carol had suggested. She had already ascertained that Norman's son and his family would not be coming down for spring break. Stephanie was seven months pregnant, and at three, little Benjamin was too young to fly by himself. The idea that Norman Grafstein would be without family during the week had influenced Carol's decision not to have herself and little Alison accompany Adam. Here was an opportunity for May to draw on Norman's assistance and recruit him for the grandfatherly role.

As it happened, Adam did not make undue demands on his grandmother. In fact, he made no demands at all. Being released from the clutches of Carol's enormous organizing power, he seemed to have fallen into a relieved lethargy; it was as though he were a spring that had been pulled taut and was now, finally, allowed to relax. Whenever May asked him whether he might like to go out to hit golf balls, or visit the science center, where the interactive computers were said to be amazing, or even take a swim in the club pool, where other boys his age were splashing each other furiously, he seemed uninterested. He was more inclined to remain on the couch watching cartoons and eating a few more of her potato latkes.

On the second day of his visit, Adam became acquainted with Amy and her friends, who had arrived to film May doing her household chores. The group had by now settled on May and Norman as the focal point of the documentary and made regular visits to May's apartment to get footage of her unloading the dishwasher and carpet-sweeping the living room. Adam immediately took to the idea of the filming, which he judged to be "really cool," and eventually Amy assigned him the role of literal "best boy." He therefore spent the majority of the time he was not lying on May's couch following the group around the club, holding the boom mike, making sure the wires weren't tangled, and, when Amy yelled "Cut," running over to give George a high five. For a child who had been diagnosed with a mild case of attention deficit disorder, his ability to remain absolutely quiet and still during a shooting sequence of half an hour or more was nothing short of amazing. He had already told Carol in a call home that he wanted to trade in his Nintendo and PlayStation for a DV videocamera and editing system, to which she had replied that she would research the matter and get back to him.

# CHAPTER FORTY-NINE

FLO FOUND HERSELF ON HER OWN DURING THE SPRING VACATION week. May was either tending to Adam or off with Norman, and Lila was busy going through Hy's effects with his son and daughter, both of whom she had taken to more than she had ever taken to Hy.

"And what's wrong with that?" Lila asked Flo in the rhetorical mode she used when she was trying to convince herself of something. "Why can't I find myself a pair of kids I like, even if they are in their forties? I'm a late bloomer, and I don't do things in order. Now that I've had the wedding and the kids, maybe the love of my life is next." Flo suggested that Lila should stop while she was ahead.

"I don't intend another wedding, if that's what you're driving at," Lila reassured her. "But I'm not above living in sin."

"Soon you'll be burning your bra and running off to a commune," said Flo.

"Always the cynic," Lila said, shrugging. "One day, I'd like to see you go off the deep end over someone. Okay—so Mel Shirmer wasn't the right one. I'm still waiting. It would do you good to make a fool of yourself."

"I'm afraid that's not in the cards," said Flo. "I get too much pleasure watching other people behave like fools to want to assume the role myself. Just let me sit back and watch."

Flo did watch as a bevy of grandchildren of various shapes and sizes wrapped their besotted grandparents around their fingers. She noted that her neighbors seemed perfectly willing to buy the candy, video games, and sundry junk that they loudly decried the rest of the year.

"You've got to give them what they want," said Pixie Solomon as her ten-year-old grandson proudly displayed the DVD of *The Matrix* she had just purchased for him. "It's for their parents to lay down the law; our job is to make them happy." And with such philosophical skill, Flo realized, her peers managed to reconcile any contradiction that happened to emerge between theory and practice.

She had even run into Roz Fliegler and Mel Shirmer near the pool one day—Roz's granddaughters, ages six and seven, in tow. It was Flo's first direct encounter with Mel since the marriage. Though she had seen him and Roz from a distance in the clubhouse, they had not been close enough to exchange words. Now, having come out to the main pool to meet Lila at the porch restaurant, she found herself face-to-face with the happy couple.

Mel greeted her with only a trace of stiffness and quickly assumed a genial tone when he saw that she was prepared to be friendly. Roz, for her part, took an attitude of exaggerated noblesse oblige, having heard that Flo had preceded her in her husband's affections. It was a pose hard to maintain as the two little girls pulled on her Chanel jumpsuit and whined for ice cream.

"You've met my husband," drawled Roz, extending her left hand to stroke Mel's arm and thereby display a humongous diamond ring (purchased by Mel through access to Roz's bank account). She used her other hand to pull little Bathsheba, the six-year-old, away from a piece of gum that she was trying to pry off the pavement.

"I've been hoping to run into you," said Mel ingratiatingly. "As you can see, I have now remedied my lack of grandchildren. These little angels are keeping me very busy." Lillith, the seven-year-old, had begun to pull on Mel's Rolex, and he struggled to free it from her viselike grip.

"You seem to have found your element," noted Flo, sweetly. "Perhaps not as elevated as you anticipated, but certainly adorable."

"Certainly adorable," agreed Mel. He had finally wrestled his watch free, though the child had now begun to play with the tassels on his Italian loafers.

"Mel is wonderful with the children," said Roz. "They adorrrre him, as you can see."

Flo agreed that she could see this, but little else was said since the younger child suddenly began to scream loudly that the older one had kicked her, and Roz hurried them off to the snack bar while Mel went to find a Band-Aid. Overall, Flo thought that Mel had gotten more than he bargained for with Roz—which is to say, Roz was getting her money's worth out of the arrangement. The meeting, in any case, had been painless. Future encounters would no doubt be increasingly comfortable—and amusing. In point of fact, she looked forward to them.

# CHAPTER FIFTY

MANY OF THE GRANDCHILDREN VISITING DURING SPRING BREAK were indeed adorable, and some even appeared to have genuine affection for their *bubbies* and *zaydies,* but though Flo knew that her neighbors pitied her for not having grandchildren to show off, she was secretly content to be left alone. One morning, she was sitting on a chaise longue near the pod pool reading Saul Bellow's recent roman à clef, *Ravelstein,* a book that brought vividly to mind the qualities that annoyed her in its author. It was her impression that the book was less a disguised jab at Bellow's old friend Allan Bloom, as critics would have it, than it was a more vicious attack on his second wife—or was it his third or fourth?—a Romanian mathematician whom Flo remembered traipsing through the library as though she owned the place. No doubt she had traipsed through her marriage to Bellow with the same air of confident entitlement and done a job on her husband's self-esteem. It was just like a Jewish man to use his literary gifts to get back; hadn't Roth done something similar in one of his earlier, self-aggrandizing tomes? Given her annoyance at such things, she wondered why she kept on reading these men's books. She supposed it was to confirm for herself that the battle of the sexes still raged undiminished as the fuel for literary creativity.

She had been reading near the pod pool for a while with no one to distract her. Very few people frequented the pod pool, except when there were pod meetings or when someone had reserved the pod cabana for a private party. Most Boca Festa residents preferred the more social atmosphere of the main pool, where gossip and people-watching were the major attractions. Once, it is true, she had seen a man reading a book near the main pool, marking in it assiduously with a yellow highlighter. On drawing near, she had discerned its title—*How to Satisfy a Woman*—and had brought Lila and May out to look. The man had peered up at them over his bifocals, considered them for a moment, perhaps contemplating whether he might want to satisfy *them,* and apparently deciding otherwise, returned to his highlighting. That was the only occasion, as far as Flo could recall, of a book making an appearance at the main pool.

Flo occasionally liked to sit by the main pool with May and Lila, but she found the shady tranquillity of the pod pool more to her taste, especially because no one else did. This morning she had been engrossed for close to two hours in translating the fictionalized pieces of Bellow's book into their real-life counterparts, when she looked up to see a rather rumpled Stan Jacobs walking toward her on the little path that connected the parking lot to the pool. His appearance was a surprise.

She had seen him fairly regularly since May and Norman had become what Boca Festa matrons winkingly called "an item." She sometimes drove May to his house to garden (though May would occasionally take Norman's advice to call a cab, she still found herself averse to what she termed "taking advantage"). When Flo did drive May, Stan generally made a point of going out to the backyard to help her friend. Flo preferred to stay in his study and browse through his books. She had once caught a glimpse of him watching her silently from the hall—he must have entered the house very quietly, since she had heard nothing—and she quickly put down the volume she was looking at (a collection of stories by Isaac Bashevis Singer), remembering his reaction when she picked up a book the last time she was there. But when she turned around again, he was gone.

Whenever she joined May and Norman for lunch or dinner

at Broken Arrow, he was usually present, though he rarely said much. She continued to catch glimpses of him looking at her when he thought she was unaware of it. It had made her careful about chewing with her mouth closed and holding her knife properly. Once, catching his eyes on her as she reached across the table for the salt, she proclaimed fearlessly:

"I realize I'm reaching across May's plate for the salt and should ask her to pass it but, say what you will against me, I'm a reckless and uncouth character. And I continue to use salt in flagrant disregard of dietary wisdom."

Stan had muttered that he saw nothing wrong with reaching for salt or using it, but Flo was convinced that he had filed the lapse away as another mark against her.

She had also seen him, though he hadn't seen her, in the Publix supermarket parking lot on several occasions. Publix was another Boca wonder. Not only did the employees do an impeccable job bagging one's groceries (in New York and Chicago, you bagged yourself or risked the lettuce and Brie at the bottom of the bag), but there was always a friendly and efficient individual waiting nearby to wheel your cart to your car and unload the groceries for you—tip refused. It was the kind of service that even the ten-year veterans of Boca still found astonishing— proof, if any were needed, that they had attained to heaven on earth. On three occasions, the last only a few days ago, she had seen Stan speaking to one of the young Hispanic women who helped wheel carts and unload groceries. Flo was struck, as she had been when she saw him talk to the waiter at the Valentine's Day dance, by the earnestness and duration of the conversation. What, she wondered, could he be saying to someone so far outside his conventional social circle? None of these individuals looked remotely like Florida Atlantic undergraduates. It was a mystery that, had she had any interest in him at all, she would have pondered more closely.

If he was looking for Norman and May now, she was at a

loss as to why he would look here, since May was in pod 3 of Crestview. Then it occurred to her that the couple was not at the club today but had left early in the morning to take Adam to the beach, with Amy and her crew accompanying. Stan doubtless didn't know this and was seeking information as to their whereabouts. He approached in what Flo thought was a shy manner for him, though glancing at her book, he immediately commented dryly, "A disaster."

Flo was more or less of this mind about the book herself but, feeling a welling of loyalty to Bellow and a natural inclination to disagree with Stan Jacobs, responded with equal dryness, "Not at all. I'd say, rather, a confusion of genres. With a few minor adjustments, it would make a first-rate memoir."

Stan was silent. He seemed uninterested in arguing the relative merits of Bellow's book at this time.

"May and Norman went to the beach with Adam," said Flo, assuming that this was the information Stan was after. "They should be back around two."

"I know," said Stan.

Flo lifted her left eyebrow. She had highly expressive features, but at moments of extreme puzzlement, her face remained immobilized and the full burden of reaction fell to this eyebrow, which had an impressive ability to lift itself high above its neighbor in an effect that would have been right at home in a thirties screwball comedy.

Stan moved forward and seated himself at the wrought-iron table near her lounge chair. Flo noticed that he was sweating almost as much as when she had beaten him at tennis.

"I came to see you."

Flo stared, and Stan, though looking uncomfortable, plowed ahead, though not without taking a handkerchief out of his pocket and mopping his face.

"The fact of the matter is, I'm having a hard time getting you out of my mind. Believe me," he continued, more rapidly now,

"I find it strange, stranger than you can possibly imagine, this . . . infatuation. My wife was nothing like you. She was a warm, domestic sort of person. Loved to cook, garden, a really wonderful woman. I adored her." He paused. Flo's face remained impassive, though she could feel her neck turning red as she struggled to maintain her composure.

"This makes it all the more mystifying to me," continued Stan, putting his hand through an unkempt mop of white hair, "why I would find your particular brand of, uh, humor appealing. And it's not as though I have a problem being alone," he added. "I enjoy my own company, and I don't mind being a third wheel with Norman and May."

Flo had hardly moved since Stan had begun this speech, and she now waited in a state of coiled alertness for him to finish.

"So that's the story," he said, putting his hands on the table as though he had just finished teaching a particularly brilliant seminar and was waiting for her to congratulate him on it.

Flo turned and pulled herself to a sitting position in the lounge chair. Then, as though thinking that even in this position the force of her words might appear insufficient, she rose to her feet. She now stood directly facing Stan Jacobs's seated figure.

"Your monologue," she said, in a measured tone that barely repressed her rage, "has been enlightening. I knew you were an arrogant boor, a man who, for all his book-learning, had failed to master the rudiments of polite conversation and etiquette. I knew that you had a jealous and malevolent streak, that you had been instrumental in ruining a job prospect for Mel Shirmer. Whatever his failings, and I admit he has many, he didn't deserve your slandering him to his friends and destroying the possibility of a job at Florida Atlantic. I never dreamed that, given your treatment of him and your incivility to me, you would still have the audacity to approach me as you have. I pride myself that I never led a man on—and in your case, I think, I have been clearer than I needed to be in indicating that I find your snobbish, superior manner insufferable and that I only tolerate it out of affection and respect for Norman and May. That you could come here and tell me that I lack all the qualities you admire most, that I am the antithesis in all respects of your wife, that you like me despite your good taste and better judgment—and then expect me to respond with gratitude—seems not only arrogant beyond words but stupid. Whatever else I had taken you for, I had not taken you for a stupid man, Stan Jacobs, but now, I'm afraid, I must add that attribute to the others."

Stan looked as though someone had given him a quick but powerful punch to the stomach. He was sitting down, but he had bent forward, his face lowered, as Flo continued her harangue. He had not felt so devastated, so thoroughly mortified, since his twenties, when he had received back from a publishing house where he had submitted it his effort at the Great American Novel with a letter advising him to take up woodworking. He had chosen a middle course and become an English professor. He reacted to Flo's words now as he had reacted to those in that long-ago letter. They struck him as harsh and surprising, but as he listened, he also found them to be true. It was a tendency of Stan Jacobs to weigh evidence, even in the most trying of circumstances, and to arrive at reasoned judgments. Watching his colleagues over the years, he had noticed that some of the most astute literary critics were the most blind to their own obvious failings—the ability to read well and to have insight into oneself being two very different skills. But he had never thought to apply this observation to himself. He had been blessed for forty years with a wife who adored and indulged him, and he had continued to see himself through her eyes even after she was gone. It came as a shock and a revelation to realize that the world at large did not necessarily see him this way. Listening to Flo and seeing the extent of her anger, he realized that his attitude toward her—and toward people in general, even his own friends—had been condescending and rude. He saw now that what he had taken to be the obvious marks of his superiority, his gift for critical observation and analysis, were not attributes at all, but signs of an often ungenerous and intolerant snobbery. There was only one area in which he felt she had been unjust.

He stood now and mopped his face again with his handkerchief. "I'm sorry," he mumbled. He was too mortified to look her in the eye. "I'm sorry to have . . . pained you. I can see that I have. I understand everything you say, but on the subject of Mel Shirmer, I feel compelled to set the record straight, though I promise not to say anything more after that. Mel Shirmer"— Stan was clearly trying to control the emotion in his voice—"is a consummate liar and con artist. He pursues women for their money. My cousin in Boca West was 'in love' with him—the phrase sounds sophomoric, I know, but it seems that such things still happen, even at our age." Despite the attempt at satire, his voice faltered here, and he paused, then continued more briskly: "They were going to get married. Date set, caterer, everything. Then he discovered her late husband's money was in trust to the children—her idea, I might add—and he hightailed his way out of there as fast as you please. She hasn't gotten over it yet, and no doubt never will. When I first met Mel, I sensed inconsistencies in his stories but put it down to nothing more than self-promotion—that is, until conversation with a friend who edits one of the weekly newspapers in New York set me straight. A good education, good mind, squandered through greed and irresponsibility. There was never any job at Florida Atlantic, so I did nothing to him on that score. The man has never had a steady job to speak of. He worked as a stringer on a number of papers over the years, low-level positions that he couldn't hold on to. Until recently, he did piecemeal work for some small PR agencies—writing press releases, public service announcements, that sort of thing. He's been through a fortune or two already. He soaked his first wife for every penny before he divorced her, and he's been on the prowl for a suitably wealthy replacement.

He thought he found one in my cousin in Boca West, and when that didn't pan out, he laid low for a while. When I saw him with you, I realized he was back for another try. I wouldn't have thought you'd have sufficient funds to attract him—excuse me, you certainly didn't seem showy that way—but perhaps he has his sources. I know, as you probably do, that he has since married a wealthy widow in your club. Perhaps she deserves him or can handle him. But to most decent women, he's a menace. On that subject, at least, you've been wrong about me. The rest—" He broke off. "If I've insulted you, forgive me. I won't—I promise—do it again."

Flo stared at him. What he said about Mel rang disturbingly true. There was no denying that his interest in her had waxed and then waned in accordance with his perception of her net worth. The final proof of his character, if any were needed, lay in his covertly arranged marriage to Roz Fliegler. But that was Mel. As far as everything else, she stood by what she had said. And yet . . .

He was gone before Flo had a chance to register his leaving. As she looked at the empty area surrounding the pod pool, she felt at once excited and desolate. Stan Jacobs's visit had rattled her, there was no doubt about it. And though she tried to return to *Ravelstein* and to summon up the memories of the old Chicago haunts that had entertained her a moment ago, she could not do it. Her mind was elsewhere.

# CHAPTER FIFTY-ONE

A DECISION HAD BEEN MADE TO MEET FOR DINNER THAT NIGHT at Pete Rose's, the popular sports bar and restaurant off Glades Road. The choice had been in deference to Adam, though it was Norman as much as Adam who wanted to go. Norman had been eagerly awaiting the time when his own grandson would be old enough to take there, and was pleased to be able to make the trip sooner than expected.

Flo tried to be tolerant of whatever fell under that lively rubric known as popular culture. Yet she found it hard to appreciate the appeal of restaurants like this one. There was a great deal of sports memorabilia on the walls, which the men and boys examined dutifully, and there were numerous television sets positioned above the tables, which seemed intended to fill any of those embarrassing gaps in conversation that so often afflict men when women aren't present to ease the transitions. She could see that a number of boys about Adam's age had been brought by their grandfathers, who were busily cutting up their meat, buying them souvenirs, and explaining some arcane baseball lore, while the boys gazed over their heads at the progress of a golf tournament or wrestling match. The sound of "Take Me Out to the Ballgame" was playing insistently in the background, and there were large bowls of popcorn and pitchers of Coke on the table. Norman, in the manner of the other grandfathers present, was trying to explain to Adam about the good and bad points attached to Pete Rose's career.

"Pete Rose was a great player," explained Norman, assuming

the familiar grandfatherly pose of imparting information while also relaying a valuable lesson, "because he never gave up. He wasn't the most talented player; he didn't have the natural ability of a Willie Mays or Mickey Mantle. But he gave it his all. He set his mind to being a great player, he practiced, and he succeeded. That's something you should keep in mind in whatever you do."

Adam, familiar with this tone and bored with it, pushed on to other things. "Is he in the Hall of Fame?"

"Well, no," answered Norman, pleased that Adam had stumbled onto the precise question that would lead him into the second part of his lecture. "You see, he did some bad things that had nothing to do with how well he played. Now, you can work very hard and be good at something, but that doesn't necessarily mean that you behave yourself in other areas of your life. One thing doesn't have anything to do with the other." Norman felt he had expressed this well until he realized that Adam had lost interest and was watching the golf game on the television above their table.

Flo, however, had been listening, and stepped in to continue the conversation. "I don't know about that," she said. "It seems to me that all behavior is related, and that Pete Rose must have had flaws as a player that were reflected in his weaknesses off the field."

"It's an interesting point," said Norman, giving it some thought. "He was feisty and volatile, I'll grant you that, but he was solid. One hell of a good ballplayer. I wouldn't say that he gambled with his talent on the field, if that's what you're trying to say."

"I just think that we generally reflect who we are in everything we do," said Flo, insistently. She wasn't sure what she was driving at or why she was being so insistent about it.

"That's a mighty high standard, then, that you hold up for human behavior," said Norman. "If all our mistakes are to be taken as marks of our character, I'm not sure many of us could survive that. I sure as hell couldn't."

"I'm not saying that we shouldn't forgive mistakes," said Flo, frowning. "It's just that they're helpful tools in judging character. They're markers or signposts of what there is to work with."

"But I couldn't disagree more," said Norman, now taking to the discussion with relish. "There are many people whose surfaces don't reflect their true natures. Shyness, for example, can get in the way"—he glanced at May—"or gruffness. Take Stan, for example. Who'd know from the look of him what a kind, generous man he is? He has students at Florida Atlantic who still make pilgrimages to see him, and he tutors half the Hispanic population of Boca in English three nights a week and doesn't charge a dime for it."

Flo felt a lump in her throat. So the Publix supermarket mystery was resolved, and, she acknowledged, it shed quite a flattering light on Stan Jacobs. He was out there making things better for people, she realized, while she was judging the tone of his voice. For a moment she felt angry that he hadn't told her, so that she could have had a reason to think better of him all this time.

"I didn't know that," she said to Norman quietly.

"Well, Stan doesn't like to toot his own horn, you know. He's got a heart of gold and he's as loyal as a dog, but he's sensitive in a graceless sort of way—though I've seen him be graceful, too, in a manner of speaking. He and Elsa used to go out dancing all the time, you know. Not that Stan was a great dancer. He just put his heart and soul into it, and he and Elsa had this loveliness about them. They used to read poetry together, for godsakes. The way he took her death—I've never seen such grief, and hope never to see it again. There's a depth of feeling in the man; well, it's beyond me to even comprehend."

Amy, who had been setting up the camera with George and

chatting with some of the waiters, aspiring filmmakers it turned out, had heard part of the conversation and now burst in with her own take on the subject. "I'm surprised at you, Aunt Flo," she scolded. "You, of all people, should know that surface manners mean next to nothing. You scare to death half the people you meet, though I know what a pussycat you really are."

Flo was silent. She felt deeply humiliated and regretful. She had misjudged Stan Jacobs based on a few instances of surface behavior, all of which could be explained in ways that exonerated him from charges of mean-spiritedness, and suggested instead kindness and sensitivity. It was not in her nature to think back and review what she had done too minutely. She had always acted with the confidence that she had behaved the best she could given the circumstances, and that there was no point regretting the past—it was better to move forward. Yet she couldn't help feeling that had she been more careful in forming her judgments, things now might have been very different indeed. The thought made her feel uncharacteristically depressed. She had initially been relieved that Stan had not joined them this evening, as he so often did when Norman and May went out, because the sight of him would have annoyed her. Now she was relieved not to have to face him in her new state of regret. Obviously he couldn't want to be around her after her self-righteous tirade that morning. She winced, remembering it.

"Couldn't Stan make it tonight?" asked May. She had a gift for posing questions that Flo had in mind but chose to keep to herself. May, Flo knew, had developed a special feeling for Stan Jacobs and professed this frankly, even though Flo continually mocked her for it.

"Well, he'd planned to come, I think," said Norman, "but I stopped in at his place before I came here, and he said he had a headache. He looked, if you'll pardon the expression, like shit. Maybe he's nervous about having the bunch of us in his course next term. The prospect, I have to admit, is scary. I wouldn't want to try teaching Flo anything. She might bite my head off."

Flo, who was normally amused by Norman's characterization of her as sharp-tongued and critical, suddenly felt uncomfortable being portrayed that way. "I don't know if I plan to sign up," said Flo. "I think you're right. I'm too argumentative, certainly for an undergraduate classroom. It wouldn't be fair to the other students"—she paused—"or to Stan, to have me putting in my two cents all the time."

"Don't be silly," Norman laughed. "We need you there. You keep Stan on his toes, and you give us something to chew on. If you don't sign up, half our fun is gone."

"I don't know," said Flo, remaining pensive and distracted. She didn't feel like pursuing the subject. The prospect of sitting in on Stan Jacobs's class, which would have entertained her a week ago, now seemed like a daunting prospect. She certainly would feel self-conscious, and she assumed that for him the experience would be uncomfortable and unpleasant in the extreme.

"I hope he's all right," said May, returning to the subject of their friend's health.

"Well, I'll stop and look in on him on my way home, if it'll make you feel better," said Norman, looking affectionately at May.

Flo also wondered how Stan Jacobs was, and if he would ever consider being in the same room with her again.

# CHAPTER FIFTY-TWO

WHENEVER A BOCA SENIOR NEEDS ASSISTANCE, A PROFESSIONAL IS called in to do the job. Professionals are theoretically much in demand in Boca Raton, but they also pose problems. The residents of West Boca are educated consumers, but the phrase goes far beyond anything that Sy Syms might have had in mind. Boca residents judge their professionals with extreme suspicion and generally find them to be wanting, or at the very least, in need of correction and retraining. Thus, a plumber will find that he can't work on unclogging the toilet without having a knowledgeable matron nearby suggesting that another size plunger would be better. And a wallpaper hanger, in the business for years, will be told by a woman in mules and a head scarf that he is applying the paste in the wrong direction and if he doesn't change his technique, the paper will peel off in a week, take it from her.

If plumbers, painters, and washer and dryer repairmen are driven to distraction by Boca residents who claim to know these jobs better than they do, doctors face far greater problems—the stakes, as it were, being higher. While most people expect, realistically, that illness and death are inevitable, Jews, perhaps as a residue of their status as chosen people, have a deep-seated conviction that they are entitled to live forever, and that they share with the washing machine, the dryer, and the dishwasher a rock-solid warranty designed never to expire. Doctors, as they see it, are specifically licensed to guarantee this.

When illness does occur, the doctor must be minutely questioned and generally harassed to rectify the situation. Once a diagnosis is delivered, these patients seek not just a second opinion but a third and fourth. They walk into their doctors' offices and study the diplomas on the walls as though they were valuable works in an art gallery. They continually impart treatment tips gleaned from *The National Enquirer* or a third cousin (a dermatologist in Baltimore) that they expect to be implemented on the spot. Only the most cunning of physicians (sad to say, not necessarily the best) can be expected to survive in this atmosphere. These are the few who manage to combine flattery with an unwavering air of certainty. A woman suffering from acid reflux reaction might visit three or four doctors, each of whom might prescribe a standard medication to treat her condition but whom she will dismiss as useless because they treat her "like a piece of furniture." A fifth doctor, however, charging twice as much and prescribing the same medicine, will be judged a genius because he nods empathetically when she describes her difficulty properly digesting a nice piece of roast beef, which, by the way, she eats rare, and then tells her that her stomach is a sensitive organ in keeping with her poetical nature. He will conclude by fixing her with an authoritative stare and declaring that she must—if she values her life—do exactly what he says. It helps, of course, that this doctor has been on *Oprah* and performed colonoscopies on Goldie Hawn and Steven Spielberg.

The same basic consumer practices that Boca's senior citizens apply to doctors also inform their approach to education. They want to learn, but they suspect that they know as much, if not more, than those they might consult to teach them. This dilemma emerged once the population began to take advantage of the area's premier educational institution. Florida Atlantic University, located in the center of Boca Raton, is one of that vast number of academic institutions that, each year, flood the market with confused young people prepared to compete for amorphously defined white-collar jobs, usually involving computers.

Some years ago, in what looked at the time to be a brilliant PR strategy, the university began to encourage senior citizens to audit classes. There were several seemingly innocuous stipulations accompanying the policy: The seniors were expected to pay a fee (substantially less than that charged to the average matriculating student); they were expected to sit toward the back of the classroom so as not to make their appearance among the undergraduates too obtrusive; and they were expected to curtail their comments so that the regular students, notoriously hesitant and inarticulate, would have every opportunity to air their views and receive the full attention of the instructor. The then-head of university relations, since let go, believed that the area's seniors citizens would add a new dimension to the classroom and, further, be the source of substantial bequests. Given that most were in their seventies, the benefits were likely to be realized sooner rather than later.

On paper, the idea was a good one. In practice, there were problems. For one thing, the seniors, savvy consumers that they were, soon began to complain that the fee, though reduced, was too high. After all, they did not get the benefit of the teachers' comments on papers and tests—since they didn't write them or take them. There was the additional problem of classroom dynamics. With a critical mass of five to ten elderly people seated together at the back of a room, the temptation to speak became, at times, irresistible. Violent arguments began to erupt over topics like whether the Pilgrims were anti-Semitic or whether the so-called sweatshops on the Lower East Side were really so bad. The undergraduate students, whose attention spans were fleeting under the best circumstances, lost interest once the skirmishes were under way, and the professors, though they tried to regain control, were swatted away by the disputants as too young to know anything. What did a thirty-year-old *vantz*, Ph.D. or no Ph.D., know about Guadalcanal, anyway? What did he know, for that matter (since we're really going back in time), about

Renaissance poetry? The provost was soon fielding complaints from all quarters—from students and professors, angry about being disenfranchised in their own classrooms, and from the elderly auditors, complaining about tuition, handicapped access, and the need for better-quality soap in the bathrooms. When university relations went through the books, it discovered that not one of the auditors had given so much as a dime to the university since the program began. They had reserved their bequests for Harvard and Yale, in the hope of facilitating their grandchildren's admission to these more august institutions.

A meeting was held, and the provost put his foot down. It was determined that no more than fifty seniors be allowed to audit each semester, with no more than two in any given class. ("How much trouble could two of them cause?" the provost is quoted to have said, a naive conclusion that some attributed to his being a Presbyterian.) This was the policy communicated to Norman Grafstein when he called to inquire about enrolling in Stan Jacobs's class for the spring term.

May and Lila had been badgering him about the course for over a month now, and though Flo had been silent on the subject, Norman had assumed that she, too, was eager to take part. Stan had been noncommittal, but Norman suspected that his friend was secretly pleased by the idea of doing whatever it was he did in front of his friends. Norman himself was no reader, and Jane Austen, as he proclaimed several times to May and Flo, was Greek to him, but he wasn't one to close the door on a challenge. If his friend and *machuten* Stan Jacobs said that Jane Austen was hot stuff, then by God he was going to give it the old college try. It would be especially appealing having May making the attempt with him. May seemed to have the ability to enjoy almost everything. Limited in experience and education though she was, her mind had an openness and generosity of spirit that, in a quieter and gentler way, matched his own.

The news that Florida Atlantic had closed its doors to them

was therefore a disappointment. Norman was told by the dean's secretary that the quota had been filled two weeks earlier, and that there was no possibility of further auditing by seniors during spring term. They might, if they chose, put themselves on the waiting list for fall; that term had already filled its quota as well, but the waiting list was shorter. Norman had tried to explain that his friend Stan Jacobs wouldn't be teaching then, but the secretary wouldn't budge. That was the policy, period, she said.

He brought the news to his friends at dinner that night in the Boca Festa dining room, and May was instantly the most vocal in her response. "Quotas!" she declared huffily. "I thought they went out in the 1960s! It's disgraceful to think they won't let us in when we're willing to pay money just like everyone else."

"It's a matter of a few rotten apples spoiling things for everyone," explained Norman. "At least that's what the secretary told me."

"But that's discrimination," proclaimed Lila, taking up the cudgel from May. "It's a case of age discrimination, pure and simple. We can sue. Hy's daughter is a lawyer and can maybe help us out."

"Carol told me about a sit-in they had at Adam's school," added May. "The mothers were against selling soda in the cafeteria. They would have won, only the children held a demonstration, too, in favor, and the mothers caved in. We could try something like that."

"May the firebrand," said Flo. "You'll storm the president's office. But I'm afraid you'd be dusting and straightening up in no time."

"Flo, this is serious. They can't keep us from taking the course."

"It's a private university," explained Flo, who knew about these things from her days at the University of Chicago. "They can keep out whomever they want—within reason."

"But it's not within reason," declared May. "And it's Stan's class. He has the right to let us in."

"He's an employee of the university," Flo responded. "He can't very well make his own rules. If he admits us, he could get in trouble and lose his position."

"Well, we wouldn't want that," said May in a more subdued tone. "I suppose we just have to accept it—and be sure to sign up early for next spring," she added, sighing.

At that moment, Stan Jacobs, a pile of papers in one hand, entered the dining room and walked briskly toward them.

"We were just talking about our unfortunate fate at the hands of your employers," said Norman.

"I heard," said Stan. He leaned over and kissed May on the cheek, nodded to Lila, and then turned to Flo. He seemed unsure how to greet her. They hadn't met face-to-face since the encounter at the pod pool. For a moment, she thought he was going to reach over and shake her hand, but he eventually nodded instead. "I'm appalled," he continued, "though I admit I understand the principle involved. Our people can be quite disruptive. I once had a woman from Boca Lago quarrel with me for twenty minutes, claiming that William Wordsworth was Jewish and had written a treatise on fairy tales. She said that her daughter, who was working on a degree in comparative literature, had said so. She wouldn't let it go, so I finally called the daughter. She'd been talking about Bruno Bettelheim. The woman refused to apologize; she said William Wordsworth and Bruno Bettelheim sounded a lot alike, and that it was a natural mistake. A good deal of class time was wasted, as you can imagine."

May suggested that they might try instituting an interview process to weed out the troublemakers.

"That," laughed Norman, "would be sure to create more trouble. Can you imagine your friend Pixie Solomon handling a rejection notice?"

"Dorothy Meltzer was just telling me," added Lila, "that when her son was rejected from MIT, she drove all the way to Boston and gave the admissions officer what-for."

"It wouldn't be pretty," agrèed Stan. "The university is trying in its way to do the right thing by limiting the number of seniors in classes. I'm just sorry that you can't take my course this term. I know you were counting on it"—he looked affectionately at May—"and it would have made me teach better"—he looked at Flo. "Anyway, after I talked to the dean, who said there'd be no exceptions to the rule, I came up with an alternative. I wanted to get your reaction before I did anything. If you're agreeable, I'll speak to the activities committee and the club president and get these things put up." He laid the papers he'd been holding on the table. They read, in a nice graphic presentation that had obviously taken him some time to produce on his Macintosh: " 'Jane Austen and Her Adaptors,' a course offered by Stan Jacobs, Professor Emeritus, Florida Atlantic University, open to all Boca Festa members, admission gratis." This was followed by a paragraph in smaller print: "The class will engage in a close reading of Jane Austen's most famous novel, *Pride and Prejudice*. We will discuss how Austen's romantic, domestic plotline has been adapted to bestselling novels, television soap operas, films, and facets of our daily lives. All interested are welcome. Please contact Stan Jacobs at (561) 456-9355 for more information."

Lila clapped her hands, and May leaned over and kissed Stan on the cheek. Norman said he was flattered that his friend would teach a course geared specifically to them. Flo remained silent. She felt touched and chastened. She recalled the vituperative force of her reaction the other day. It occurred to her that for someone like Stan Jacobs, an expression of affection of the kind he had attempted was understandably difficult and awkward. No doubt he would never want to approach her that way again. Still, the course was a gesture of reconciliation and friendship.

She smiled, catching his sideways glance as he picked up the flyers.

"I look forward to taking the class," she said. "But didn't Austen have some Jewish blood? Something about missing a good potato knish while her family was vacationing in Bath?"

# CHAPTER FIFTY-THREE

WORD OF STAN JACOBS'S COURSE SPREAD QUICKLY, AND INTEREST turned out to be greater than expected. The idea of having a genuine professor, not (as was more usual in the case of Boca Festa cultural events) an amateur enthusiast, leading the discussion was part of the draw. So was the fact that Stan was related by marriage to Norman Grafstein, who was generally known to be linked to May Newman, a club member. This gave added romantic spice and connected the course in an appealing personal way to the club. Finally, most people had seen the Greer Garson/ Laurence Olivier film version of *Pride and Prejudice,* and therefore were either inclined to want to read the book or were convinced that having seen the film, reading the book would be unnecessary.

The course had originally been planned for the small lounge off the card room, which held about ten comfortably. But with an enrollment closing on twenty, it was moved to the Fairways pod 9 clubhouse, near Lila and Flo's apartments, where there was still a stock of folding chairs in the cabana near the pod pool, left over from the Levinsons' fiftieth-anniversary reaffirmation-of-vows ceremony. For the course, the chairs were arranged in front of a small table where Stan would sit—he had nixed the idea of a lectern as too formal—and Lila and May had set up a refreshment table in the back. May had made her chocolate truffles and Lila her "surprise" punch (orange juice, ginger ale, lemon sherbet; the surprise: a dash of Manischewitz wine). Rudy Salzburg, who had seen marketing possibilities attached to launching Boca Festa as a cultural center for the area (the Paris of Southeast Florida), had worked out a deal with the local bookstore and arranged to stock discounted copies of *Pride and Prejudice* in the pro shop in a prominent display alongside the Bollé sunglasses and Vuitton tennis bags.

Everyone arrived at the first class with a copy of the book in hand, though how many had actually opened it remained a question. Lila and May had both dutifully read through chapter 23, as assigned, and had found the reading easier than expected.

"Once you get used to the Old English," noted Lila, "it reads very fast."

May said with her usual astuteness that the tone of the book put her in mind of Flo. "I didn't know they were sarcastic back then," she commented, "but I guess being sarcastic isn't necessarily modern." Flo told her to raise the point with Stan in class—it had possibilities for interesting discussion.

Norman had read a page or two but said he would wait to be inspired by Stan's lecture. Of the group, only Flo had read the book before. Reading it again, she was struck by certain resonances with her own case that she preferred not to think upon too deeply.

Stan began the class by giving some social background on the period and some details about Jane Austen's life.

"In Austen's time, middle-class women had almost no opportunity for a paid occupation," he explained. "They were dependent for their support on fathers, brothers, or husbands. Property was inherited through the male line, and the home in which a woman grew up often had to be turned over lock, stock, and barrel to the closest male blood relation when her father died. So you see why having five girls was such a problem for the Bennets," he continued. "When Mr. Bennet died, all the property, down to the furniture, would automatically pass to their distant cousin, Mr. Collins."

When he described these circumstances to his undergraduates,

Stan was used to getting a reaction of astonishment and sympathy for the women of the period. Here, however, the situation produced less shock and more identification.

"It reminds me of how my mother felt when Grandpa Abe left the bakery to his cousin Leo, who didn't know white from rye," said Gert Kaufman. "The business went down the drain in six months."

"When I married Saul, I had to move out of a nice house and into a dump," offered Fran Levy in a mild non sequitur. Stan discovered that, generally speaking, the group held to a very loose line of reasoning, but that, if he concentrated, there was always a logical filament connecting one comment to the next.

"I had four sisters, too," noted Pixie Solomon. "My mother didn't stop *shvitzing* until we all were married. I feel for that Mrs. Bennet."

"What do you think Jane Austen thought about her?" Stan interceded hopefully, though he could feel the class getting away from him.

"What are you talking about?" asked Pixie Solomon in an offended tone. She was clearly not ready to take a meta-perspective on the action. "What has she got to do with it? I say that woman Bennet had her work cut out for her, marrying five daughters and with a husband always hiding away in the den."

"Herb was like that with the children," noted Dorothy Meltzer, whose deeply tanned visage was decorated with several Band-Aids marking the removal of the latest basal-cell skin cancer. She wore these as proudly as a German officer sported his saber scars. "He went into the den with a sandwich whenever Melissa and I would start screaming. Even now, when there's noise, he can't digest."

Several women nodded. They, too, had known men to hide in the den with a sandwich. Mrs. Bennet had their sympathy.

"But don't you think that Jane Austen wants us to see her as a very silly woman whose values are mixed up?" urged Stan, trying to steer the conversation in a direction more in keeping with the book's aim and tone. "What, for example, do you make of this description of her on page three?" Everyone dutifully picked up her copy of the book to follow along. Stan read the passage slowly, to make sure that they grasped the full force of Austen's satire on the subject of Mrs. Bennet: " 'She was a woman of mean understanding, little information, and uncertain temper. When she was discontented she fancied herself nervous. The business of her life was to get her daughters married; its solace was visiting and news.' " Stan looked at the group inquiringly.

"That's a nasty description," said Pixie. "That Jane Austen doesn't know what she's talking about."

"She didn't marry or have children, did she?" queried Dorothy Meltzer. "So how would she know what it's like to have five daughters that need to get settled if you're going to have any peace of mind? I can't tell you what I went through waiting for my Sheila to find someone."

"And now it's waiting for the grandchildren," proffered Lily Posner. "I lie awake at night wondering what they're doing. Every time I call, they're out to dinner. Why aren't they home *shtupping*? Janet is thirty-six years old. They say the eggs start turning into raisins by the time they're thirty-five."

"Don't worry," said Dorothy reassuringly. "My Sheila had a healthy boy at thirty-seven, a difficult pregnancy, yes, half the time in bed, but everything turned out fine, knock wood."

"I think it was very nice of the cousin—what was his name? Cutler?—to offer to marry one of the girls," offered Lila.

"Collins," corrected Stan. "Mr. Collins. Elaborate a bit on that, will you, Lila?"

"Well," Lila continued, clearly pleased that her comment had elicited the request for more, "it wasn't his fault that the law gave him the property. He tried to do right by the family."

"I understand Elizabeth turning him down," added May. "He wasn't her type. But he should have asked one of the younger girls. Mary, for example, would have been right for him."

There was general agreement that Mr. Collins and Mary Bennet would have been a good match.

"And Charlotte?" continued Stan. "Do you think she was right to accept him?"

"What choice did she have?" observed Lila. "And she did get her own room, which is important."

"Herb always lets me decorate the house however I want," noted Dorothy. "One thing, when your husband doesn't want to get involved, you get to pick out the wallpaper. I tell my friends whose husbands are always saying they like this color and not that color that at least with Herb, you know, whatever you do, he'll accept it. So he naps a lot. It's a small price to pay."

"You take the good with the bad," noted Pixie Solomon philosophically.

"I do feel sorry for Charlotte," offered May. "She had so much to offer that I don't think Mr. Collins could appreciate."

"She had her friends," said Lila. "What more did she need?"

"And what's your impression of Elizabeth Bennet?" asked Stan, hoping to take advantage of what seemed like a tenuous return to the events of the novel. "Do you like her?"

"Too sarcastic for my taste," noted Dorothy. "I can't say I'd be friends with her."

"I like her," countered May. "She sees things everyone else doesn't, but it doesn't keep her from joining in."

"I agree with Dorothy," said Pixie. "She's stuck-up. Very snooty."

"No," said Lila, who clearly had begun to enjoy the discussion and fancy herself something of a literary critic. "It's the rich one, Darcy, that's stuck up. He's proud, she's prejudiced. There's the title: *Pride and Prejudice*." She looked expectantly to Stan for approval at this feat of analysis.

Stan nodded at Lila, but before he could respond, Dorothy shouted: "No! She's the proud one, and he's the prejudiced one. He's the one who looks down on her for not having enough money. That's like Christians looking down on Jews, or whites looking down on blacks."

Pinkus Lotman, who had taken a course at his synagogue on the roots of anti-Semitism, now felt himself in his element, which he hadn't during the discussion of domestic relationships. "Prejudice," he intoned in a slow and pompous tone of voice, "is when one individual or group of individuals labels another individual or group of individuals based on generalized qualities assumed to apply to all. We say," he continued, and Stan feared that once begun he might never relinquish the floor, "that Jews have big noses and are cheapskates because of certain unflattering generalizations that have emerged over many years based on fears and the positions held by Jews in the societies in which they find themselves. These stereotypes breed prejudice, which in turn—"

Pixie Solomon, who had no interest in Pinkus's definitions, interrupted. "She's the prejudiced one because she thinks he's a bad person based on a few not-so-nice things he says, but she doesn't really know him. She *pre*-judges." Pixie gave the group a significant look.

"I agree with Pixie," said May. "She's judged him incorrectly, and his pride gets in the way of appreciating her."

"No," insisted Dorothy, still attached to her theory and determined to make it prevail, "her pride gets in the way of seeing him, and his prejudice against her family gets in the way of seeing her."

"And he's right," proffered Milt Tarkoff, until then silent but now finding an obvious point of identification. "You don't marry a woman, you marry her family."

"Well," said Stan, "I think you all have a point about this pride and prejudice thing. It's certainly been subject to different interpretations over the years, so you follow in a long tradition of debate. I wonder what you think, Flo," he said, looking over to where she was sitting in what she had hoped was unobtrusive silence toward the back of the room. His voice, far from being sarcastic or challenging, sounded genuinely interested in her opinion.

She paused, thinking how she would put it. It was a question to which she had actually given some thought already, though she hadn't expected to have to air her conclusions in public.

"I think the two ideas go together," she said slowly now, keeping her eyes on Stan, who seemed engrossed in her response, "and that both characters suffer from both defects. When you're too proud, you generally don't see things—good things—in people because your pride blinds you to them. That makes you prejudiced, because, then, you're likely to jump to conclusions about what these people are like based on insufficient information. Darcy and Elizabeth both suffer, in different ways, from this problem, but they're both intelligent and sensitive enough to learn from their mistakes. I don't want to give away the plot, though." She stopped, embarrassed, since Stan was listening to her more intently than her words seemed to warrant.

Everyone agreed that Flo had come up with a good compromise: Pride and prejudice referred to both characters and did not need to be parceled out between them. This resolved, the group could return to the question of whether Mrs. Bennet was right to let her daughters hang out with soldiers in Meryton. Daughters at that age, it was agreed, generally have a mind of their own, though certain limits must be set.

After another fifteen minutes spent discussing what a terrible job their own children were doing bringing up their grandchildren and how they would never have stood for being talked to the way their granddaughters talked to their daughters, Stan intervened with the announcement that the class was formally over. They would meet next week at the same time and place to continue the discussion. He urged those who could to finish the book, and those who felt they weren't up to it, to rent the latest BBC production. The Garson-Olivier version, he explained, though charming, was not faithful enough to the book to serve the purpose. "Well, I love that movie," responded Norman, "and I think that Jane Austen could take a lesson from it."

Everyone converged on the refreshment table in the back and continued the discussion about how to manage and marry off daughters. Stan gathered his notes, which had gone largely unconsulted, and was putting them into his bookbag when Flo approached. She didn't really know, as she walked up to him, what she was going to say, but she did know she would say something. The class had had a strangely invigorating effect on her.

"I'm afraid the discussion wasn't quite what you had in mind," she offered as he glanced up at her with a mix of pleasure and embarrassment.

"Not at all," he said, sitting down behind the table and looking at her directly now. "I feel there's a lot to be learned from this kind of discussion. There's digression, of course, but there are surprising nuggets of profundity. These people have had the life experience that my college students—and even the best graduate students—haven't had. The point about Mrs. Bennet, for example, is really quite insightful. I think the feminists were taking her part a while back, but they didn't say it in a way that convinced me as well as your friend Dorothy did. I'll have to reread all of Jane Austen now through the lens of Boca Festa."

"That sounds like quite an undertaking," laughed Flo. "I think you might want to work up to it gradually."

Stan said nothing, but continued to look at her.

She looked back at him. "I see there's punch here, but no coffee," she finally said with the deliberation of someone who had thought on this at some length. "I wonder if you'd like to come back to my apartment for some."

There was no need to take the car. The pod clubhouse was only a few steps from Flo's apartment. She unlocked the door and let Stan go in ahead of her.

"Well?" she said as he stood there, his shirt looking like it needed a good pressing, his hair disheveled, and the beads of perspiration, the familiar sign of his anxiety, beginning to form on his forehead. But before he could respond, she walked over, and standing in front of him, very close, brought one hand behind his head and her lips up to his in a swift, sure movement.

It was a kiss that lasted a very long time. But it wouldn't be right, given the age and dignity of the subjects, to describe anything that happened after that.

# EPILOGUE

AMY'S FILM ENDED WITH MAY AND NORMAN'S WEDDING CERE-mony. It was a discreet affair held in the pod clubhouse, where Carol *kvelled* as though she were the mother, not the daughter-in-law, of the bride. The wedding was an accomplishment, she acknowledged to herself, perhaps her greatest accomplishment to date, but she was not one to rest on her laurels. Her eye was on Lila, who, she decided, looked lonely, though very well dressed in an Oscar de la Renta gown and a necklace and earrings that weren't chopped liver, either. Stan and Flo were present, informally serving as best man and matron of honor (no special attire required). They were, to adapt Lila's phrase, "living in sin" in Stan's house, where Flo was gradually putting Stan's books in order.

The film did not win an Academy Award, but it did win second place in the NYU Student Film Festival, and Amy and her friends took it to Sundance, where Robert Redford himself, during a few moments at a cocktail party for student directors, said that he liked it, particularly the use of the elderly romance as the film's structural hinge.

Adam, as "best boy," had been invited to go with the group to Utah. Carol had originally been against it—he would miss a week of school and hockey practice—but he had thrown a tantrum that had lasted two days, and impressed by his stamina, which she felt reflected energy and initiative, Carol had yielded and jetted off with him to schmooze with the beautiful people.

Indeed, the festival proved to be a marvelous forum for

Carol's networking skills. Along with hawking Amy's film and arranging auditions for Adam for the latest film about a child prodigy (this one battling Nazis during World War II), she managed to meet Steven Spielberg. She explained to Alan on the phone that she hoped to engage him for the annual fund-raising dinner of the North Jersey chapter of Hadassah. Spielberg had a new film in production and was very busy, but Alan had no doubt that, whatever the obstacles, his wife would prevail.

# Discussion Questions for Reading Groups

1. How does *Jane Austen in Boca* combine satire with romance? Is the tone of the novel primarily critical or affectionate (or both)?

2. The novel deals with older people in a retirement setting. In what ways is this fundamental to the plot and in what ways is it incidental? How do you think different age groups would respond to the novel?

3. How does the use of Yiddish and the particular focus on customs and ethnic humor ground the book in a specific cultural group? How might some of these aspects—for example, food, shopping, child-rearing—be translated to other groups?

4. The book deals with romance, but it also deals with friendship. It's been said that May, Flo, and Lila resemble high school girlfriends. Why might aspects of friendship that we knew in high school get revived at this later stage of life?

5. The book contains many dramatic scenes or set-pieces (the Valentine's Day Dinner Dance, Hy and Lila's wedding, Hy's funeral, May's birthday present, Flo and Stan's confrontation, the final seminar, etc). Discuss the dramatic nature of these scenes and their function in moving the plot forward. You might also consider how these scenes might be staged in a movie—and who might play the key roles.

6. There's no sex in the book (excluding of course the Viagra scene—which is recounted rather than dramatically represented). Is the absence of sex a function merely of discretion, given the age of the characters, or is it fundamental to the novel's kind of romantic plot? Some people have said that the absence of sex in a book or a movie can be sexier than its presence. What do you think?

7. *Jane Austen in Boca* draws on the plot and, to some extent, the satirical style of Jane Austen's *Pride and Prejudice*. What do the two books have in common, and what are the differences? What does this say about changes in society over nearly 200 years?

8. One of the themes of *Pride and Prejudice* is that first impressions may be misguided. How do our views of the characters and community change as we read *Jane Austen in Boca*?

**For more reading group suggestions visit www.stmartins.com**

*Get a* **Griffin** 🦅     St. Martin's Griffin

## ABOUT THE AUTHOR

PAULA MARANTZ COHEN IS DISTINGUISHED PROFESSOR OF ENGLISH
at Drexel University in Philadelphia. She lives in Moorestown,
New Jersey, and her in-laws are snowbirds in Boca Raton,
Florida. She is the author of five nonfiction books, including
*Silent Film and the Triumph of the American Myth* and *The Daughter
as Reader: Encounters Between Literature and Life.* This is her first
novel.